A Lot to Ask

by the same author

—

SOMETHING TO ANSWER FOR
ONE OF THE FOUNDERS
THE PICNIC AT SAKKARA
THE BARBARY LIGHT
TEN MILES FROM ANYWHERE
A JOURNEY TO THE INTERIOR

A Lot to Ask

P. H. NEWBY

FABER AND FABER LTD
3 Queen Square, London

First published in 1973
by Faber and Faber Limited
3 Queen Square, London WC1
Printed in Great Britain by
Latimer Trend & Company Ltd Plymouth

ISBN 0 571 10293 X

1

The possibility he might drop in caused Head of Chancery to have a word with the Ambassador who said, "That's all it needed."

But when his plane put down at Damascus Poumphrey stayed in his seat and went straight through to London, so the alarm was unnecessary. Cooper said he wasn't housetrained. He rubbed Arab statesmen up the wrong way without being aware of it but he was too important for leaking the kind of misinformation that would cause Arab states to refuse him a visa. Hints were dropped to the Chairman of his company. These were so vague they were not understood.

Another useless ploy was when Gutteridge, boss of the East Dene Conservative Association, was lunched at the Travellers Club by a bald man in a faded Daks suit and a Parachute Regiment tie, who said, "We hear Fred Scott isn't standing at the next election and you've got your eye on Poumphrey of Murex Oil. A frightfully nice chap. We just wanted you to know he's a *frightfully* nice chap. His opinions are listened to."

Gutteridge had a stammer. When he was angry he was incapable of utterance and he spent most of the meal in silence because he was very angry indeed. Who did this Foreign Office colonel think he was, presuming to put in a word for a prospective candidate? All these so-called Intelligence men were liars. What's more, they were only interested in foreign parts, no great concern to the electorate in East Dene.

Gutteridge went off that much clearer that Poumphrey was not the man for them. From the Foreign Office point of view this was a pity. With a seat in the House Poumphrey might have stayed away from the Middle East altogether.

He never hurried, particularly in the heat, so he was last of the first-class passengers to board the plane. In the seat next to his was a normal-sized man. He's a good fifty pounds lighter than I am, Poumphrey thought, so maybe it's right and proper he should be sitting against the window and that much farther from the plane's centre of balance. But, for God's sake! he was not all that fat. Weight was getting an obsession.

They had been flying for ten minutes when Poumphrey saw this normal-sized man's name on his brief-case, H. Collison, M.P. "I expect you're on some free, sponsored, fact-gathering tour. Can't expect M.P.s to pay their own expenses these days."

"Have this one on me," said Collison. "What'll it be?"

"First-class passengers have free drink so it isn't on anyone. Champagne! A chap's got to keep going somehow. Mind you, I'm not against M.P.s travelling. They've got to be educated. It's the bare-faced way they come up and ask you for free trips. I've had quite prominent M.P.s come up and ask me. I could name names."

Poumphrey drank off the champagne and held the glass out for more. After ten days of enforced abstention in a tee-total Arab state he was making up for lost time. By the time they flew into Heathrow he would have put on three or four pounds. "I wouldn't mind being an M.P. myself. I've been thinking about it seriously."

They were five miles up. The Gulf was behind and somewhere below (Poumphrey thought) was Babel, and Accad, and Calneh, in the land of Shinar. He wouldn't mind betting this M.P. had never heard of the places. Well, Babel of course. But he could not have quoted Genesis. Culture was just falling apart.

"You know, you and I have met before," said Collison. "Don't you remember?"

Poumphrey shrugged.

"But it really is rather an extraordinary coincidence," Collison insisted.

"I meet lots of people. How old are you?"

"Fifty."

"How old were you when you first went into the House?"

"Thirty-two."

"I'm forty-five. That's too old to think of going into politics, at least for the ordinary sort of chap it is. If you've been a back-bencher for eight years and still done nothing you've no future in politics. I mean, you can't have done anything or I should have heard of you. You've never been in the Government. If I'd been in the House for eight years I'd never have been satisfied with that. What lot do you belong to?"

"Labour."

"You see what I mean."

"I am sure you'd have done well."

"Of course I would have done well. And it's not too late. Not too late for me to start, I mean."

"One thing a politician's got to have and that's a thick skin," said Collison.

"I'd thought of that. And determination. And if there's anything to inspire determination in a man it's the sight of the kind of people who get into the House these days. Third raters the lot! Labour—wet dons and trade union officials. The Tories are a frightful lot of has-beens. They're not the sort of people I'd care to mix with. Something's got to be done. You think I'm joking, don't you? I expect you think I'm some sort of romantic anarchist."

"Not at all."

"Or a Communist?"

"No."

"Well, somebody against the system, then. You'd be wrong. I'm not against the system. I just want to improve it."

They had lunch flying over Cyprus. Poumphrey had taken a liking to Collison. But then, he always liked intelligent men who spoke their mind and argued without fear or favour. He never had time for small talk himself. No blather about the weather. He enjoyed good conversation. He liked an argument.

"Our local M.P. is retiring. You know him? Fred Scott. Majority twelve thousand. Safe Tory seat. I don't mind telling you the local party officials have got their eye on me. I wouldn't be an orthodox Tory. I'm a maverick. They know that. They'd take a bet on me. But you know what it is with the Tories? It isn't what you stand for it's who you are, who your wife is. My wife's such a silly bitch I don't think she'd even want to be an M.P.'s wife. I'm not embarrassing you, am I?"

There was a three-quarter of an hour wait at Athens, enough time for Poumphrey to stroll across to the duty-free shop and buy some ouzo. A seat on the starboard side, against the window, was now vacant. Poumphrey sat there, looking out. Nobody else came on board. There were just the two of them. Collison and himself, sitting in the first-class section. Collison had loosened his tie and was dozing.

Poumphrey called over, "Hey! Like a nip of this ouzo? I've just been out to buy a bottle."

Collison snored, rather noisily.

"It's a very good digestive," Poumphrey shouted.

A few minutes after take-off Poumphrey was peering through his window, and saying, "Christ, it's clear. There's no haze. It's all sharp and sparkling."

Immediately beneath was the cobalt stain of the Gulf of Corinth. Poumphrey looked down at the lion-coloured low-lands and snow-splashed heights. He knew Greece. He swore he could pick out Thebes itself. That great white splodge was certainly Helicon. And there, a moment later, was Delphi. At this height and position he was three miles in a straight line from Delphi, so naturally he could pick out the temples and the stadium. The stone had the sun on it and he could see the dark flank of Parnassus light up at this spot. It was early April and snow hung on Parnassus like some gipsy's washing on a bush.

That spring afternoon the atmosphere over all Greece must

have been unnaturally clear because when Poumphrey raised his eyes he saw this washing hung out into the remotest distance. Due north, a long way away, perhaps every one of a hundred and twenty miles, was a pale, gleaming presence that could have been nothing but Olympus itself.

Tears came into Poumphrey's eyes. He would never see anything more moving. Because of some trick of the weather he had seen—well, what had he seen? He could not put it into words. He was sailing in the blue air like some Greek god, like Mercury. No, not Mercury. He was sailing through space like Phaeton. Down there was the cross-roads where Oedipus killed his father. He could see from Hellas across Thessaly into Macedonia.

"Come and look at this." He turned and called to Collison but the brute went on snoring. "These mountains and valleys and plains," Poumphrey said. "Look at them. It's all so clear. We're looking down on myth and legend and religion and history. This is where we came from."

He actually went over and shook Collison by the shoulder. "You'd never forgive me if I let you miss this. To see Olympus from this distance is unheard of."

Collison came and studied Greece. Poumphrey was so stirred the tears were actually running down his cheeks. "It's wonderful. Don't you see? We're actually looking at something the Greeks could only imagine. We're riding like Phaeton in the heavens."

Poumphrey wiped his eyes with a big white handkerchief and blew his nose. "There are not many men nowadays who would understand why this is all so moving and so sad. I've always thought I might have Jewish blood. You never know. It isn't just the Greek in me. There's something more. Then you wonder why I want to go into politics."

"I don't see what this has got to do with politics. You work for Murex, don't you?"

"Sure."

"Isn't there some sort of kerfuffle over the way Murex is

selling crude oil to the Americans when Parthian can't get enough of the stuff?"

"Sure! We sell crude oil to Parthian's competitors and Parthian has forty-nine per cent of our equity. That's nineteenth-century liberal economics. I'm against that sort of confused system. We're at war with the Yanks but nobody likes to say so. If you really want to know, that's why I'm going into politics."

Collison went back to his seat and produced a book and a pencil. He said his hobby was studying unusual languages because of the insight they gave into the way people thought. He just liked grammar. This was a Turkish grammar. He'd had a go at one or two Red Indian languages too.

As the aircraft floated out over Epirus and the Straits of Otranto, Poumphrey talked about the way people seemed only interested in exotic and barbarous matters nowadays. They seemed to have lost their sense of history and tradition. Changes were decided on not because there was any reason but simply for the sake of change. So-called western liberal values were the luxury product of the society they were in process of destroying.

"There are times when I just want to pack everything in and breed horses," he said.

"Horses?" Collison looked up from his Turkish grammar. "I'd never have guessed you were interested in horses."

"I'm interested in everything. You thought I was some aloof intellectual, I suppose. Sorry!"

"Didn't speak," said Collison, "I was just listening."

Some days later Poumphrey was talking about his trip to his new girl friend, Mitty Flavers, and saying there was this interesting M.P. on the plane but for the life of him he could not remember his name or even what he looked like. If he met him tomorrow he simply would not recognize him. This was disturbing. It was a symptom of the stress he was under.

He had gone through a lot. He was going through a lot: domestic rows, Board room rows, death in the family, more money. Because of this confusion he temporarily forgot people's names and appearance. But other senses were sharper. The fried sausage he had eaten for breakfast had a piquancy and flavour of the sausage he had eaten as a boy. The London air was clean and tingling. The daffodils in Mitty's garden had the shivering brightness of flames in the wind.

And Mitty herself! She was a little thing; about a hundred and twenty pounds, melancholy green eyes, a slightly flattened nose and a mouth that hung open to reveal crowded, crossed teeth in her lower jaw. She had a lot of brown, frothy hair and a complexion that was pale and pink in turns, depending on the temperature of the room and the state of her feelings. She came from Shropshire. Although she worked as a secretary she had money. This little terrace house in Maida Vale was hers, for example. The other girl who lived there with her probably did not pay any rent. Mitty was fascinated by him. Why? He used to ask.

"Oh!" she said, "Well, I mean, you can't sort of——" her face going very pink, her eyes brightening and looking very boldly into his. "That's not the sort of question a man usually asks."

"I'm not vain." Poumphrey looked at her with amazed delight. He adored this mixture of innocence and brassiness. "And what I see is a pretty young girl and a middle-aged man. What's in it for you? You're not mercenary. You don't really think you're in love with me, do you?"

"In love with you?" She looked at him with tears of laughter in her eyes. "Well, what a question!"

He knew she was just crazy about him. He just wanted to make her say so. He wanted her to give reasons. Go on! he implied. I'll believe you. You can't tell me anything I don't know.

He did not feel forty-five. She made him feel twenty-five. They went to night clubs together and he was still dancing at four in the morning, running with sweat and sober enough to drive her home and so to Hampstead, never making excuses to Jinny, never explaining. No doubt Jinny guessed. He did not care. Mitty made him feel young. It was not all rapture. To be honest there were times when he was melancholy. He put it down to frustration. Mitty would never make love. Kissing and fondling was as far as they got. After a bout of this hot petting he would go home and lie in the spare bedroom. To be forty-five and feel the spring-time rising in his blood was frightening. Mitty had the conventional effect; she made him feel he was alive. But, wondering too, for the first time whether it was entirely good to be alive.

"Do you know what this fellow was doing?" he said to her.

"What fellow?"

"This M.P. on the plane. He was studying a Turkish grammar. He said it was his hobby. He said he didn't actually want to speak the language. He just wanted to know how it worked, what sort of tenses they had. Because that would give you an insight. Very interesting man. He'd studied Red Indian languages."

"He seems to have made quite an impression on you." Mitty could ask what time it was and make the question sound arch. "I sometimes think you're more interested in men than you are in women." She perched on the arm of his chair and sipped sherry. She giggled. "You're terribly observant, Gogo. You know that? In the Tube, there was this man sitting opposite——"

"Mind you, I know how to draw people out. It's a matter of being interested and asking the right questions, I suppose. No, I'm not really observant, Mitty. Otherwise I'd remember this man's appearance, wouldn't I? What man in the Tube?"

"He was looking at my legs."

"Oh, bugger him! I do wish you'd listen. I said to this M.P., well, I see you're learning Turkish; and *he* said, no, he was studying the structure of the language because it was a way *out* of his own mind and his own, sort of, society: and *into* quite alien minds. That's why he went for Red Indian languages. He said there were languages with no future tense. He said there were European languages with no future tense; well, a Sicilian dialect actually. That's really something! He said if dogs talked they'd have no future tense. They live in the present."

"Gogo," said Mitty plaintively. "I'm hungry."

"But then he went on to say other things! I can't remember! I'm cracking up. I'm getting old!"

"I'm hungry, Gogo. Would you like me to cook you something?"

"Sorry, darling. I'm thoughtless. Let's go out."

There was warmth and life in the spring evening and Poumphrey paused, with his hand on the handle of the cab door, thinking that just as the year was changing, so his life was changing; the life of the country at large, that was on the verge of change too, he could smell it. People were on the point of realizing they were bored by the permissive society. They did not know it at the moment, but tomorrow they would wake up to the fact they did not want naked actors on the stage (not men, anyway), nor legalized pot, and abortion. That M.P. was a figure out of the romantic past. It was entirely typical of the world that was dying to think there was something praiseworthy in studying the mental processes of utterly alien people. You ended up by identifying. This was the great liberal fallacy. The more you studied the structure of remote foreign languages the less certain you were of the bases of your own conduct. For "foreign languages" substitute "psychopathic behaviour", "Marxian theology" or indeed any other alien world—cultural, social, economic, or psychological. By a natural process of imitation and sympathy you entered *into* these worlds. You stopped being yourself. That was why psychiatrists were unstable. Now, the British people were getting tired of all this.

"Quo Vadis," he said to the cab driver. "The restaurant in Dean Street, you know?"

As was his habit he dropped his hand on to Mitty's knee and as was her habit she removed it.

"Mitty," he said, after he had smothered his customary resentment, "what would you say if I told you I was going into politics?"

"What as?"

"It isn't a fancy dress competition, you know."

"Gogo, what shall we talk about?" she said, as though they had been sitting in silence.

In the three months since they met he had told her things he had confessed to no one else. She was not inquisitive. She did not ask questions about his life and background and did not seem particularly interested when he gave her his life history. But she listened. She knew about his bastard and even Jinny didn't know about him.

There were quite a few people sitting about in the vestibule where drinks were served. Poumphrey and Mitty had deposited their things in the cloakroom and were looking round for seats when a man in a dinner-jacket got up and came over with his hand outstretched. "What a coincidence! How nice!" he said.

Poumphrey was amazed. The two thoughts came to him, quite simultaneously it seemed. "I have never seen this man in my life before," and, "Why is *he* always following me around?" They were contradictory. But instead of cancelling each other out the two convictions (he was convinced both thoughts reflected basic truths) seemed to fight each other, to rear up in his mind like grappling animals, and grow huge. He stood still and said nothing.

Mitty looked up into his face and then at this man.

"Well?" she said, and giggled.

The stranger had a simian face under that prominent two-lobed forehead. His black hair was silvered and coarse. It stood up strongly on each side of a clean parting. At the level of the eyes, which were brown and close together, the face was narrow. It was underhung by a wide jaw. The nose was short, the nostrils large, the upper lip long. It was the face of a man who had lost weight.

"Wouldn't you join us for a drink?" The fellow, not having been introduced, looked uneasily at Mitty. "Oh, Liz," he said to the pale, elderly woman he had been sitting with, "this is Mr. Poumphrey."

"This is Miss Mitty Flavers," said Poumphrey.

"Elizabeth Brewster, Mr. Poumphrey——"

"I didn't get your name. I'm sorry," said Mitty to this man in the dinner-jacket when Poumphrey said no more.

"Collison, Humphrey Collison," he said. "Only the other day Poumphrey and I were flying back from the Middle East together and now we bump into each other like this. Extraordinary coincidence."

"Gogo was telling me all about you this very evening. Now isn't that remarkable, running into you like this!"

"I'm sorry." Poumphrey had fixed his attention on the man's companion. He still could not bring himself to admit the fellow really was Collison. Perhaps this woman would help in some way. She had a habit of shutting her eyes when information was being given, no doubt, the better to concentrate; and when she did this the face was corpse-like. She appeared not to have much hair under that little black hat she was wearing.

"Humphrey keeps his friends in compartments," she said in a pleasant baritone.

By now they were sitting and drinking.

"Quite a coincidence," said Collison. "I saw Edric Todd today. I told him we travelled back from the Middle East together."

"Edric? He's on the Murex Board. He's an old colleague."

"But you've never actually met, I understand."

"Board meeting this week. You really were on that plane?"

"Yes, of course."

"Sure you were on the plane. You just look sort of different. Maybe I was tired. We had quite a talk, didn't we?"

"Miss Flavers," said the Brewster woman, "do you think there is any limit beyond which they are prepared not to go on the London stage? Humphrey is taking me to the theatre. We are, I understand, to witness a public copulation."

"What of?" asked Mitty.

"An actor and an actress, I suppose. What else?"

"When I said 'what of?'," remarked Mitty, "you mustn't

imagine I don't know what the word 'copulation' means."

"She doesn't, actually." Poumphrey had ordered a second round of drinks and recovered some of his composure, "worse luck!"

"Vulgar brute!" said Poumphrey as soon as Collison and Miss Brewster had gone into the restaurant. "He's a Labour M.P., you know. Absolutely typical! I don't like it the way he's in cahoots with Todd, I must say."

But was he a Labour M.P.? Was he Collison? The man who had travelled back with him in that plane from the Middle East had not really looked like this intellectual monkey. Poumphrey was annoyed that surprise and shock had prevented him from taking the fellow apart. Turkish grammar, he ought to have said. Red Indians! What has a man with an interest in languages that lack a future tense to do with a woman who looked like the angel of death? The brown eyes were the same. Poumphrey had recognized those all right.

"You never take me to the theatre, Gogo. Why's that?"

"Too much to talk about."

"You're not talking much this evening. I expect you'd rather be with your wife."

Poumphrey laughed. "If somebody said to you, 'You know, Poumphrey, don't you? What sort of a chap is he? Would you say he was right in the head?' "

"Right in the head?"

"Yes! Sane!"

"I'm hungry, Gogo. I don't like it when you start talking like this. Can't we go in and eat? Of course I'd say you were sane. What are you talking about? I don't understand what's come over everybody this evening. That awful woman! Fancy *him* taking *her* to dirty plays! It isn't natural, but then I suppose that's half the pleasure to some people, being unnatural, I mean. *Of course*, I'd say you were right in the head. What next!"

"How would you know?"

"When I'm with you, Gogo, I have such a sense of security."

"Don't let's eat here. It's Italian food and I fancy something

Greek." He went off to the cloakroom and returned with their coats. "We'll go to the White Tower. I'll get the doorman to call a cab."

Later that evening Mitty mentioned Collison and Poumphrey said, "Oh shut up about him, will you? He's precisely the sort of man who's responsible for all this rot in society."

"I liked him."

"You know very well we came here to get away from him."

"Gogo, that was an absolutely frightful thing you said about me to those people." Mitty was smoking a cigar. A little cigar, certainly, and Dutch, but a cigar nevertheless; and Poumphrey did not approve, because he knew it was just to show off. Cigarettes were what she really liked. There were times he had the illusion smoke came out of her eyesockets.

"What frightful thing?"

"I didn't know the meaning of copulation, worse luck."

"Who gives a damn what they thought?"

"That's not the point. You were sneering at me."

"No, you mustn't think that. I wasn't sneering at you. I was correcting a wrong impression you might have given. Maybe in my wish to be emphatic I gave your innocence too much prominence."

"What *are* you talking about, Gogo. I understand long words as well as anybody, almost. I'm not a prude."

"I just wanted to be sure they didn't think you were some tart, see? I don't mind telling you that was a *very strange* encounter. You notice the way he mentioned Edric Todd? What was the significance of that? I wasn't my usual self. You notice?"

"So you think I look like a tart! Thank you *very much*, Mr. Poumphrey!"

"Todd has no justification for consorting with left-wingers. There's something behind all this."

"Aren't you going to apologize?" said Mitty.

"I didn't recognize that chap. He was on the plane with me

but I didn't recognize him. I'm slipping. I mean, we'd actually been talking about the fellow earlier in the evening."

Mitty took a sip of wine and held it in her mouth, judging by the way her lips were pursed up. And, judging by the way she was looking about the table there was something wrong with the wine and she wanted a receptacle to spit into. Or perhaps she was just still very angry and wanted to find a plate she could smash.

She swallowed. "It was a real coincidence, wasn't it?" she said in a tinny little voice.

"By the time a man's forty-five he ought to be thinking of a new start. The more successful he's been the more important it is to chuck everything. Women can't do this. They can't start new families, for one thing. But men can. Cromwell was a farmer who became a soldier. Now, that's what I mean by being reborn. Man is born and there comes a time when he has to be reborn."

"You can't be born without a mother, so you can't be reborn without a mother either, I guess."

Poumphrey thought about this for some minutes. "You've said something important, there. It's one of the reasons you fetch me, the way you blurt things out like that."

Mitty softened. "Seemed sort of obvious to me, Gogo."

"You're right, clever little Mitty. I'm going out of my slightly bloated mind. I must find my mother and set about getting reborn properly."

Mitty giggled because she did not really know what he was talking about.

* * *

His father had been a good man and his step-mother had been a good woman but they were both dead now and there was no reason why he should not get reborn. It would not be disloyal. Not that his father had ever suggested there was an issue that involved loyalty. His mother had gone off. There was a divorce. They had heard no more of her. She had left her husband and young son for some fellow who had caught her fancy. Years later his father said, "She was a bit of an actress. She had to dramatize and exaggerate everything. I believe she was very happy." But he almost never mentioned her.

Then, of course, *he* had married again and was happy. They were all happy. Then he died. Then his wife died. And among his papers Poumphrey found the legal document making the divorce absolute and a yellow newspaper cutting, dated 7th July 1925, reporting the court proceedings and quoting an extract from one of his mother's letters. "Love", she said, "was everything and there was no resisting it."

The man she went off with was a mining engineer, an American. They lived for some years in the States. This was one of the reasons mother and son never met. When the mining engineer died in 1947 she came back to England and bought a house in Sidlesham. Poumphrey knew this because soon after she wrote him a letter at the Company saying she had seen his promotion reported in the *Financial Times* and that she was now, after all these years, "filled with an overpowering wish to see him". His father had never stopped him from having any dealings with his mother. He was not that sort of man. But his step-mother might have been hurt, and that was the point loyalty entered into the calculation. He had ignored this letter.

Where was his mother now? Dead, very likely.

He shouted down the stairs to Jinny who was in the kitchen. "I'm not going into the office today."

"You working at home?" she shouted back.

"No, I'm driving down to the country."

"Will you be back this evening?"

"Don't nag! Yes, I'll be back."

"You're not taking that girl with you, then?"

"I'm going to see if I can find Mother."

"Sounds innocent enough," she yelled. She was a tall, thin, golden-haired woman with very pale, perhaps brown eyes and a heavy-looking nose which used to swell up and become red when she had a cold, which was often. She had been born in Kenya where her father had been Director of Education and now, in the post-Imperial era she still had the interests of black Africa very much at heart. The house was always full of black men and black women drinking his gin, eating biscuits and talking about *négritude*. "It's rather pathetic, isn't it?" she said over breakfast. "Middle-aged fat man looks for mother."

"Don't sneer. I said I was going to look for my real mother."

"Where?"

"I had a letter from her twenty years ago. It was sent from Sidlesham."

"Then she's bound to be still there. What do you want her for anyway?"

"It's unnatural not to try and make contact."

Soon after ten he was in Chichester. It was early enough in April for a lot of the country to have a grey-green winterish dullness upon it in spite of the sun. The trees were still naked. Primroses glittered. The cold, clear brightness made him think of that aerial view of Greece; and when he found the village of Sidlesham and drove down to the silted-up harbour he was still carrying this Greek memory. He switched the engine off. Nobody about. Everything was very quiet. The sun shone brilliantly. He climbed out of the car and sat on the harbour wall. At that point there was no wind and it was really hot in the sun, so that he undid the top button of his shirt and slackened his tie. When you're fat you sweat at the neck, he thought. He wiped his throat with a handkerchief. Immediately below the wall was a stretch of water; and beyond the water were the fawn acres of reeds, quite still and pale.

Sidlesham? Perhaps he had made a mistake. Well, it was Sid-something. Sidbury? Sidcup? Sydenham, even? It could be anywhere. By the time he had smoked a cigarette and tossed the end into the water he was beginning to find the heat and the silence too much for him. Gulls appeared and floated across the empty sky. The Greeks would have understood this silence and had a temple on the nearest high ground. What was twenty years in this numb silence? He was fatter now and sweated more. Otherwise there would not be much change to notice. The same reeds, the same water smells, as if he had come twenty years ago.

A pity he'd not kept that letter. Then he would have known her name and address. Mrs. *What*? What was her name? He would go into the post office and say, "There was a woman came here from America just over twenty years ago. She bought a house."

Is she dead? Did she leave? Where to?

He thought of the post office because that was the obvious place to ask. He would not mind asking anybody he came across. But there was still no one stirring. All the windows and doors of the pub and the houses were shut. It all looked as phoney as a stage set and the loudest noise was his own breathing. He was sorry now he had told Jinny what he was up to. He would never live down this fiasco.

Most of the houses were some way back from the harbour. He was walking towards them when he met a woman who walked lamely, and with the help of a stick. He asked her if she was his mother.

* * *

Another thing, this talk of rights for women. The notion that women were really *just* the same as men, except for certain physiological differences, he was against it. Once you conceded the physical difference you conceded all the emotional and psychological differences that flowed from it. Women needed cheering up. They needed taking out of themselves, they needed a good laugh, they needed to be reassured and fondled. You had to keep telling them you loved them. Sure it was a strain! But you had to face it. No woman had ever been unhappy because of the way he treated her. On the contrary. He had the knack of making women laugh and enjoy themselves and bear no resentment when it was all over. Women he had forgotten would come up to him at parties and remind him of good times they'd had. They were always happy about it. Tears of laughter. He liked a bawdy joke. Women liked a bawdy joke too. They pretended not to, some of them, but a lot of women liked a bawdy joke and a bit of sex on the side. Promiscuous he might be but he was not a philanderer. He genuinely loved these women. He gave good presents, nothing cheap. He was very attentive. He flattered them like hell and when it was all over he was clever enough to make them think they were breaking it off, not he. He was never jealous. He was too out-going to be jealous.

Made you wonder why he had ever married, when he had this gift for going from one affair to another, and the women always delighted and grateful about it all. A businessman needed a wife, that was all there was to it, not so much for the entertaining. The importance of entertaining was exaggerated. A man just needed a wife to show he was not a homo and that he had a family and that kind of solidity behind him. Bachelors found it that much harder to get on the Board.

There were too many long-faced buggers about who just wanted to be loved. Men, he meant, men who wanted reassurances and devotion. You could see them sucking the vitality out of their wives and girl friends. Nobody could accuse him of exacting that kind of tribute. He was a giver not a taker. He was generous, exuberant, prodigal. He gave them presents and he jollied them along and they had a good laugh. He was a sort of saint, really. He gave without calculation of any reward. He did not mind whether these women loved him. What mattered was that he loved *them*. If anyone said to him, "You're an enigma. You're difficult to know," he would say the real secret is I've got this compulsion to love and give and forget myself. Love whom? Women, of course. Pretty women.

The sight and smell of a pretty, well-perfumed woman could make him quite tiddly, particularly if she was clean, well-lit and near enough to touch. The touch of soft fur on a fine woman was as good as champagne. Light and strong colours were important. At a night club there was some bearded entertainer who wanted Mitty to help in his act. He wanted to sing some damn silly song, kneel at her feet and pretend to woo her. Mitty went to the middle of this brilliantly lit floor and stood by the side of this bearded chap (he had a guitar, come to think of it), laughing and showing her little crossed teeth and gums that were very red in that light. She was transfigured. Her flesh gave off a pink radiance. She looked healthy. She was like Eve before the Fall. The bearded guitarist sang his song and pranced about while Mitty clapped and took a few steps herself. She was so happy and certain of herself Poumphrey had to stand up. He had a glass of champers. "Hurray! God bless us all," he had shouted drunkenly, or some such nonsense. Then he and Mitty started dancing. Everyone was dancing.

That was what he meant by love. He had only to look at Mitty that night to feel the inhibition drain out of him. He became gay, responsive, uncalculating. O.K. so you had a little orgy. And what was wrong with that provided you didn't get so stinko you couldn't work next day? You had to work. You had to be a success. And he was a success, wasn't he? You had to be a really big man to play and work as he did. If you had a girl like Mitty to love you could, dammit, work all the better. Sexy excitement gave you a lift like a jet. Love was flight. As you left the ground you saw the buildings get smaller and smaller. Cars on the roads were like ants in track. Momentarily you were in cloud, but you burst through into the dazzling heights where Mitty moved her thighs and threw her head back to laugh. You became a really big man at that height. The human personality expanded. You were so big you could do anything you damn well please.

Not that he would ever let anyone guess.

Nobody in the family, so far as he knew, had ever behaved as he did. They were respectable and unsuccessful. He owed nothing to his father. The gene must have come from his mother's side. When he had spoken to Mitty about being reborn the question of genetic inheritance had been much in his mind. He would be happier if he could attribute his capacity for euphoria to *somebody*. He wanted to be a natural successor and not a sport.

* * *

"It's a bit unlikely, isn't it?" The lame woman had a soft, puffed-up, large-eyed, pussy cat's face under that floppy straw hat. She even had little silvery whiskers on her upper lip. She had seemed to take his extraordinary question as a matter of course. Perhaps she thought he was an escaped lunatic who had to be humoured. Anyway, she wasn't frightened. Grey eyes, he noted. His own were brown. "You're too fat to be any son of mine."

"Thin women can have fat sons. But you're not thin."

"What a very rude man."

"I'm sorry. You must think I'm drunk or off my head."

"I did have a son once." The woman was examining him carefully. "He did not look much like you."

"When did you see him last?"

"A long time ago."

"I have no recollection of my mother," said Poumphrey. "I was a year old when she left."

"I can't stand still. You see I have this gammy leg and I have to use a stick. About this time of year, you know, little lizards come out of the sea wall. I was just on my way to see if the sun had roused them. I have to sit or keep walking."

"Do you mind if I walk with you?"

"Tell me about your mother."

"I didn't know her."

Her legs creaked as they moved. Or, more probably, it was just one of them. Poumphrey looked at the firm hollows she was squeezing in the mud with the big black rubber ferrule of her walking-stick. She wore ordinary brown walking shoes and thick stockings. Her long rough coat made Poumphrey think of some story he had heard of a woman who had woven cloth out of the hair of her pet dog. This would not have been dog. Goat, maybe. It was that colour.

"I'm sure it's too early for lizards. I saw them on Ascension Day one year for the first time. And I remember Ascension Day was early, right at the beginning of May. There'll be no lizards for two or three weeks yet. I hope you won't be disappointed."

It was even possible she had an artificial limb.

"How did you lose touch with your son?" Poumphrey had to step out to keep up with her. "Or perhaps I shouldn't ask."

"What age are you?"

"I'm forty-six next birthday."

"That is just what he would have been. I didn't lose touch. I just broke off the relationship."

"You mean you quarrelled?"

"How could one quarrel with a baby? No, I did not care for the role of young mother. I had to assert myself. I never regretted it. You say *your* mother left too. Why?"

"Usual thing, I suppose. There was a divorce anyway."

"Could I suggest that you do not know what the usual thing is? Take my case. I am intelligent. I was educated. I could think for myself. It was intolerable to me that I was dependent on somebody else for my standard of living, very largely for the company I kept, and almost entirely for my general expectations from life. What made it the more humiliating was that this other human being, a man, was physically different. So I couldn't pretend to understand or control him." She pointed with her stick at the nautical gear outside the pub overlooking the harbour. "It was like being First Mate on some ship where the Captain was unpredictable and possibly insane. It was worse than that. A sailor can always get a different ship."

"So you got a job?"

"For a time. Then another man. It was either that or become a man myself. I discovered there was no honourable escape from being female."

"My mother married an American and went off to live in the States for some years."

The woman spoke with no hesitation or surprise. "So did I. It was there I discovered men are victims just as much as women are. When I was a girl I used to think women were much put upon. Why should women be the ones to have the babies? It was so unfair. Why couldn't husband and wife take turns at childbearing? Snails do it."

"I did not know snails were bisexual," said Poumphrey.

"Oh yes, my dear, I'm sure certain snails reproduce themserves without fertilization. On the human level I can see this would bring problems of its own, if it were ever introduced, as God knows it probably will be; only the point I was trying to make was that I was against the system."

"But you are no longer?"

"On the sex issue I had to cave in. Physiology was too much for me. Politically I'm an anarchist. What are your Christian names?"

"Edward Arthur."

"That's right. My son's name was Edward too. Would you like to walk back to my little house with me. I am a diabetic. I have to give myself an injection. That square white house just round the bend is mine. You might like a cup of coffee."

"You're not really an anarchist are you?"

"Ha! Ha! Sir, so you *have* got a sense of humour!"

"I'm thinking of standing for Parliament as a Conservative."

"I think it should be every man for himself, too," she said with an obvious wish to be accommodating. "Why should you look for your mother in Sidlesham?"

He explained and she said the only woman who fitted his story was herself, which was most mysterious. She walked just that bit too fast for him to keep up with for comfort. Creak! Creak! Creak! like a bloody automaton. He said he had better collect his car and she told him to drive straight into the yard. There were white painted railings in front of the house and the entrance to the yard was just beyond them. She swung on up the road with her dove-grey gloved left hand smack on the crown of her hat. A breeze had sprung up and was trying to blow it off. "So, you're a politician, are you?" she called out.

She was sitting on a chair with her skirt up and the needle of a syringe in her thigh when he entered the hall. An even older woman stood watching her. Neither of them took notice of him until the lame woman withdrew the needle, replaced her dress and said, "I'm kept quite busy on the Citizens' Advice Bureau, you know. Poor Mrs. Collier's house is going to be pulled down for road widening."

Poumphrey wondered whether he ought to apologize for coming in and glimpsing her white thigh. She seemed unembarrassed.

"I'll burn it down first", said Mrs. Collier, "and everything in it." Her face was tiny and white behind the thick-lensed, steel-rimmed spectacles, which she now turned on Poumphrey. She wore a fluffy brown overcoat and a white woollen cap with a green bobble. Certainly she was eighty, possibly more. Her voice scratched away. "Nobody takes me seriously."

"I take you seriously", said the lame woman, "and so I am sure does this gentleman. We just met down by the quay and have had a most interesting conversation. He is the same age and he has the same name and very much the same background as a son I once had. Now, I am sure, Edward", she said, turning to him, and smiling her big pussy-cat smile, "that if Mrs. Collier's house has to be set on fire you would do it for her. If she did it herself I couldn't be sure she'd get out in time."

"That would be arson." Poumphrey was uncertain how serious she was.

"It's the half-timbered cottage at the cross-roads. Absolutely filthy and uninhabitable. The Council is right to condemn it, but that doesn't alter the fact Mrs. Collier is going to burn it down rather than surrender to this demolition order. They are going to pay her four hundred pounds, this is the fair value of the site, so that they can make a traffic roundabout; and Mrs. Collier will be offered a place in the old people's hostel. The authorities are reasonable and humane. But Mrs. Collier thinks differently and rather than see her accidentally burn herself to death it would be a good idea if someone took a box of matches out of the kitchen and set fire to the cottage for her."

"At 11 o'clock in the morning?"

The lame woman reflected. "Yes, you are right. The fire would be extinguished before it really took hold. You had better stay the night and go and do it in the hours of darkness. Mrs. Collier could be up and dressed and slip away quietly."

"Snapper would bark," said Mrs. Collier.

"Snapper is her dog," explained the lame woman. "You'd have to make sure he was safely out."

"I don't agree the house is what you said, filthy," Mrs. Collier went on. "I've always been clean in my habits."

"It's like a pig-sty, let's face it, Mrs. Collier," said the lame woman. "The official view of the Citizens' Advice Bureau, and it is this I am now expressing, is that you are totally in the wrong and that you ought to do as the Council require. Now don't start crying. It won't make two-pennorth of difference to the Council if your cottage is burned to the ground. They're only interested in the site. So if the idea of a bonfire gives you any satisfaction I am not going to stand in your way, except to the extent that I insist you are safely off the premises when Edward strikes the match." She was so serious about it she was almost angry.

"But what about the neighbouring property?" Poumphrey could not think of any better question, though he tried.

"No danger at all. The cottage is detached and one can reasonably expect it to be consumed without danger to the other cottages thereabouts. Unless, of course, the flames rose high and there was a strong wind. In that case we might have a general conflagration." She was calm again.

"I'll set fire to it and come to an end there," said Mrs. Collier. "It's what they want. They want my death."

"Nobody wants your death, dear. Sit down and we'll all have a cup of coffee." The lame woman removed her hat and revealed a lot of shining white hair, cut in a mannish way with a parting that showed the pink scalp on the left-hand side. "Burning to death would be very painful. Though perhaps", she went on after a pause, "the fumes would cause you to lose consciousness first. It might not be so bad."

"They say as I can't 'ave Snapper in the old folks' place. I don't want to be with a lot of old people."

Five minutes later they were sitting in the kitchen drinking some old coffee the lame woman had warmed up in a saucepan. As they talked she did the crossword puzzle in the *Daily Telegraph.*

Poumphrey was dazed by all this and thought he would go back over the tracks and establish just where the bewilderment had started.

"Didn't you ever try to get in touch with your son?" He ignored Mrs. Collier, and this crazy talk about setting fire to her cottage.

The woman filled in a word in her puzzle and then raised her head to look through the south-facing window at the neglected lawn, the elms on the other side and cows moving behind a hedge. "I know it would be too much for me to meet him now. I'm not as ancient as this old girl but she'd last me out in the normal way. I really am right at the end. I want my mind quiet."

She said she would like to show him the house and the garden. She was proud of it. All the modernizing had been her work. It was a seventeenth-century house. She had spent thousands on it. The picture window in the sitting-room was her special joy. She was a widow and lived there alone. Mrs. Collier came in three mornings a week.

"May I ask what your name is?"

"Abel," she said. "It will stand high, if not first, in the obituary column. I hope no Scandinavians with two As at the beginning of their names die that morning. Anyway, you'll know roughly where to look."

When they returned to the kitchen Mrs. Collier had gone.

"Strange," said Mrs. Abel. "How everything is strange and come too late."

Poumphrey wanted to rush away. She confused him. He still thought it would be wrong for him to set fire to that cottage. But he wasn't sure.

"May I call you Edward?" she said. "We could pretend a little."

"Yes, if you like. Though I'm usually called Arthur."

"What about your father?"

"He's dead. He wasn't a success."

"If my son *really* came it would finish me off."

"The old man was all right. He just wasn't what you'd call a success in the end," said Poumphrey. "He had a beard."

"Unusual in that generation."

"It was quite a small beard. He kept it neat and business-like."

"I might write to you, Edward."

"My name's Edward but I'm known as Arthur."

"I shall call you Edward."

"Good-bye."

"Good-bye, my dear."

She had nothing to do with him. He could have clinched it by asking what her name was before it was Abel. She'd have wriggled. It would have been embarrassing. But he left her one of his business cards because, after all, she had said she might write.

2

The Syrians shut down the flow of oil through the pipeline that crossed their territory with the idea of upping the toll and—as Poumphrey pointed out—putting a squeeze on the Baghdad government into the bargain. Murex was not directly involved but the Board was in a state of high excitement. Poumphrey increased this excitement by bringing out his pet theory that Murex was too small to stand many political shocks in the Middle East on its own, that its future lay with a Parthian merger, and that this merger would lead to a vast saving in staff, directors not excepted.

He had another reason for not rushing off to the Middle East as, no doubt, the Board expected him to do. He was fed up with the Arabs. "I've done my best for them. I've looked at problems through their eyes. Years of dedication. I'm no Zionist. I told them so. I told them they weren't going to drive the Jews into the sea. Do you think they'd listen? Cultivate your own interests, I said. Iraq alone could support a population of 40 million. How many have they got now? Eight! I've had enough of them. You can't shout across the centuries."

When the Board was worried about some great problem Poumphrey loved introducing a quite different one, insisting that it was the same, and that this new aspect needed priority treatment. He brushed aside the behaviour of the Syrian government. The F.O. and the Iraq Petroleum Company would handle the Syrians. If only the Board would start positively thinking about a Murex-Parthian merger while the other companies were up to their ears in Middle East politics that would be a great step forward. Poumphrey was obsessed with the

Murex-Parthian merger, it was one of the reasons why the Board was glad when he was abroad. They could then have meetings where the idea, which the Chairman and most of the other directors were against, was not mentioned.

"All the same", said Lowther, who was Chairman and a Scot with big, sandy eyebrows, "you'll be away to Damascus to see how the land lies? We want first hand observation of the negotiations."

"No, it's a waste of time. There's nothing going on the I.P.C. can't let us know about on the phone. I'd rather stay and talk to Todd about Parthian. Where is Todd, anyway?"

"Oh dear! Didn't I present his apologies? He couldn't make it."

"Does he exist? I've never met the man."

"He was here in October." Lowther's eyebrows were going up and down. "You must have been away, Arthur. Yes, you were in Brunei. It doesn't really matter, you know. Shareholders' director."

"It's bloody discourteous, if not offensive. Hercules Assurance!"

"Thirty per cent of the equity," another director, Nightingale by name, pointed out. "That represents obligations and duties. He ought to be here."

"We know what he thinks." Lowther gave the impression he was quite pleased there were directors who knew their place sufficiently well to put in an appearance only rarely. "He's all right."

The telephone rang and the Chairman's secretary answered it. There was an understanding no member of the Board took calls during a meeting but when Mrs. Straik said it was for Poumphrey he jumped up without apology.

"Yes?" He stood looking out of the window on this twenty-third floor, still thinking about Todd who had been put in by Hercules as if Murex were some tuppenny company in need of sorting out. The fact he made himself so scarce hardly supported that view. Hercules were shrewd operators. It had not struck him before how odd it was their nominee director should be such an absentee. If Poumphrey had been in the Chairman's place he wouldn't stand for it, but Lowther was plainly not up to the job.

He could do Lowther's job. He could do it on his head. He could do Nightingale's job as well. There wasn't a single job on the non-technical side he couldn't do better than the particular director who happened to be holding it down; and even on the scientific and technical side he'd be more than adequate. At their particular level you didn't need to be a real boffin. Lowther was a prime example of the chap who kept a dog and still wanted to do the barking himself, a bloody chemist who thought he could not only check the details of new technical installations but negotiate with governments in person. He had never learned to delegate. Poumphrey was without that kind of arrogance. In Lowther's shoes—or Wainwright's, or Peel's—he'd be getting better results with less effort because he had this confidence in himself, and this modesty, this readiness to delegate; and enough energy to chase the lazy bastards up if what had been delegated wasn't done damn quick.

"Who is that?" he said.

It was a man's voice, heavily foreign, globular. "Mister Bum-free, well, you know, I just wanted to tell you——"

"Who's talking?" An Egyptian, he thought, judging by that throaty laugh and the thick P. "I'm in the middle of a meeting."

"We have decided to shoot you."

A pause. "Who's talking?"

"We do not threaten to kidnap you. We would not like to find ourselves in your company, so we will just shoot you down. Not here in London."

Poumphrey looked round for another phone he could use to get in touch with the switchboard. There ought to be some way of tracing this crazy call. But there was only this one phone in the Board room. He could have put his hand over the receiver and said something to the Chairman. He just did not want to involve anybody else though. There would be such a cackle of conflicting advice. He kept his voice down so that the rest of the Board could not hear what he was saying.

"Is this a hoax?"

"You will see if it is a hoax. You are an Israeli spy."

"Then it's a bit idiotic of you to warn me, isn't it? It's a lie I'm anything to do with Israel. I've never even been there. My business is with the Arab world."

"When next you set foot in it we'll shoot you down."

"How did you get on to this extension? Were you transferred?"

"Just a warning. You don't have to go. Why not stay alive?"

Poumphrey heard the throat laugh again and the rattle of the receiver as it was put down.

Not a heavy smoker himself, Poumphrey really could not put up with all this cigar smoke. It made him feel physically sick. At that very moment, standing there, looking out south and west over sunlit London, he experienced a wave of the most disquieting nausea.

It was a brilliant morning. All the sky, from the dome of St Paul's on the left to the remoter post office tower, was cloudless; and there was a silvery brightness over the Surrey hills, as though light were being thrown up by a great stretch of water below the horizon, the sea maybe. Out of the corner of his eye he could see a green playing field swim, actually swim about, down there among the roots of the steel, glass and concrete towers.

"You all right?" said the Chairman when he had returned to his place.

"Why do you ask?"

"No bad news I hope."

Poumphrey hesitated. "Sorry about the interruption. My secretary had no business transferring the call."

They were all looking at him and the cigar smoke seemed thicker than ever, so he went on talking. "Tory Central Office."

"What's biting them?"

"Nothing to do with the company. Just personal. As you know I'm seeking nomination."

He supposed that breathing in all this cigar smoke had made him look a bit green and that was why everybody looked at him. But when the discussion on Syria started up again and he began to explain why so-called left-wing Ba'ath governments, one in Damascus and the other in Baghdad, did not necessarily see eye to eye, he felt better. The black coffee helped. It was natural that men in his position should, from time to time, be threatened with assassination. This caller had been absurd, though. He couldn't have been fiercer if he'd caught him selling Arab oil in Tel-Aviv. Perhaps that is what he thought Poumphrey had been up to.

He regretted his lie. He did not tell lies. It was out of character. There was no reason why he should not have put the phone down with a shrug, said, "Some bloody madman," and gone back to his seat without invoking the Central Office. It had been the first thing to come into his head. But he must have lost colour to have excited the curiosity he had. And if, looking wan, he had said, "Some bloody madman threatening to shoot me!" and tried to shrug it off they would have asked questions and created a lot of fuss. The truth was that nothing could be done about threats of that sort. The police were useless. The Board would have insisted on calling them in and that would have led to the Press getting hold of the story. It would appear in the Arab newspapers. The moment he set foot in some Arab country he would be the focus of attention. Bad! The trouble about keeping his mouth shut was the Board might think he'd been upset by what the Central Office had told him. They would suppose he had been informed the Office did not propose putting him on their list of approved candidates.

He had no illusions about the Board. With the exception of George Drew they would give him no mercy if they thought he was at some disadvantage. He'd be pecked to death like a sick hen. Drew would not be quite so ruthless because, for one thing, he was Hungarian by origin. Drew was not his real name. He came from some near-patrician family and could be relied to behave like a gentleman. More important, though, he was the director nominated by the parent corporation and this conferred on him a very special kind of independence. Not so independent as Todd, of course.

These thoughts were going through his head when Poumphrey said, "That's no bloody good," in answer to some question put by Nightingale. "There was a time when commercial attachés had at least a certain amount of information. Not any more. They learn more from me than I learn from them. You've got to talk to the top man, whoever he is, in Damascus. And John is right", Poumphrey nodded and smiled in Lowther's direction, "—about the need for conversations on the spot." He wanted Lowther to see that friendly justice was being done to his point of view before it was swept aside. "But we haven't reached that moment yet. I've got this session at the Foreign Office this afternoon. I expect to learn nothing. No doubt I shall be able to restrain them in some folly."

"Perhaps we can leave it all to I.P.C., as you suggested Arthur," said Lowther.

"In the light of the Board's observations", Poumphrey went on, not wishing them to be left with the feeling they were entirely useless—a demoralized Board is worse than no Board at all—"I think I'd better go. I'll report after this F.O. briefing and if you still feel I ought to go, of course I will. You must forgive me for blowing off steam. The thought of a fortnight or more in the New Ummayad hotel with the Dawn Prayer from the minaret amplifier next door at a high rate of decibels is enough to make me an old-fashioned jingoist. Or missionary. I could never see what was wrong with having a Bible in one hand and a sword in the other."

"I.P.C. would welcome Arthur's presence," said Drew.

In the bar afterwards Poumphrey picked up the *Evening Standard* and saw the report of Fred Scott's death. He handed it to Drew.

"There you are," he said. "You can see what's on my

mind." Fred Scott, who had been sitting on a 12,000 majority, had collapsed and died in the street. Poumphrey thought it quite likely that the Conservative Central Office would immediately think of getting in touch with him. The coincidence awed him. When he had lied to the Chairman there must have been some telepathic process in operation.

"I can see this means a lot to you," said Drew.

"You're damn right it does."

* * *

He was, quite deliberately, so late for the briefing at the Foreign Office that he had to be given a special briefing all on his own by a man called Cooper in a fine room with two large windows, double-glazed, commanding a view of St. James's Park. There was a marble fireplace, the colour of barley sugar and a white bust of Canning on a column of porphyry. The Victorian mahogany desk probably weighed half a ton. From offices like this Britain had spoken across the world; opium wars, Don Pacificos, bombardments, Fashodas. In 1870 a man like Cooper could look forward to—what? The Embassy at Constantinople, say, with all the freedom of manoeuvre a knowledge of being always in the right naturally brought. Nowadays, an Arabist, he would end up in some Latin American state busy with trade fairs and visiting football teams. Confidence had gone. The assertion of national interest had gone. People like Cooper would spend their official lives accommodating themselves to claims from a lot of foreigners that were based on nothing better than naked self-interest.

Cooper was a fine chap, though. Accommodate himself he might have to but he would always remain the same Cooper. He was nearly seven feet tall and, properly greased, could have been slid through quite a small-bore drain pipe. He had a big, thin nose, a line of black hair on both cheek bones and enormous, amazed blue eyes. It would have been impossible to travel back from the Middle East in a plane with him and then fail to recognize him some days later. Poumphrey particularly liked the blue eyes. It was the brown-eyed people who confused him. They might look quite different but there were certain brown eyes that gave the impression they were operating under a special intelligence; indeed, a special *central* intelligence. It was as though the same individual was looking out through a variety of masks. Damn silly, of course. Collison had these brown eyes.

"Have you ever seriously contemplated suicide," Poumphrey asked Cooper after ten minutes of the Foreign Office version of what was going on in the Middle East. "Because a first in Oriental Languages, or whatever it is you've got, won't help you to understand the Arab mind unless, like me, you have your suicidal bouts."

"Don't talk like that, for God's sake," said Cooper in a bored sort of way. "Don't joke about such things."

"Mind you, I wouldn't want to kill myself just now," said Poumphrey. "For one thing there are people ready to do the job for me."

Cooper looked at him sharply. "Somebody threatening you?"

"You've got to watch yourself at your age. All that responsibility and not enough staff to cope with the routine. I know! You married?"

Cooper reared up out of his seat, rather cross. "I have never contemplated suicide and I understand the Arab mind very well."

"Will you promise me something?" Poumphrey would have liked to reach up, catch hold of Cooper's watch chain and drag him to his knees. It was a mistake trying to frighten such a tall man from a sitting position. "If ever you did feel pushed to do something desperate you'd give me a ring. I'd come. It wouldn't matter what time of night."

"Let's leave my supposed difficulties out of it, shall we?" Cooper had a remote, echoing tenor voice. "If somebody's been threatening you we'd be very interested. A number of chaps have been threatened."

"Thug on the phone with a bogus Egyptian accent."

"What did he say?"

"He'd have me shot if I turned up in Arab territory. It wasn't you, was it?"

"Look, Poumphrey, this is serious. We don't understand it, of course."

"Of course not. Well, I've got this personal assassin who rings me up. If you really do assure me it wasn't you then I'm bloody scared, boy. I think I'll give up oil and go into politics. Who knows what might happen? Could be your political boss one day."

"What are you talking about?"

"Fred Scott's dead and I've had an understanding in that constituency for some time. Could be Foreign Secretary one day. I'd be good with the permanent chaps. I'd notice anyone under strain."

"If you're going to Damascus our advice is to take this murder threat seriously. You're not the only one to have been telephoned in this way. Now, is there anything more I can do to help you?" Cooper had seated himself and placed his legs on the desk. He was so tired even his ears looked limp.

"I don't think you could have understood what I said." Poumphrey rocked from one buttock to another, so happy that he could have sung. Certainly he was going to Damascus. Certainly he was going to observe the tariff negotiations. And he was going, basically, because some clown had threatened him and he liked the feeling of defying a threat. But more important than all this was the East Dene seat. An M.P.! He'd not been joking about taking over the Foreign Office. Once in the House there'd be no stopping him.

"My weakness as a politician will be my directness and simplicity," he said. "I say what I think without regard to its effect on other people. Now, a really clever man knows what his objectives are and he manipulates people so that he can attain them. I'm too independent for that. I'm not really clever. But I've got money. I've got getting on for half a million."

He could see Cooper was taken aback by these confidences. "My step-mother left me property in Brighton worth a hundred thousand. She had a big holding in Channings. Then she left me a lot of miscellaneous stock. I don't mind people knowing I've got money. I've got a small estate in Cornwall worth fifty thousand. I've got a company running it as one of these nature cure establishments."

"Well, at least your step-mother must have been fond of you", said Cooper, "if nobody else was."

"I'd be glad to have you as my guest in Cornwall if you ever got to snapping point."

"I'm fast getting there."

"Now, now! You're looking at a thrusting, independent, maverick Tory M.P. You'll thank God you knew me, Cooper. What job would you like when I become Foreign Secretary?"

"A transfer to another ministry, I'd say."

Poumphrey shouted with laughter and said it might come to that, but the main thing was not to take life too seriously; Cooper should enjoy himself while he was still on the right side of fifty and make some women friends.

"When I get into the House", Poumphrey said, "I'll make the sods sit up."

* * *

Clear feminine writing in debased copperplate on a blue envelope. Inside, the writing was not so clear. Words had a way of breaking up into the individual letters and some of them had long tails that curled through the line below. Probably written with an old-fashioned steel nib. Black ink.

Dear Edward,

I'm glad you left your name and private address because

I am not sure I spoke with sufficient clarity or directness and I should be sorry to think that, looking back on our meeting, you should have of me and my point of view anything but a precise recollection.

I do not, except on a journey, as it might be in a railway compartment or an aeroplane, easily fall into conversation with strangers and never on such intimate subjects as my own family history. Your appearance and air of harmless vacuity were not, however, immediately offensive. And what old woman could fail to respond to the particular question you threw out?

All my life I have accepted responsibility for my actions. What I have done and will do can only, by me, be considered as the result of deliberate choice. What about you? I suspect you are a bit of a drifter. You are certainly overweight. What about your health? Many diabetics do not suspect their condition.

Unless I do something myself I have no confidence that it is done properly. Of necessity there are certain areas where I have to accept I lack the first-hand knowledge that will permit me to form my own conclusions and, ideally, act on those conclusions, as in international affairs or the treatment of certain extreme social problems like race, drugs or recidivism. But in matters where I possess experience and an interest I always consider I am most myself when persuading other people to my point of view or even pressing them to give way.

It is unlikely that you have achieved your business position without being ruthless or a trimmer. The latter, no doubt. An encounter between an old woman who insists on having her own way and a middle-aged man whose natural propensity for reaching an accommodation is reinforced by the courtesy he would wish to show a female diabetic cripple is bound to be unsatisfactory. And, indeed, ours was. We did not talk to one another intelligently and no basis was provided for any future relationship. Frankly, I was embarrassed. The strange way in which our respective family histories appeared to interlock was not examined. The purpose of this letter is to enquire whether, in your view, such an examination would be mutually profitable. If you should reply that you do think there is room for further conversation I should like to make it clear I hold myself a perfectly free agent. If I should wish to show you the door I would expect you not to resent it.

What is the opposite of a trimmer? No, not a fanatic. I am too sceptical to be a fanatic.

Yours sincerely,

Edith Abel

He read the letter twice, the second time very slowly but still he could not understand it. Not that it was obscure.

This letter was a different sort of attack from the threatening phone call but it left Poumphrey with the same slight breathlessness. It seemed to hint at something alarming. But what? His father would have known how to deal with it. "Penis envy," he would have said. He had always thought one of the old man's many weaknesses was the way he ignored unpleasant or disturbing facts in the hope they would go away. Maybe this supposed weakness had something to be said for it. "Don't over-react," he could imagine the old man saying. "Write a brief reply, mainly about the weather. Then she'll write again, perhaps more revealingly." No, the letter was too queer to be brushed off like that. Poumphrey thought he would come back to it when he had had something to eat.

"You going to Fred Scott's funeral?" said Jinny over the dinner table.

"Cremation, I expect."

"Better than nothing."

Jinny loved funerals, particularly the old-fashioned kind with a deep hole in the ground, but she was beginning to appreciate the crematorium.

"Don't you think that's an extraordinary letter to get?"

The letter, back in its envelope, was flipped across the table and when Jinny had read it she looked up, surprised, and said, "What's extraordinary about it? You mean she doesn't call you Arthur?"

This annoyed him because he knew she was not speaking honestly, that she was contradicting him for the sake of contradicting him, that he ought to have realized this would be her reaction and not exposed himself in this way. Now it was too late. "What's it bloody well mean, for one thing?"

"The language is a bit stilted but I don't see it's actually *obscure*. Why shouldn't she call you Edward? I mean, she's naturally guarded. Who wouldn't be, meeting somebody like you? The real question is whether she is your mother or not."

"We didn't actually discuss the question."

"She only wants to, that's all."

It was Jinny's bright-eyed, pitiless detachment that enraged him. She had less feeling for him than for these blacks who were always about the place. It was remarkable two or three were not sitting with them at the table that very moment. Perhaps they were all at some Black Power meeting Jinny was excluded from because of her colour. She'd get to blacking up. She liked blacks because they were vulnerable. He was not vulnerable. Whenever Jinny and he talked and he was the subject of conversation he thought of her as some murderous thrush breaking a snail on a stone. There was the same glint in her eye of greed and curiosity. She put her head on one side too.

He reached out a hand for the letter and read it again. Those remarks about being overweight and a trimmer were uncalled for. As for the crack about diabetes that was not unsurprising, coming from her. She seemed to be laughing at him, though, and there had been too much of that sort of thing lately. She'd laughed at him over setting some damn cottage on fire. He could not quite remember the detail but she had certainly tried to make a fool of him. The assassination threat on the telephone was somebody trying to make a fool of him, too. And Collison, disguising himself on that plane and subsequently turning up, looking quite different, that was all for his benefit. Did they think he did not notice? He wasn't paranoic. There really had been too much giggling behind his back.

"I don't think she's my mother," he said. "I'll write back and say I'm certainly not a trimmer or a drifter and that she entirely mistakes the sort of man I am."

"Wouldn't that prove her point?"

"What?"

"It would be just the thing a trimmer or a drifter would do. If you were serious you could establish whether she was your mother or not quite easily."

"Do you think I'm a trimmer or a drifter?"

"I think you're totally unprincipled."

"Show me a man who has principles," said Poumphrey, very angry now, "and I'll show you somebody who is mean-minded. Have you ever known me do anyone any harm? Do you know what, Jinny? Life, you've never even so much as put your toe into it. You don't know what a queer bloody jungle we live in. Most people are a bit touched. I sometimes think I'm touched myself."

She served sherry trifle. Poumphrey went to the sideboard and came back with some Bristol Cream which he began splashing on to the trifle as Jinny watched carefully.

"You're out of date," he said. "You're narrow-minded. You have absolutely no conception of the way the human mind is confused. To you everybody is either sane or sick. To me, everybody is staggering on the edge of some bloody psychic bog."

"It's boredom, really."

"Boredom?"

"Yes, everybody's just bored. They're not crazy."

"I didn't say they were crazy. I said everybody was on the edge. You've only got to use your eyes. Bird watchers, people cutting their throats in bed-sitters, train spotters, hippies. Now me, I'm aware of this thing. I've got it under control, like not recognizing people. You know I don't remember faces. I don't know who the hell I'm talking to half the time. I accept this about myself and worse."

"She's just lonely, that's what I think."

"Anyway, I'm never bored."

She looked at him. "No, that's true." She sounded surprised. "But you think every day is going to bring its lovely big surprise."

"I don't know about that," he said, "but there's something odd going on behind the scenes. That's the way I feel. I just want to be happy, that's all. I want you to be happy."

"Oh sure, I'm less of a bother to you then," she agreed. "If we're going to that funeral you'll have to find out where it is, won't you? Too bad if he turns out to be a North Briton and left directions he was to be buried in Aberdeen."

"Scott was a Londoner. I knew him. He was a Cockney. Member of the Humanist Association."

"Sounds like Golders Green then. Goody, goody."

"I don't want to give you the idea I'm going round the bend," he said. "If there's anything wrong it's not in my mind."

"Do not adjust your mind, whatever you do," said Jinny. "There's a fault in the universe."

Death! he thought, two days later. Goody, goody! She only talked like that to frighten him. It was a grey morning with rain and a bitter wind cutting through the crematorium forecourt. There were so many cars that Poumphrey had to park way up the hill. He wore his heavy gun metal blue overcoat and a bowler so he ought to have been warm enough but he shivered as he walked and Jinny, who had a Paisley scarf over her head (odd for a funeral, he thought) and was hugging her short beaver coat to herself, said her father had died from a chill contracted at somebody's funeral.

People were getting smartly into the chapel to escape the cold, looking about to see who else was there, and women were wearing hats they seemed unaccustomed to. Titheridge was there, he was Shadow something. Shadow what? Pensions? Poumphrey raised a hand but Titheridge did not see him and shuffled, his flat feet splayed out, hatless and coatless, under the Edwardian redbrick portico, smoking his heavy pipe to the last.

Jinny wanted to go right down to the front where the coffin was displayed on a sort of platform but Poumphrey would have none of this. He wanted to sit where he could stretch his legs and that would be to the left of the entrance. For the last time, then, Scott was the centre of attention. Poumphrey looked about him, conscious of a slight resentment. He did not want to be dead himself but he never went to a funeral without feeling neglected.

Safe Conservative seat. No reason, once he was in, he need ever be out. He would do better than just hold it. When his time came, thirty years or so ahead, with a bit of luck, he would have had jobs. He would have been in Government. He would have been a Minister of the Crown. Prime Minister? Stranger things had happened. Look at Neville Chamberlain entering the House in his forties. He would do better than Chamberlain. He had more ability, more character. Chamberlain was a Liberal wet and it was unpleasant to think of him as any sort of precedent. Might be the twenty-first century, Poumphrey thought, before he pegged out. An ex-Minister, an ex-Prime Minister, would have a bigger turn-out than this; the same number of local party workers and officials, but a bigger representation of both Houses, industry, foreign governments, the Armed Services. The Crown! In the Abbey, of course. Or St. Paul's.

In the corner under the plaque commemorating the founder of the crematorium was a big man, fifty-ish, very solid, close-cut hair and a Kitchener moustache who wore a black jacket and a shirt with a stand-up stiff collar. He was straight out of 1920. Yet he could not possibly have dressed in this elderly way when he was in his thirties. It was sartorial regression. Poumphrey noticed it everywhere. Recently he had seen an old lady in a bonnet. So, at *his* funeral, it was possible people might not look so very different from this mob.

They sang "Onward Christian Soldiers" which was a funny

sort of hymn for an atheist. Jinny held the book six inches from her nose and sang piercingly. Way up front was the neat grey figure of Mrs. Scott. She chose this hymn. That would be it. Whatever her husband might have been she was a Christian and she had chosen this hymn and decided the form of the service. Everything calculated to annoy. Why did wives hate their husbands so?

Poumphrey realized that he was crying. The coffin was sliding sideways into what looked like a baker's oven and the narcissi in brass pots that stood on the altar gave a wintery flicker. He just could not go on singing. Tears ran down his face. He could taste them at the corner of his mouth. Jinny wanted to die but he didn't. He did not believe that phone call was a hoax. As he left his Damascus hotel the man with the plum in his mouth would gun him down. Death was a solitude beyond bearing.

"Mitty", he thought, "you wouldn't leave me, would you? Jinny would. She would leave me and laugh about it. I must ring her up, Mitty, and perhaps we could go away somewhere." The taste of the tears made him think of Greece. That's where he would take her. They'd go to Delphi and just sit about in the sun.

"Catch your death at a funeral," he joked to Pennithorne who was the local association treasurer. "That's what my father-in-law did." He wiped his face with a handkerchief and blew his nose. "Terrific turnout. I must go and present my sympathies to Mrs. Scott."

The wind jostled them towards the cloisters where people were already filing past Mrs. Scott, who stood sheltered by a wall encrusted with memorial tablets and surrounded by wreaths and bunches of spring flowers. Beyond was a rough field with patches of naturalised daffodils. Poumphrey would shake her hand gently, say how glad it would make him to be of some service to her, and add something polite and flattering about the honour of following Fred as the member for East Dene.

"If the Association decide to put me up," he would say, smiling.

The rain came down so heavily that when the wind blew it swayed like great gauze curtains over the field and the daffodils. Jinny, with her head scarf and red nose, looked as though she had been gutting herrings in an east wind.

"Keep my place, will you?" Poumphrey had caught sight of Redman who'd been a Junior Minister in the Douglas Home administration. He was about to step over and have a word with him when he felt a hand on his arm and turned to find the Association chairman, Gutteridge, begin a slow, stammering introduction to some other fellow. It was all the more exasperating because Gutteridge had this speech defect.

"A-a-a——," said Gutteridge, with his eyes shut.

Poumphrey waved to attract Redman's attention. He was bound to get a job in the next Tory government.

"Gug-gug-gug," Gutteridge went on, tightening his grip on Poumphrey's arm.

"Very, very sad," said Poumphrey. "Sixty-eight is young these days. He served the party and the constituency well though my own view is that he'd have been more at home ideologically so to speak in the Liberal party. Course he wouldn't have had a seat."

He kept his voice down so that Mrs. Scott could not hear. He knew Gutteridge had not entirely approved of Scott who had a habit of quoting Disraeli and fancied himself as something of a Tory intellectual. Gutteridge was a man who had started life as an estate agent and auctioneer and then made a fortune in property development; for him the essence of conservatism was enlightened self-interest and a distrust of human nature so deep that even Scott's modest idealism where the liberty of the individual and the evils of poverty were concerned had caused him concern. As he stood there, holding his head up, his cheeks blue and puffed, his grey moustache lying back rather flatly against his upper lip, looking vaguely like the blind face of a stone lion, it was probably too much to say he was glad old Scott was dead but Poumphrey guessed he was hoping the Association would not make that sort of mistake again. Besides, Scott had always been hard up. An impoverished M.P. was no good to the party. He spent too much time wondering how to make both ends meet.

"I-er, I-er, I-er," said Gutteridge. Then he opened his blue, watery eyes in an appearance of wonderment and brought out a whole string of words with a rush. "Want you to meet our candidate in the impending by-election. Poumphrey. Nice young man. A lawyer. Name of Grice."

"Grice?" Poumphrey started a snarling sort of laugh and looked everywhere but at this young man. He looked at the queue of mourners and the ink running purple and black on the cards the wind was lifting from the prim wreaths. One moment he had been swimming in that deep sea of awareness, fighting the sucking tide of death; crying, and, thinking to himself, "By God! I want to walk on the mountains of Hellas again," weeping actual, salt tears. And then to be gutted! So unexpectedly and expertly there was no pain. Like a shark gutted but still snapping the air.

"What impending by-election?" Poumphrey still did not look at this young man.

"W-w-w-w——"

Obviously it was not East Dene. Even the bone-headed Gutteridge would not have the tactlessness to use old Scott's funeral as an occasion for such an introduction. It must be some other constituency.

"East Dene, of course," said Gutteridge with sudden lack of effort.

"You knew very well I regarded myself as the prospective candidate?" Eviscerated sharks can be thrown into the sea and still have so much fight in them they are caught again on hooks baited with their own guts. "We knew Fred wasn't offering himself at the next election."

"S-s-sorry, old chap, must be some misunderstanding."

"No misunderstanding at all. I warn you, Gutteridge, I'm not a boy. I'm not going to be eased out."

"Thought you knew. Didn't I write to you? Y-y-y-you must have had my letter."

"What is he, a Powellite?" Still Poumphrey would not look at the fellow. He was hoarse with anger. "You thought you'd tell me here so that you could boast you'd given me the information in person. You chose your moment. You chose a time when you thought there'd be no fuss. You're wrong. I want to know how this selection was carried out. I reckon Central Office would be interested too."

He started waving his arms about and lifting his voice so that people in the queue and others who were walking about trying to read the cards on the flowers looked in his direction. And he knew all this. He was going to be a shit. Gutteridge was never going to forget this moment. The East Dene Conservative Association were going to find their affairs splashed over the front pages.

"Come on," said Jinny. "I'm freezing. Mrs. Scott is waiting to speak to you."

"What sort of man do they think I am?" He turned on Jinny. "I'm forty-six. Where the hell else do they think I'll get a constituency?"

"That may not be the aspect of the problem they are considering."

It always surprised him, and it surprised him even now, that Jinny had never been afraid of him. "Do you understand what I am saying?" He was now speaking quite calmly. "I mean to be the next member for East Dene and no one is going to stop me. Gutteridge has been bloody provocative. He's not going to get away with it. I will not be introduced to anyone else or speak to anyone else. We're going."

"Not until we've spoken to Mrs. Scott."

Poumphrey turned sharply and stepped off over the wreaths. Another funeral party had arrived, more wreaths and sprays were being laid out on the pavement and Poumphrey could only make his way towards the exit by hopping over them. No doubt, he was making a tremendous tactical mistake, losing his temper like this at Scott's funeral. He was too angry for reasoning of this sort. He was not an ordinary man. He did not calculate. No doubt Jinny was at the head of the queue by now, talking to Mrs. Scott who was probably disturbed and did not know anything unusual was happening to anyone but herself. So there was no need for Jinny to apologize on his behalf.

"Mr. Poumphrey," said a woman's voice. "I thought if I came round this way I might intercept you."

He found a youngish woman in a little black hat and a fur coat standing in his path.

"Who are you?" he asked.

"Mrs. Grice."

"Grice?"

"The candidate. You know, he was introduced to you." She had big eyes, reddish hair, reddish eyebrows and a long nose so she looked like a little fox and Poumphrey wanted to put out a hand, angry as he was, and touch her. "I'd like to talk to you."

He stared at her coldly. It occurred to him he had not even looked at her husband.

"We can't stand here in the rain," he said. "Let's get into the car."

* * *

He drove north, which was the opposite direction to the one he should have been taking; and, of course, Jinny should have been with him and this woman should not. He'd quickly sized her up. She was putting in a good word for her husband. She wanted him to rally round Grice now he'd been picked by the local association. No doubt there had been more talk behind his back. Someone had tipped off Mrs. Grice to butter him up. So he'd give her the opportunity and embarrass everybody like hell. He could imagine Grice rushing around asking where his wife was. She was surprisingly calm. Perhaps she thought he was just driving round the block. Jinny would be furious, and that was fine too.

He drove through the rain as fast as the traffic and the greasy road let him with his heavy coat on, with the heater on, the radio on, giving the weather forecast, and this sharp-faced, big-lipped, red-haired woman full on too, waving her hands and smiling at him sideways.

"Reggie's great! You'll like him." Her voice came from deep down, from somewhere behind that big bosom. "The only boy out of four children. And the youngest by ten years, so he was mothered and made a fuss of and spoiled. You can imagine. I suppose it sort of sapped his confidence. You're not angry with him, are you?"

She wore shiny lipstick. He caught sight of her face in the driving mirror from time to time, and the image seemed to bleed. But it was not blood. It was some pain welling up and made visible. Or was it the voice that gave her away? In spite of the cheerful talk there was a slurring sulkiness in the voice as though, in spite of appearance, she too had been humiliated and disappointed. She was a failure. What had she tried to be? She was in her mid-thirties, and she had a way of talking about Grice as though he was younger and she resented it.

She sat up. "Where are you taking me? Reggie will wonder where I am."

"Does that matter?"

"Of course it matters."

The rain eased and the northern sky was breaking into cloud shapes, some of them yellow rather than grey; so there was sun up there after all. He edged across the road and pulled up at the kerb opposite a newsagent confectioner's with Easter eggs and adverts for ices in the window with a grey, sleeping cat.

He switched off the radio. "You can get out."

"In this rain?"

"It isn't too bad now. I'm fed up listening to you talk about your bloody husband."

"Charming!"

"You're not shocked," he stated flatly.

The thermometer said eighty-four so he pushed open a side

window and struggled out of his overcoat while she unbuttoned her own coat, threw back her collar and undid her scarf. No, she was not shocked. She even unwound the window on her side down a few inches. He flipped the heating off altogether.

"I was told you were a bear but not as bad as this. You're driving me to a Tube station now, aren't you?"

"Who's been talking to you about me?"

"Mr. Gutteridge, and others. They didn't actually talk to *me*."

"I can't stay here. There's a yellow line. Are you going to get out or aren't you?"

"Where are we?"

She peered about. They were in one of those north London streets of 1930-ish semi-detacheds, traffic lights and signs, and stores with the neon lights going all day. "I'm not getting out. You're going to drive me home and I'll introduce you to Reggie."

"I'm not driving you home. I'll take you out into the country. We'll go and get drunk."

"O.K." She was totally unsurprised.

So he drove north again and eventually hit the North Circular where traffic was crawling; and then struck up the A1, following signs for Aylesbury, Hatfield and the M1.

"You're not making for the motorway?"

"What'll Reggie do? Lie down in a dark room?"

After a bit she asked him what speed he could get out of the car. "It's a Mercedes, isn't it?"

"Don't talk!" he said. "Do you know what? You annoy me!"

"Actually", she said softly, "I think you're lying just a little teeny bit, aren't you?"

He drove faster than was safe. The rain came down hard again, and he noticed that she was moving her head, very slightly, from side to side in time with the windscreen wipers. He was sweating about the face and neck, which was probably why he felt so thirsty; though funerals always made him thirsty. He had noticed that. "I don't know what you overheard Gutteridge saying. But the only way I figure in this story is as a candidate myself. Why the hell should I stand down in favour of your husband? I've had encouragement. I've put work in. I've been nursing the bloody constituency."

"You can easily get another one."

"I don't choose to."

"But it's entirely up to the local Association, you know that."

"Then why am I being placated? There's something going on. I suppose you've been put up to buy me off. How far are you prepared to go? Bed?"

"I don't think you have *that* much influence." She lit a cigarette and did not offer him one, a detail he noticed. "You're a really vulgar man, aren't you? I've known lots of vulgar men. I've discovered it always pays to be open and honest with them. I want Reggie to be successful. D'you see? In spite of himself. He's not the ambitious type. I am determined he'll become a public figure. I'm quite rich."

"What do you mean, rich?"

"I've got a lot of money."

"How much?"

She hesitated. "Maybe a hundred thousand. Not in cash, of course."

"I don't call that a lot of money. I've got more than that."

"How much more?"

"Mind your own business!"

He decided not to take the M1 but drove through Bushey and by-passed Watford, so that soon they were in the constituency that had been snatched away from him. He had not deliberately chosen to drive there but they had arrived, impelled by some homing instinct, with mud from a van in front spattering the windscreen. It was a convenient constituency. You could pop down from Westminster at any time.

"Where did you get your money from?" he asked.

"If it's such a trivial amount is it worth talking about?"

"I was only trying to make polite conversation."

"Relax."

If he was to make a public scandal a good place to choose for it would be a pub smack in the middle of the constituency with the wife of the prospective candidate; and with some such idea in mind he was shouting and laughing in the saloon bar after a single Scotch.

"We've been to a funeral", he said to the bar-tender, "and we need cheering up."

But for them the bar was deserted. The fact there was no one to argue with or quarrel with or buy drinks for sobered Poumphrey considerably and he took Mrs. Grice to a window seat where they went on talking, fairly quietly. He didn't want her to think he was upset by what had happened, he said. She was quite right about the ease with which he could get another constituency. If it hadn't been for the rather emotional state normal in any decent man immediately following a cremation he would have behaved quite differently. Oddly enough, weddings upset him in much the same way.

"Weddings?" She had two big gins in quick succession. She drank them like water, throwing her head back.

"I heard a speech at a wedding reception in which the father of the bride said he loved her. He wanted to take this occasion, he said, to say how much he loved his daughter."

Poumphrey had another Scotch and Mrs. Grice another gin.

"That was very nice of the father," she said. "Was the bride a relation of yours?"

"Funerals and weddings," said Poumphrey. "I can't stand them. They upset me. They open up——" he paused—"great perspectives!"

"But what the father said was very nice."

Poumphrey could not remember how he had brought this subject up and he spoke very slowly, watching to make sure he was not moving unwittingly into yet another disagreeable area. "This man said his own father and mother had died without his ever having said to them, 'I love you.' Now it was too late. People don't speak out, he said. So he was going to speak out, and that was why he said he loved his daughter."

"Fathers don't speak at wedding receptions. Mine didn't."

"This one did. He's quite right about people not speaking out, but I've always spoken out. I enjoy myself, you know. I like life. I like food and drink and women and a bit of power. I'm not a hypocrite about all this. Certainly, I'd get another constituency if I'm eased out of East Dene. But my point is that it doesn't worry me if I don't. There are more important things. What does it all matter deep down? We don't live for ever."

When Mrs. Grice put her cigarette down there was lipstick on it. "I'm getting worried about Reggie. Do you think I ought to phone him?"

"There must be somebody in your life", said Poumphrey, "whose happiness is more important than your own. What this chap actually said at the wedding was if ever he was chained in some circle of hell while rats devoured his entrails——"

He paused at the mention of entrails. Sharks caught with the bait of their own guts. Now this!

"This fellow said if he ever roasted in hell but he knew his daughter was happy then he'd be a soul in bliss himself. Now, that upset me."

"Do you think I ought to give Reggie a ring?"

"Yes, he'll be wondering where the hell you are. I expect they can give us something to eat here. I'm feeling peckish. I don't know about you."

"What about your wife?"

"To hell with her!"

"Oh no, you don't really mean that, Mr. Poumphrey. I'm sure you love her very much. You talk about hell too lightly."

She ate with a real animal appetite that made her sweat and go red, smoked trout, a helping of old-fashioned steak and kidney pudding, steamed under a suet crust, with Brussels sprouts and braised celery. Poumphrey had no more to drink because he wanted to keep awake but she drank a small carafe of red wine, then black coffee. She was just as greedy with cigarettes. By that time the dining-room had filled up and they had to raise their voices to make themselves heard over the buzz of conversation.

"I don't get drunk," she said. "The stuff has no effect on me." He believed her because she was talking precisely and looking at him from time to time to see how he responded. "My father used to talk about the war. What a laugh! I suppose the past always seems safe and secure, however dreadful and uncertain it was at the time. I don't feel safe and secure. I don't feel my present is going to be my past. I feel we're all just making things up as we go along."

He supposed she must be a bit dotty to allow herself to be picked up in this way and taken out into the country. No good as the wife of an M.P. No good with the constituency work, worse even than Jinny. It was a wonder Grice had got as far as this.

"I know where I'm going," he said.

"When I look back on this meal it will mean something to me, I suppose. But I don't get this sense of occasion now." The tip of her nose quivered as she hesitated for a word. "You know, you were beastly to me earlier on. But I think you're sweet! There!"

He did not really like her but he had studied her carefully by this time; a pretty, delicate featured woman with greeny-blue eyes and a child's complexion. Solid, though. Up to twelve stone. He wondered if she had any children.

"I could have had the pick of any number of seats. But it isn't the end of the world for me if I don't go into the House. I may decide not to."

After a funeral people are either calmed down or excited and it so happened that this woman and he both came into the same category, the ones who are excited. To be honest, he'd been stirred up over the nomination of Grice, but it was Scott going into the furnace that really excited him.

"There are more things in life than just having a good time," he said. "In the midst of life we are in death. I've had an assassination warning."

"Assassination?"

"I've been threatened over the telephone."

"It was the word 'assassination'. Private people are just murdered."

"I'm not a private person."

"Of course not, darling. And don't let anyone persuade you that you are."

"I'm not afraid to die," he said. "But I haven't this feeling of improvising all the time you say you have."

"Well, soon Reggie will be in the House. And then perhaps life will be more *considered*."

"Excuse me, will you?" He thought it would be cooler in the lavatory and sure enough there was quite a breeze blowing. He sat there some time with his eyes shut, trying to think why this woman should have allowed him to pick her up. Was she really so ignorant she really thought he could stop her husband's nomination? Or did she just want to show she was sorry? Unlikely, that.

He went back to the lounge where they had been drinking coffee and found her chair empty, though her coat was lying over the back of it. In a few minutes she came back smelling of lilies of the valley and rummaging about in her bag.

"It is quite possible that deep down I'm not so much a political animal as a religious one," he said. "More of a yogi than a commissar."

He helped her on with her coat. Perhaps it was not lilies of the valley. Perhaps it was jasmine. The sun shone through the window, catching her face, just the right side of it; and the contrast between brightness and shadow threw her face forward, it seemed, the white of her right eye bright as silver. Her breath was sweet and because of it he wanted to kiss her. No, it was because she was laughing at him and would not say why.

"Which is not to say I haven't a political future. In fact", he said, "if it's the wife of a politician you want to be I'm a better bet."

"But I'm married already. So are you."

He shrugged. "What's your first name?"

"Elaine."

He stood watching her fingers as they did up the buttons of her coat. "If you've got as much money as you say, your parents must be dead."

"My mother's alive."

"Do you like her?"

She was astonished. "Of course! Don't you like your mother? But I'm sorry. Perhaps she's——"

"Don't know," he said. "Are you coming or aren't you?" And on the way back to town they did not say much; most of it was about his driving. He fancied himself as a safe, fast driver.

3

Recently he had on four occasions worked all night drafting agreements. His secretary thought he liked work. He hated it. He hated it so much he wanted to get it over and done with so that he could sit and let his mind go. He liked music. If ever he was asked which disc he'd take to a desert island it would be the Schubert C major string quintet. The sweetness and innocence of the adagio would wash over him as he sat under his palm tree and watched the stainless horizon. That was happiness. Poor bloody Schubert. Poumphrey would have liked to send him a message, thanks, or something like that.

"I've had a tip off from the F.O.," Lowther said. With those blue eyes, those sandy eyebrows, the long jaw and the black suit he looked like some dignitary of a respectable but vaguely heretical sect: the Old Catholics, for example, whatever they were. "The Foreign Ministry in Damascus seem a bit unhappy about you as negotiator. They've got some idea you're a Jew."

"A Jew?"

"Said you looked like one. But, I mean, there are *thin* Jews!"

"I'm not fat."

"I mean, you're *not* Jewish either? Strong features, yes. Extravert. I can see all that. If I were a dispossessed Palestinian I might make the mistake the Syrian Foreign Office is making. But Poumphrey is not a Jewish name. You're not Jewish but it's humiliating for the Company, for this sort of nonsense to come up. Perhaps we'd better leave it all to the I.P.C. After all, we shall have to accept it they're the real negotiators."

"Bloody incompetent lot," said Poumphrey. "Can't possibly

leave it to I.P.C. There's got to be somebody from the Murex board in Damascus right now. We had a church wedding with choir boys to please her mother. I could take the marriage certificate. I'll go."

He looked at himself in a mirror, the first opportunity. Where did they get the idea he was Jewish? Funny, he'd always thought he might be, a bit. It worried him that the Arabs had cottoned on.

"Listen!" he said to Jinny, "I'm going down to see this woman at Sidlesham again. It's a question of ancestry."

This was why he had the reputation for hard work. Once a problem was seen it had to be solved. Once a job came up it had to be done, because it was rest he wanted more than anything else. He had been known to set time limits. Forty-eight hours to establish whether he had any Jewish blood or not. Another twenty-four hours to ensure Grice stood down and he secured the Tory nomination for the impending by-election in East Dene. Temperamentally he belonged to the nineteenth-century cavalry. Charge! When it was all over, a booze up and oblivion.

"What do you mean, ancestry?" asked Jinny. Poumphrey explained and she laughed. "But you said she wasn't your mother."

"She's the nearest thing I've got to one at the moment."

"I'll come with you," Jinny said. "I'd like to meet her." She had not forgiven him for the way he had spoiled her funeral at Golders Green. By losing his temper he had made the occasion seem like any other party and she was still of a mind to punish him for it. By imposing her company on him if need be.

"Frankly I don't think she'd like you." Poumphrey was annoyed Jinny wanted to come.

"I am interested in your background. So I'll come, I think, if you don't mind."

"As a matter of fact", said Poumphrey, "I've no time for this sort of nonsense. I've got to fly out to Damascus the day after tomorrow and I must get this East Dene nomination problem cleared up before then. There's no knowing how long I'll be stuck in Damascus. I suppose I could speak to her on the telephone. Trouble is, people are such liars on the telephone."

Get it over and done with. He had once reorganized his life assurance policies to reduce estate duty. And when the documents had been signed, the medical examination undergone, the standing order for the bank signed, he just thought, well, that's all accomplished. Or not quite, perhaps. To wind the whole affair up completely he ought to drop dead.

And he sat there really figuring to himself that the last job of work was death itself, and even that, in spite of his being frightened of it, for a few brief moments he contemplated, like any other job to be done, with impatience.

Mrs. Abel was expecting them (Poumphrey had telephoned ahead) and she immediately set her slatey-grey eyes on Jinny and said in a langorous way, "Your husband and I had such a strange encounter. I expect he has told you about it."

Jinny was taking stock of the pretty little sitting-room. "You're Arthur's mother, aren't you?"

"My son's name was Edward."

Poumphrey broke in. "There's a cottage gutted in the village. We saw it as we came by. Is that where that old girl lived?"

"I warned you, Edward. I have never understood Cassandra so well."

"Why do you call him Edward? His name is Arthur. Call him Arthur." Jinny had already pulled a book out of a bookcase and was beginning to read. She had a trick of reading and conducting a conversation at the same time; and Poumphrey had a picture of Jinny reading and talking to Mrs. Abel about the rights of black Africa while Mrs. Abel did the *Daily Telegraph* crossword puzzle and spoke about the mating habits of snails.

"What happened?"

"I said she couldn't be trusted to set fire to her cottage. She was burnt to a cinder, I am reliably told."

Poumphrey thought that if it was true death was the last job of all, and that it was to be hurried through like any other, how strange it was he should be trying to get into the House. He wanted to say politics was drama. He wanted to get into the House because this was the one way open to him of performing in public. He was like his mother, an actor *manqué*. Histrionics was play not work. It was natural that at his age he should turn away from work, death that is to say, to *play*. He wanted to say all this, but instead he found himself muttering, "How terrible. Poor old girl! How awful!"

"I warned you," said Mrs. Abel. "You wouldn't listen."

"What's all this?" Jinny was sprawled in an armchair, taking great bites out of an apple she had found in a convenient bowl and letting her eye wander down the pages of a book called *The Complete Fruit Grower*. Poumphrey told her about Mrs. Collier and she said, without lifting her eyes, "I don't think you can really blame Arthur for not setting fire to this old girl's house."

"*Someone* ought to have done it for her. Mrs. Collier would have been with us today if Edward had done as I asked."

"Let's face it. She had to die some time. You a gardener?"

"I think it's what interests me more than anything else."

Jinny stood up and peered through the window at the garden, wiping her red nose with a man's size handkerchief. Every time she identified a shrub or a plant she muttered its name. "You won't have much frost here, being so near the sea."

"The first winter I was here the sea actually came into that far corner. Ideal for asparagus."

Poumphrey began pointing out the detail of some invisible map with his right forefinger. "Let's get this straight. You think I was wrong", he said to Mrs. Abel, "not to go out when you told me and set fire to that cottage? I want to be quite clear about this."

"The place was coming down anyway."

"It would have been arson."

"In a manner of speaking", Mrs. Abel replied, "you did not strive officiously to keep Mrs. Collier alive."

"How was I to know she wasn't bluffing?"

Mrs. Abel laughed with surprising girlishness. Her face went round and merry. "Because I told you so."

"I don't even know whether you're serious now. I can't believe that you mean I'm in any way responsible for what happened."

"Where does responsibility begin and end? that's what I'd like to know," said Jinny. "Can't we take you out to lunch somewhere, Mrs. Abel? There must be some pub we can go to. Arthur wants to ask if there are any racial factors in the family background he ought to be made aware of. And if there are any shocks I know he'd find them easier to take in a bar."

"We'll have lunch here. I never go out to lunch. My odd-job man grills a very good chop. There's plenty of drink."

"She's just trying to make you feel guilty. Do shut up," said Jinny when Mrs. Abel had gone off to the kitchen. "Anyway, I don't believe she's your mother. You don't look a bit like her."

The morning opened up with some unexpectedly hot sunshine and they all went and sat on the little stone terrace where the odd-job man, a Mr. Prossor, a grey-haired, stooping, sad-looking man of about seventy, brought sherry on a tray. He was wearing a butcher's apron and rubber gloves. He never worked with his bare hands, he explained with a melancholy snigger; canvas gloves in the garden, rubber gloves in the kitchen.

Poumphrey was still amazed by Mrs. Collier's death and he went off, leaving the two women to drink their sherry. He walked round the lawn and up and down the garden paths. From the other side of the hedge cows, plastered with mud and dung, gazed at him. The morning was sweet with hawthorn blossom and this milky reek of cattle.

He had his faults, God knows. But callousness was not one of them. If Mrs. Abel had been so certain Mrs. Collier meant what she had said surely *he* was not the only man she had told. What about Prossor? The whole thing was incredible. Mrs.

Abel was lying. She wanted to torment him. How could you ask a woman possessed of such a macabre sense of humour whether she had Jewish antecedents? Not that it mattered. She wasn't his mother, was she? Then why was he there? Why didn't he ask the kind of questions that would have immediately established she was not his mother? He knew he wouldn't. Jinny might; but not he.

He went off to the kitchen where he found Prossor drinking sherry out of a tumbler. "This business of old Mrs Collier. She really did set fire to her cottage? And she was in it? I mean, did she ever suggest you might go and set fire to the place for her?"

Prossor was just a bit sleepy with drink. "No, she wouldn't have said that."

"She really did not put it to you that since the old cottage was coming down anyway there'd be no harm in putting a match to it?"

"With all Mrs. Collier's things in it? That'd be a tidy bit of insurance. She had china ornaments and a TV set and some really nice bits of furniture. She had a very nice corner cupboard."

"You'd be the obvious man to ask." He looked at Prossor speculatively and then marched off to the terrace where the two women were talking about some new technique for bringing cows into milk without the usual preliminary of calf-bearing. Jinny was against it and Mrs. Abel was for it.

He struck the friendly note that was habitual with him when he suspected he was in for a row. "You didn't *really* think she was going to set fire to the place, did you?"

"Oh, Arthur, you *are* a bore." Jinny turned to Mrs. Abel. "One thing you've got to know about him. He does go on about things. He gets an idea in his head and he goes on about it."

"Edward, your wife tells me there has been some muddle over your standing for parliament." She waved a hand towards the sherry that Poumphrey had still not touched. Her tone was of jolly raillery, as though she had found him out in some petty deception, something he had kept from her in the misguided notion that she would think it silly or disgraceful, when all the time she thought it jolly good fun.

"I've really got to know about that unfortunate woman."

"Oh, Arthur," said Jinny.

"Edward", said Mrs. Abel, "can't you please see the subject is very distressing to me? I've known Mary Collier ever since I came here twenty years ago. She did my laundry before the laundrette came. And cleaning and bottling. She's dead and it's no good repining. The horrors of death are somewhat exaggerated in my view. It really is *not* as bad as all that. I've never really seen what was wrong with holding human life cheap. It is, isn't it, Edward? Death isn't so bad as the uncertainties of life."

"Have you made your will?" Poumphrey asked her over lunch.

"Why do you ask?"

He shrugged. Unexpectedly Prossor had walked in with a bottle of Pommard and Poumphrey had already taken two glasses. He was sweating. He undid the shirt button at his throat and slackened his tie. His father had been thin and yet he had died of a coronary in his late sixties. Mrs. Abel had her bones concealed but she was not fat the way he was. Fat men did not enjoy any prestige in Europe. Perhaps that was one of the reasons he was so happy to reach the other end of the Mediterranean. They were respected there. Fat men did not live long. He did not have morbid thoughts but, all right, he'd go on a diet. He'd see that man Lowther consulted. He'd cut out drink. He'd cut out sugar. He'd cut out starch.

"Everybody makes a will," he said. "I've made a will. Everything's left to Jinny. I took advice on how to reduce Estate Duty. The Company lawyers put me on to a chap who specializes in that sort of thing. The house is in Jinny's name. I've got a big property in Cornwall. I've taken out policies under the Married Women's Property Act. I've done the lot.

Though if you really pressed me, if you really asked me whether it was all for Jinny's benefit, I'd have to say no."

Mrs. Abel drank Perrier water. She was sharing a pint bottle with Jinny, which left Poumphrey himself responsible for the wine. "Don't you like your wife?"

Poumphrey hesitated. "It's a very peculiar relationship. Put it like this," he went on, as though Jinny were not there, "I could describe the relationship in terms that made sense in a man-run society. I utter and she obeys. But we don't live in that sort of society. So it doesn't make sense. She's never defied me. She's a bloody intellectual. Deep down she thinks I'm not good enough for her."

They were eating roast mutton, braised celery, and some extraordinary frothy mashed potatoes that Mrs. Abel dispensed with a ladle.

"I shall not make my will", she said, "until I am on my death bed and I shall act as whim takes me."

"The reason I'm against the stilboestral method of bringing cows into milk", said Jinny, "is that it is so unnatural. You ask me what the word means and I don't really know the answer. Unnatural! Natural! I sometimes think that in a world where everything is explained in terms of chemistry the only think I can cling to is this belief I have that some things are natural and others are unnatural."

"This is a very subjective approach to problems," said Mrs. Abel.

"That's all I'm capable of, to be honest," said Jinny. "It's a hell of a relief realizing it."

"You mean you think cows should have calves?"

"If you press me."

"And here we sit eating a dead sheep." Mrs. Abel sighed. "And enjoying it. I really think that in the appropriate circumstances I would find it possible to eat human flesh. And I do not mean out of extreme necessity. Anthropologists say that cannibalism has some kind of metaphysical origin. You eat a man and acquire his strength. I've even heard it said that women experience a special kind of sexual gratification from eating the flesh of a male. But I wouldn't be so silly. I'd eat it because I liked it, wouldn't you, my dear?"

"Eat human flesh?" said Jinny in horror.

"There's a lot of cant talked about behaviour," said Mrs. Abel. "I believe in doing what I like."

Prossor, still wearing his rubber gloves, poured Poumphrey another glass of Pommard. The temperature in the room was tropical. The sun blazed through the windows, the new green of the spring leaves flashed metallically in the breeze. Poumphrey said, "Are you Jewish? Or partly so?"

"You haven't once called me Mother, Edward. You've decided not to humour me."

"Mother," he said.

"Let us go and have fruit and coffee on the terrace. It is quite warm enough. The breeze has dropped. It is like summer. Jewish? Me? Let me think now."

"It isn't quite true that Arthur utters and I obey, you know," said Jinny as she rose. "Everything is altogether queerer than that, I'm afraid."

"Poor Edward," laughed Mrs. Abel, taking him by the arm. "My experience is that people are interested in the past only if they are afraid of the present. What are you afraid of?"

"Nothing at all."

"That's a very good answer." She was still laughing. "Normally the older most people grow the more frightened they become."

"The older Arthur grows the smugger he gets," said Jinny.

Poumphrey could not sit on the terrace talking to the women. There was no breeze. No, worse than that, there was no air. The sweat oozed out of him. He wished he had not taken that third glass of wine. The physical discomfort he found himself in—his clothes sticking to him, the suspicion that his light-coloured suit was showing patches of damp where it fitted tightly across his back—and yet in spite of this discomfort, an inability to stave off a dreamy somnolence, all this made him, in desperation, just want to walk about.

"Can you get out of your garden?" Without waiting for an answer he set off across the lawn and found himself walking along a path between a vegetable plot, where young peas were three inches high, and a soft fruit cage; here were black currant bushes opening their buds, it seemed to him, like so many tiny green fists.

He climbed a stile into the pasture and set off along a path so muddy his shoes were soon caked. But he took no notice. There was still no air. Vast, sepia-pocked clouds towered motionless in a white, bright, hard sky and as he walked on, wiping his face with his handkerchief, drawing it across his forehead and making a little pad to dab his throat with, he tried to think about his trip to Damascus and the possibility someone might gun him down there. Mrs. Abel would not let him think. He did not know why he had come to Sidlesham again. Because, honestly, it did not matter a sod whether she was his mother or not.

Through the flowering hawthorn he could glimpse cottage gardens. A greenhouse gave a milky wink as he passed and opened a screeching iron gate. Here, on a bank, were primroses in great clumps. Though beaded with water the pale petals were crisp as porcelain. In the heat a thin vapour was rising. He had never seen such bright flowers. The puckered, deep-veined leaves were beaded and bathed in oily light. And then he realized the sun had at last broken through and was catching this bank of primroses. The scent of wet earth, bruised grass, cow shit, milk, gillyflowers—he could not tell quite what it all was in the summery heat. Primroses didn't give off much of a smell, did they?

He took off his tie and put it in his pocket. Heat had never bothered him before, in spite of his weight. Even now, with the sun full on him in this sheltered nook, the temperature could not be more than seventy. But it really dazed him. He felt he had to keep walking. If he stopped he might fall.

The gutted cottage was just over there, at the end of a gravel path with iron railings on each side. Now he could smell charred wood and burnt rag. This was the real stink of crisis and fear. Normandy, 1944. Everything stinking of piss and burnt rag.

If he had an attack of seizure who would come to his assistance? He did not want any assistance. To hell with assistance. He was independent. He fought off the dizziness. He could not bear the thought of anyone touching him. Or observing him. Least of all Mrs. Abel. The reek of burning made him feel so ill he didn't want to know one way or the other whether she was his mother. Looking for her had been a horrible mistake. Now that he had come so far in the search he didn't want to go forward or back.

The cottage stood close to its neighbours but it was detached, it occupied a corner site. He could understand why the Council wanted it down. Drivers of cars from an easterly direction would be able to see what was coming from the south. At the moment they couldn't without nosing half-way across the street. He had walked past into the street and was looking back at it.

The roof had gone completely, the windows were out, and the interior scoured. In his imagination Poumphrey could see the flames shooting up thirty or forty feet. Draught came in through the ground floor doors. Once the bedroom floor was alight the four walls, now black and stinking, would have operated like an incinerator.

On the other side of the street was a man in a short raincoat and cap who seemed to be watching him. Something in his way of standing seemed familiar. He was under the blind of a butcher's shop and leaning forward slightly as though into the wind; but there was no wind.

Poumphrey crossed. The man was a stranger after all; but he knew Poumphrey was coming and lifted his head. He might have been in his sixties. Thin, untidy, white hair stood out between his ears and the stained check cap. It was a red, lined, crumpled face. The real man, however, seemed to be hidden away inside; the spirit could just be glimpsed through the eyes, as the prince might be made out behind the flat countenance of a frog. He looked like a creature taken unawares and thrust into mortality. There he had been, an insubstantial spirit only to be suddenly caged by flesh and bone. He didn't know why. Yet he did not take it too seriously. He had been caught, that's all.

Poor bastard! Poumphrey thought.

He felt better now, because he, of course, was not caught. In spite of Mrs. Abel he was not bewildered by mortality. He liked this phrase. In spite of old Mrs. Collier and the stink of her cottage he was not bewildered by being alive.

Poor bastard! he thought, walking on. The man in the raincoat and cap was just caught up in some process he did not understand. Whereas Poumphrey had total awareness of any situation he might find himself in.

Back at the house Jinny and Mrs. Abel had moved indoors and were playing Canasta in the sitting-room with Prossor. The old man had discarded his rubber gloves but was still wearing his butcher's apron. He said nothing. He just laughed, sighed, sucked his pipe and played his cards. But the women were arguing in a friendly sort of way about race and immigration.

"What are Edward's views?" said Mrs. Abel, suddenly noticing him. "If he's going to be an M.P. they'll have more practical importance than ours. But Jinny tells me you've been disappointed over a particular constituency."

"I've every confidence of getting the nomination."

Jinny looked up from her cards. "The East Dene lot have nominated Grice. They're not going to change their minds now."

"Grice might."

"Change his mind? It's a safe Tory seat."

"Pressure might be brought to bear."

"By whom?"

"Me."

"What sort of pressure?"

"His wife is attractive and a bit sporty. I could tell him that unless he withdraws his candidature I should take her over."

Jinny went back to her cards. "Oh, yes. I hadn't thought of that. A threat of that kind and he's bound to cave in. Mrs. Grice too, I shouldn't wonder. If your timing is right you might get the seat *and* the woman."

Mrs. Abel said she was tired of Canasta. She sent Prossor off to do the washing up, waited until he had closed the door behind him, and then said, "Wouldn't the idea of your proposed course of action cause more amusement than terror?"

"At least *you* think I'm serious."

"Why not? My first husband was a bully too."

Poumphrey remembered how his father had been fond of primroses and taken a lot of trouble to stock the banks of the garden at Grendon with wild plants he used to grub up on country walks. Indeed, he had a strong sense of his father's presence in the dark, cold room, at that moment; the big, heavy man in the tweed suit who, when his hair was white towards the end of his life, grew a beard, close to the chin and neat like George V's, but surprisingly dark. It was as though he was in the corner, smiling and watching. The room was crowded with wet primroses and wild white hawthorn, making the air tremble with sweetness. Poumphrey saw all of his own life up to that moment as a mere improvisation. Nothing had been fixed. Now it was as though he had died and was looking back on it; all, in a twinkling, was settled, permanent, decided.

"There wasn't much the matter with my father," he said. "I shall always regret that I never made it clear how much I loved him."

Mrs. Abel produced photographs of her dead husband. Although Poumphrey did not want to look at them she insisted. He felt surprisingly cross, and at the same time, contemptuous, as he looked at the spread-out, worried-looking face; it was round, almost hairless, and the eyes and mouth were pushed as far away from the short nose as possible. Poumphrey thought of features painted on a balloon.

"Here is one of us taken together."

He could not have been much more than five feet tall. He came up to Mrs. Abel's ear and was dressed in lace-up boots, riding breeches, a bush shirt and, incongruously, a bow tie. Poumphrey felt the smiling presence of his father even more strongly.

"You had no other children?" He handed the photographs back. Jinny, to his annoyance, asked to see them.

"Only the one son. But that was by my first husband."

Jinny loved photographs. She took them over to the light and asked questions. Where were they taken? When? Poumphrey knew what she was leading up to and waited for it. "Is your late husband buried locally?"

"He was cremated in Virginia."

"But you chose to live in England."

Mrs. Abel laughed and replaced the photographs in a drawer. "I always felt England was my home. I enjoyed living in the States but there is something disquieting about the way the natural optimism of the people there flies in the face of the evidence."

Poumphrey had been about to ask whether he could go upstairs to one of the bedrooms and lie down. After a nap he and Jinny would go home. He would never come to Sidlesham again. He would never see this woman again. He could not bear the sense this house, the photographs, the soft plonking sound of her voice, all gave him of the onward, wild wave of life being arrested. After this experience of heat and scent and darkness it was incredible the ostensible reason for coming down to Sussex had been to ask this woman if she had a Jewish grandfather. Poumphrey just did not want to know. She was nothing to do with him. Or, rather, he did not care one way or another. The past did not matter. He wanted to go.

"What makes you think the Americans are any worse than we are in that respect?" was what he actually said.

"The optimism. In spite of everything they still believe in the perfectibility of natural man. It just makes me want to become a Roman Catholic. But I object to organized religion. As I told you. I'm an anarchist."

"But don't anarchists believe in the perfectibility of natural man?"

"I suppose I belong to the right wing of the movement with Tolstoy."

"Politically, Tolstoy was a fool. It's all so bloody unreal, these anti-organizational, anti-society, anti——"

He could see Jinny smiling to herself. But Jinny refused to look the real world in the face too. She was a lefty-Liberal-humanitarian with a special weakness for blacks. And if what Mrs. Abel said about the Americans was true, there were too many Jinnies over there, living lives that touched only now and again, and then coincidentally, the abrasive detail of the real world. The young were worse than the old. Protesting students were the luxury products of a rich civilization, like mink-covered lavatory seats.

". . . anti the kind of set up that makes decent living possible. There is a very real drive to fantasy, and self-deception. Any time now I expect to hear about hospital patients going on strike against cancer. Well, it's there. Cancer is there. Evil is there. The Devil is there."

Mrs. Abel walked up and down the room to exercise her arthritic leg. "You don't really believe in the Devil do you?"

"It was the first time he had succeeded, he felt, in getting her to take him seriously. "I just mean life is harsh and people can be nasty. Instant Paradise isn't on."

"And no doubt you consider your entry into politics opens up the prospect of some general mitigation of public misery."

"Politicians aren't *that* important."

"You're not actually on the *side* of the Devil?"

"I'm very kind at heart."

"But you let Mrs. Collier die." Mrs. Abel supported herself with her stick and sighed, as though she was trying to generalize the reproach and, in deference to the views he had just expressed, attribute the crime to unregenerate human nature rather than to him personally. But the effort was beyond her. "I shall never forgive you, Edward."

"You silly woman!" Poumphrey jumped up and looked at her very angrily. "You have absolutely no right to talk in that way."

Calmly, not even appearing to look at him, Mrs. Abel raised her stick and poked him shrewdly in the stomach. "You're getting fat and self-indulgent. I refuse to lose my temper with you. But there!" And she jabbed him again, so violently that Poumphrey gasped with pain, stepped backwards clutching his stomach, and fell over a chair.

Jinny shouted, "Oh, I can't stand this!" burst into tears and ran upstairs.

In spite of the pain Poumphrey took note of the way she had deserted him. A man in his position ought to have a wife who at such moments rushed to his side with shocked concern on her face. But not Jinny. He wasn't black suffering Africa. He was just her poor suffering husband, lying on his back with his legs curled over a chair and his head resting on what felt like broken glass. This gammy-legged old bitch had ruptured him. If it hadn't been for the big rubber ferrule on the end of her stick she'd have stuck him like a pig.

Mrs. Abel waited for the clatter and groaning to stop and then, unpityingly, went on. "*You* talk of taking over some other man's wife as part of some political manoeuvre! My first husband despised women too."

Poumphrey rolled over on to his side. His head had been resting on a cast-iron Victorian Mr. Punch and Dog Toby door stop and he had the wild idea of picking it up and throwing it in her face. He felt his stomach. He did not know whether it was sweat or blood that was soaking through his trousers.

"Get Jinny," he said shortly.

They could hear Jinny sobbing overhead.

"These old houses," Mrs. Abel muttered. "It's an illusion

that they knew how to build in days gone by. This house is a splendid example of early seventeenth-century jerry building. I hate a room where you can hear what is going on upstairs." She raised her stick and hammered on the ceiling. "Jinny! Jinny!" she called. "Edward's hurt himself, poor boy."

She herself went out into the garden where Poumphrey, who had struggled to his feet, was able with some incredulity to watch her through the window as she supervised Prossor carry out some transplanting job in one of the borders.

"Murderous old bitch." He was massaging his belly, unaware that Jinny had come downstairs, her nose flaming under the powder she had been dabbing on.

She was hostile. "What a way to speak of an invalid."

"Invalid? What about me? Look, my head's bleeding."

"We can't leave until you've apologized. I've had quite enough of your boorishness." She did not ask about his injuries.

"Apologize? Me? She's convinced I'm lying here in my death agony. She's out there getting Prossor to dig my grave."

"Well I shall have to apologize for you."

"I'm off."

"Then you can go without *me*."

She went out to the garden while Poumphrey made his way out to the car. He sat behind the wheel thinking he was in no state to drive. He was in shock. He was a sick man. Nobody liked him. After sitting there for some time, and still Jinny did not come he backed out of the yard and drove off towards Chichester, shouting with anger and then laughter as he went. "Mad, vicious bitches."

He thought for some reason of the man in the cap and short raincoat, wondering if that is what his assassin would look like, with the same trapped smile, when he came out of the Damascus side-street.

In Damascus once he had seen a boy of about eighteen writhing in some sort of fit. He was in the Great Mosque at the beginning of the Hadj and there were a lot of Turkish peasants walking up and down. The men were in big boots and European-style suits in coarse cloth. The women were chunky and short, heavily veiled and all in white. They were all off to the Hedjaz the following week in a fleet of old red motor coaches. None of them took any notice of this boy. They walked up and down, two or three hundred of them, looking insignificant in the great pool of sunshine and the cavernous shadows. They did not so much as glance at the boy and Poumphrey began to think he wasn't having a fit at all.

Before one of the pillars a rectangle had been marked off by wooden railings no more than nine inches high; it was here the boy lay, dressed in a European shirt and grey cotton trousers. The white-bearded man who was handling him made a more striking impression and Poumphrey could remember the details of his face and dress even now. He was wearing voluminous white pantaloons, an embroidered waistcoat, and a little red cap surrounded by many turns of white cloth held by a gold pin. Three other men, dressed not quite so grandly, sat in the enclosure, watching closely and occasionally putting out a hand to hold a flying ankle. All the time Poumphrey watched, the Elder (there seemed no other word) was ministering to the boy, guiding his limbs, bending over him, trying affectionately to restrain him, lips moving in what was presumably an invocation.

Poumphrey was near enough to see the look on the boy's face. In spite of the twitching body and threshing limbs there was a kind of merriment in the eyes. He might have been playing some game. If Poumphrey had been in the place of the Elder he would have tried the effect of a sharp slap. Or a belt round the ear. Perhaps the old chap did when no one was looking. Perhaps he was not so holy and patient as he looked. And even if the boy really was having some epileptic convulsion Poumphrey would, in the Elder's place, still have wanted to belt him. He had a prejudice that people were responsible for their illnesses as they were responsible for the rest of their behaviour. A peculiarly modern prejudice, he thought, that was a damn sight less compassionate than the primitive notion of possession. Maybe the Elder believed in evil spirits and that allowed him to distinguish between the youth and his affliction. So probably he was as other-worldly as he looked and did not go in for any surreptitious beating up after all. All right! Poumphrey wasn't as holy as the Elder, he had never been a sucker for any of those ideas that transferred responsibility away from the individual. You are what you are because that's the way you want it to be. Telling this boy he'd chosen epilepsy was a bit harsh but deep down it was how Poumphrey felt about the world; and in that Elder's place he'd have wanted to try, at least, the effect of a little shock treatment.

He had never been a whiner. He was as ready to face this problem in himself. Something odd was going on, wasn't it? It was unlike him to fail a challenge. To run away. Who the hell was this old diabetic woman? Why had Jinny cried. Why did his guts ache? His mind was not focusing with its customary precision. There was some dislocation in reality he could not account for, not even when he reminded himself that, if he was to be consistent, he must believe he had brought about the dislocation himself.

By five he was back in the office with a throbbing belly and a headache. His secretary, used to his irregular hours, smiled calmly even though she knew he would now probably work through to midnight and try to keep her there too.

"There are quite a few messages for you, Mr. Poumphrey. The Chairman wants to see you. And Mr. Cooper at the Foreign Office wants to have a quick word. A Mrs. Grice telephoned."

"Mrs. Grice?"

"She's having a few people in for drinks and wondered whether you and Mrs. Poumphrey would like to pop round. It's this evening. Bit short notice, isn't it?"

"Had a row with Mrs. Poumphrey. Will you bathe the back of my head and put some plaster on?"

He had a theory that if a secretary was to function properly she ought to be aware of her boss as a human being. This meant she had to know about his private life. This one—what was her name? Judith!—had not taken the interest in his private life her predecessor had. Poor Pittikins had *loved* hearing him talk about his girl friends and money and what he thought about euthanasia and holidays and so on.

"If my wife rings tell her I'm busy." He sat in his little private wash-room while Judith went to work with the first-aid kit. He liked his wash-room. No other director had one. On the other side of that partition there was a shower and toilet. And here, in front of him, was the comfortable little couch where he had slept many a night after working late. The wash-basin was pink. The tiles in the shower were pink too.

"I left Mrs. Poumphrey down in the country. She's near Chichester. If she rings tell her I'm not here. She can come up on the train. There's a good service from Chichester. I'm not going home tonight. She'll be hopping mad. I'll just stay on here and work. I could sleep on that settee. I shall just go out for a meal perhaps. Somebody might want to come with me. You might ring Mitty. I'm very upset. Look at my belly!" He undid his shirt to show her. "You can't see much. Too much hair, but I had a real bloody thrust there. I thought she'd ruptured me. But I expect it's only bruised. Would you like to feel?"

"Mrs. Poumphrey did that?"

"No, it wasn't Mrs. Poumphrey." He didn't like Judith's tone. She might have shown more interest and sympathy. Was she as bored as she looked? Impossible. Her mind was on that idiotic husband of hers. Poumphrey had met him once at a party. He worked in London Transport and earned less than Judith did. Extraordinary mésalliance! Poumphrey had advised her to leave him more than once.

"On second thoughts I'll ring Mrs. Poumphrey," he said. He gave Judith Mrs. Abel's number. "I'll take it on the phone by the drinks cabinet."

He was drinking Scotch when the call came through, but it wasn't Jinny, it was Mrs. Abel herself and Poumphrey put his hand over the receiver while he shouted through to Judith, "I didn't want this old bitch. What did you put her through for?"

Judith did not reply.

"I want to speak to Jinny," he told Mrs. Abel. "She hasn't left, has she?"

"She's lying down. She's not well."

"There's nothing the matter with Jinny. Tell her I want to have a word with her."

"I'm not going to disturb her."

"Look, Mrs. Abel, I'm setting off in a few minutes to drive down and pick Jinny up. If she's unwell her place is in her own home."

"She won't come."

"Why not, for Chrissake?"

"She needs a little rest and attention. I wouldn't let her leave."

Poumphrey put the receiver down on her and went through to Judith's office. "Did you hear that? She's holding Mrs. Poumphrey prisoner!"

After a long silence Judith said, "I don't know what to say, Mr. Poumphrey. Is that the woman who struck you? She sounds very fierce."

The whisky seemed to have made him sweat. His heart thumped along like a robot in gum boots. If, instead of sitting in this bloody office, he was on one of those Japanese jets now one of those Nip hostesses would be mopping his brow with a hot scented cloth, and then maybe a cold scented cloth. Everybody was having sauna baths put in these days. He'd have one put in next week where that shower was. He'd have the whole wash-room torn out and a sauna put in. But he'd seen some chunky Finns in his time, some really fat ones, and they were supposed to take saunas all the time. They did not live any longer for it.

"Get Mrs. Grice on the line for me, Judith."

"Look, Elaine," he was saying some time later, "I've just had a row with my wife so we can't come."

"Reggie's away. It was just a few drinks for two or three people. Why not come by yourself?"

"Jinny's down in the country too."

"I'm very sorry to hear there's been a row."

"Some other time. I don't feel too well. Been in a bit of a shindy. Might go straight home to bed."

"It seems a shame, you being on your own and me being on my own——"

"Some other time, darling."

Going home did not seem such a bad idea, now he came to think of it. He lay on the couch for half an hour or so, getting his breath back and hearing the pace of his heartbeats slacken. He was cooling off. By now he realized it wasn't the whisky that had made him sweat, it was what Mrs. Abel had said on the phone. When he opened his eyes it was dark in the wash-room and he had to shout for Judith to come and switch the light on.

"I'm driving down to Chichester to get my wife," he said.

"What about the Chairman? And Mr. Cooper?"

"See you in the morning, gal!" he said with a show of blustering gaiety.

"Are you sure you shouldn't see a doctor?"

He had some idea of calling at the house to pick up a few clothes and other oddments for Jinny just in case she did turn out to be really unwell when he reached Sidlesham. But when it came to looking in cupboards and drawers he was baffled. He did not know what to take. He did not understand women's clothes. He found a nightdress, slippers, dressing-gown; and he was pulling a coat out of a cupboard when he thought, "What the hell, I'll bring her back here," and he replaced the night-dress, the slippers and the rest. He went down to the kitchen and fried himself some bacon and eggs.

He liked to keep two bottles of Scotch in the sideboard, a Bell's and a Glenfiddich, and the bottles were there, both empty. Jinny must have had another discussion group. They drank so much whisky, these blacks, he figured they actually needed hangovers. If it weren't for the hangovers they'd be leading gay, relaxed lives. If you were some kind of disaffected black intellectual that must be bad. You needed hangovers. You needed to keep the fires of resentment smouldering. He just wished they'd stick to their own national liquor, palm wine or whatever it was. He went off into the larder and found one last bottle of Bell's in the carton. He'd wait a couple of hours until the roads had cleared and then, with a bit of luck he'd be down there in not much over the hour.

Not tonight, though. He was too tired.

* * *

He was not surprised, driving straight into the yard at Sidlesham, to discover the side door open and to be able, as he had wanted, to enter the house without warning. He had an easy run down the A3. All the lights went green when he approached. Not much traffic about either. He felt better than he had all day. Not tired. He drove with both back windows down a couple of inches, enjoying the cool.

Mrs. Abel had lied about Jinny because there they were, the pair of them, in the sitting-room apparently playing Canasta. They were holding cards in their hands and other cards were spread out on the table in front of them. But the two women were motionless.

Poumphrey studied Jinny's eyes and Mrs. Abel's eyes but the lids did not so much as flicker. The light came from a standard lamp at Mrs. Abel's side. He looked at her big, swollen fingers and switched the light off abruptly. Then he realized there was a wall light. He found the switch for that, and then there was such silent blackness he might have been anywhere. No sound, not even of breathing.

He switched the wall light on again, and there they were, two seated figures in the palace of some Sleeping Beauty he had no idea how to find and waken.

"I'm here," he said. They seemed not to hear. Only he could speak. Only he could move. Doors opened for him but for no one else.

He picked up papers, ornaments, books, a pencil, and put them down again. "Nothing moves or changes. You understand?" He lectured them. Jinny had her lips parted as though to answer. Mrs. Abel had the beginning of a smile. It occurred to him they were sitting slightly differently.

A bowl of daffodils stood on a side table. He drew one out and took it, the stem trailing water across the card table and Mrs. Abel's forearm, to the light and studied the detail of the flower. It glowed. He prodded the stamens with his little finger and drew it out again, frosted with yellow.

"You're stopped," he said to Jinny and Mrs. Abel. "You're not going anywhere. There's no destination."

Naturally he worried about the reality of the experience but always in terms of why he had wanted it that way. He knew he was not dreaming. He was much too aware of himself physically for a dream. But he had just as much responsibility for what he had experienced as if it had been a dream.

He took a lot of pleasure in the way things looked. Flowers, shadows, hands. Because of the pleasure the experience seemed all very interesting, like a puzzle of some kind. He looked round for clues. Perhaps the pieces had to be moved. Perhaps a thread, if pulled would cause some masking fabric to fall away. But he just couldn't figure it out. He really was there in that house, and those two women were there too. But he was just too amazed to think straight. He felt Jinny's pulse. It did not beat. He tried to close one of her eyelids. It would not move. She was warm.

"Bugger you then," he shouted. "If that's the way you want it."

He walked out of the house, got into his car and drove straight back to London. Whatever this experience meant he was going to face it. But what did it mean? Why had his mind bent reality in quite that way?

There seemed even less traffic about than when he had driven down. Then he realized that what there was had stopped. Cars and trucks were all over the place, some right in the middle of the road, some half-way out of side streets, all with their lights on, quite normally. And there were people in these vehicles. When he realized nothing else could hit him he drove fast, thinking not of the frozen traffic and whatever apocalyptic explanation there might be for it but of Jinny. The night was clear, cold, dry. He was over Kew Bridge into Chiswick and on to Kensington, the Park, the West End. One thing at a time. When he had dealt with Jinny he would turn to the rest of the Universe and solve that problem too.

In front of his own house a porch light was burning.

The first moving object Poumphrey had seen for some time was his own front door. It opened in response to his ring (he could not find his key and rang even though he knew there was no one in the house) and the man who now stood in front of him was the same size as he was, on the fat side, with an untidy brush of greying hair, watering brown eyes, flushed face and an uncertain tremor in his voice.

"Ah, there you are," he said. "At last! Come in."

"Who the hell are you?" said Poumphrey. "This is my house. Is there something wrong?"

"The most extraordinary dream I've been having," said the man. "I'll tell you about it."

By now they were in the study and the man was just pointing to one of the leather chairs, as though inviting Poumphrey to sit there, when the door bell rang again and off he went to answer it. There were voices in the hall and Poumphrey stood watching the man and the visitor, a woman, through the open door of the study.

The woman who had come in was turning her excited face up to his—the man was so much taller than she was—and to the light. It was a long, almost boyish face. The hair was a bit dark to be called red, but it was red enough in contrast with her brown fur coat to make him think of a hunt; yes, the fox. Vixenish. Explosive.

"I told him I won't answer his questions. A man who questions his wife about her sexual behaviour can have no respect for her, or for himself for that matter. The least I expect is trust of that sort, and confidence in me."

"So you've had a row too."

Clearly the man did not want Poumphrey to meet her because he took her off to another room from where, after a while, he could hear them laughing and the clink of glasses. For something like half an hour, he supposed, he sat where he was, keeping the hall under observation; and sure enough they eventually returned, the woman no longer wearing the coat. They had their heads together. In fact, he had his arm round her waist and she had been trying to respond in the same way but her arm was not long enough. She just had to grip the back of his coat with her hand.

"Within the limits of what is humanly possible," the man was saying, "I try not to refuse a challenge or a relationship."

"Sounds a bit twentyish to me," said Elaine as they moved towards the stairs. "I like to be a bit more discriminating."

"As long as you realize my motive is not political."

"I don't think Reggie cares one way or the other. He's just the cold sort."

Poumphrey walked into the hall and looked up the stairs after them, jealous, angry and now—for the first time—frightened.

"Love," she said, a very, very, long time afterwards. "You call this love?"

No doubt it had been a mistake—tactless at the least—to mention love to her but he had wanted to preserve the usual courtesies.

"When you came in last night", he asked as they lay in bed, "did you notice anybody else in the house?"

"I thought you said your wife was away."

"Not a woman. A man."

She just rolled away from him and sat up, the red hair down over her ears, her breasts hanging. He did not cover himself either. He was still a bit sleepy and watched her through half-closed eyes.

"Why are you talking like this?" she asked.

"There was nobody here?"

"I didn't see anyone."

"The individual mind", he said, "is the last bit of nature left for us to tame."

She sat gently stroking her breasts and watching the nipples wobble. "I think that's silly. There's a drug for everything nowadays."

"No drugs for me."

"You're just fine," she said.

4

Damascus was dry, bright and warm. The weather suited him. He was fit and cheerful, to such an extent England seemed unreal. He had been through a rough time there, but he was all right now. Years since he had a nightmare but that is what he felt like, that he had wakened from some sweaty dream and he even thought of ringing Jinny in England to say he was all right. He'd had this idea she left him.

That evening the Embassy gave a reception for leading members of the Syrian Government, the representatives of I.P.C., of Murex, and for a small group of visiting British businessmen who happened to be in the city. No members of the Government put in an appearance. The Ambassador said he was sorry about this. It had happened before and would probably happen again.

"The President's an old friend of mine," said Poumphrey. "I'll give him a ring."

The Ambassador asked which President he had in mind. When Poumphrey gave a name the Ambassador said he had ceased being President six weeks before.

"Well, I'm bound to know the new one. Who is it? I know all these chaps."

"Any phoning that's done is done by me. No phoning will be done."

"I'll give my old friend Raouf Omra a ring."

"Who's he?"

"You don't know Raouf? Old friend of mine. Nice bloke. You know, that Palestinian lawyer in the Foreign Ministry. Cambridge graduate. Sister teaches in the American University in Beirut. Knew their father. I'm surprised you don't know Raouf, because he ought to have been invited, you know, because he's one of those men who are fairly junior on the face of it, but in reality——"

The Ambassador was taken over by a director of I.P.C. Poumphrey tapped him on the shoulder. "Jimmy, did I tell you there'd been a threat on my life?"

"Then you must look after yourself," said the Ambassador. "We don't want to lose you." And he walked down the room with his head close to the I.P.C. man's.

Poumphrey went off to the room where the switchboard was, looked up Raouf's number at the back of his diary, and gave it to the operator. "He's my Arab brother. I've lots of brothers in Arab lands but he's my special brother."

"I am your brother too," said the Chinese-looking operator who had a white fringed shawl over his shoulders. One eye was closed because of the smoke from his cigarette. "Take your call in the waiting-room, sir. It should come through in a matter of minutes."

"Hallo, Raouf," said Poumphrey a quarter of an hour later. Even when the number had been answered there was difficulty in locating the man. "Hi, there! What goes? This is Arthur Poumphrey. We've got a party on here at the Embassy. Why don't you come round? Hey, do you know what? Some bugger's threatened to shoot me."

After some hesitation the voice at the other end of the line said, "I am sorry I do not know you."

"Raouf? That is Raouf, isn't it? This is Arthur. You know. Murex."

"You must have the wrong number." His English was excellent. Not the slightest doubt it was Raouf Omra.

"It is not the wrong number. What's the bloody game? You are Raouf, aren't you?"

"Yes."

"Well, this is Arthur Poumphrey."

"I've never heard of you."

"Look, you are the Raouf Omra whose father was old Dr. Omra of Jerusalem?"

"He was my father."

"Then you're the Raouf Omra I mean. You know me."

"There must be some mistake," said Raouf, and put his receiver down.

Tired of sitting in the waiting-room Poumphrey had come out and seated himself at the switchboard operator's side. The man had gone on smoking his cigarette and reading. He must have known what was happening but he took no interest. This, to Poumphrey, seemed symptomatic of the Embassy's plight. Extraordinary that Jimmy should sit down under that snub from the Syrian Government. Extraordinary that a switchboard operator should be indifferent to what, quite plainly had been an intriguing conversation. The British in Syria were, diplomatically speaking, incurious and passive. They had infected this Mongol at the switchboard with their indifference. Or was he, Poumphrey, the one with the wrong responses? Maybe that voice on the other end of the line had been right. Maybe he didn't know Raouf Omra. The old, confusing, vapours began to rise about him.

They made him feel so unwell he had the fleeting, desperate idea of walking straight out of the Embassy on the chance this personal assassin he now thought so much of would be hanging around. If it was the last thing he did at least he'd have some assurance his senses were not playing entirely false.

He consulted his diary again and saw that in addition to Raouf's telephone number he had his private address. Raouf was a Christian and they exchanged Christmas cards. What the hell was the fellow playing at? They were old friends. They had been on binges together. Poumphrey just had to confront him and say, "Look, you can't mess me about like this. What are you trying to do? Are you trying to confuse me?"

The Ambassador did not live in the Embassy. His private residence was some distance away. This meant that his Rolls was parked outside, waiting to take him home (Poumphrey had noticed it on the way in) so he now made for the front door. He took a whisky from a convenient tray on his way through the party, swallowed it neat, and pressed on, out through the double doors and down the steps to the Rolls. The driver was half asleep behind the wheel.

"I want to go to this address in Salihiye. Take me there and wait for me. We shall be away no more than half an hour."

The driver took it the instruction had come from the Ambassador himself and a few moments later Poumphrey was being driven across Damascus behind a small Union flag fluttering on the radiator cap. If he ever became Foreign Secretary flags on ambassadorial cars would be twice as big.

There was difficulty in finding the address. The driver tried one street and then another. The night was black, moonless and starless. No street lighting in this part of town. After a while the driver said he thought he had found the place and Poumphrey, staying where he was, sent him to make inquiries. They had pulled up at a modern block of flats with a light over the entrance. Christ! he thought. If I look at him and know him, and he looks at me and doesn't know me, *and I know he doesn't know me*, then I'm in trouble. I'm in a psychic skid. I just won't know how to control it either.

Poumphrey looked up from where he was sitting in the back seat of the Rolls to see Raouf walk across the hall, push open the glass doors followed by the driver, and walk towards him. He was saying something in Arabic.

Poumphrey wound the window down. "What the hell d'you mean by saying you don't know me, Raouf?"

Raouf put his head inside the car. "Clear off, will you," he said in English. "You want to get me into trouble? Go away."

Poumphrey was just purring that Raouf knew him after all. So he wasn't crazy! Jinny hadn't left him. He'd had a rough time but everybody had a rough time and the main thing was the way he was now coming out of it. He wanted Raouf to climb into the car and drive with him out to Jebel Qassiun where they could sit and talk until the sun came up. From that height they could look down on the city and its oasis. Imagine the dawn coming up out of Arabia. Marvellous!

"This is the Embassy car." Raouf, suddenly realizing it, stood back. "You must be crazy to compromise me in this way."

"Why did you say you didn't know me?"

Raouf walked away, a bit drunkenly. He really might be tight or high and that would explain his behaviour. Poumphrey was on the point of opening the car door and going after him when Raouf turned. He pushed Poumphrey back into the car, climbed in beside him, and spoke to the driver in Arabic.

The driver turned and addressed Poumphrey. "He says drive to Prime Minister's office. O.K.?"

Raouf lost control at this and began shouting in Arabic and English. "To the Prime Minister! To the President! To the General Officer Commanding! I have nothing to hide! I will take you to the Government!"

He didn't seem tight or high, just frightened.

"You know me all right, Raouf," said Poumphrey confidently.

"I don't know who the hell you are! Why do you persecute me?"

"Well, maybe my brain is operating in some super-creative way. Maybe I've just invented the whole history of a relationship between us. Next week I'll invent a whole new universe." Poumphrey laughed noisily. "Take us wherever the gentleman wishes us to go," he said to the driver. "You stick to your story, Raouf. Maybe you're right. Maybe I'm a new psychic type being tested to destruction."

He wondered how Mrs. Abel would take it if an old friend said she just didn't know her. Fell him with her walking-stick, no doubt! Not immediately. She'd play along for a while, agreeing that, yes, they probably didn't know each other; it was all some curious mistake on her part. And then Mrs. Abel would test this friend. She would—oh, God knows what she'd do! Something frightful. And when this other person complained, Mrs. Abel would just say they weren't friends anyway, were they? And that would be the moment she'd fell him with her walking-stick. She'd jab him in the guts. Or her. Why wasn't he jabbing Raouf in the guts?

The night was so dark and the city so ill-lit Poumphrey could not pick out any familiar buildings until he saw the little domes of the Tekkiye floodlit on the other side of the Barada; and then, the driver turning down a side-street, they were lost among blank walls and huge, shuttered windows that seemed to rise out of the night like great kites as the headlights of the Rolls struck them. Raouf had lit a cigarette but refused to utter another word, so Poumphrey talked away and laughed.

The car pulled up in front of a cavernous doorway with a sand-bagged strong-point just inside. A soldier with an automatic rifle was talking to a girl, also in uniform. When he saw the Rolls he brought his automatic weapon up to his waist. The girl produced a small automatic with an enormous bore, apparently from inside her blouse, and they both strolled out on to the pavement. Other soldiers had appeared in the doorway. Poumphrey saw two armoured cars a little way up the street and guessed he must be somewhere near the seat of government. By this time Raouf was talking to the soldier and the girl. He obviously knew them.

"Come on in here," Raouf said to Poumphrey.

Poumphrey climbed out and shut the door of the Rolls behind him. "The Ambassador is going to be annoyed if he sends for his car and it isn't there. How long are we going to be?"

"I'd send it back if I were you."

Side by side they walked through the doorway, followed by two soldiers who seemed to be under instruction to kick Poumphrey's heels without actually bringing him down. They crossed a courtyard and walked down a succession of bare corridors lit at intervals by jumping neon strips.

"I'm sorry about all this." The apology from Raouf struck Poumphrey as odd, remembering the angry funk he was in, and that they weren't friends.

After some argument with go-betweens, all in uniform, Poumphrey found himself in a brilliantly lit room. Men wearing earphones were buzzing about and talking. A television screen in the corner showed what looked like a court martial in progress, but no words could be heard only military music—"Colonel Bogey", actually—on a tape that was being run a shade slowly. A drop in voltage, Poumphrey thought.

A Military Figure, wearing uniform, even to the cap, was sitting behind a huge desk, reading a newspaper and drinking coffee. No sooner had one of the attendant officials spoken in his ear than the Military Figure looked up, saw Raouf approaching out of the shadows, smiled and began clapping his hands. The talk stopped but "Colonel Bogey" went on.

Raouf held himself stiffly and looked at the ceiling. "Colonel Asraf, I am going to speak to you in English because this gentleman does not understand Arabic and it is important he should understand what I am saying."

The Colonel had a pillar-box red hatband and pillar-box red lapels. He had a golden cord and a tassel over his left breast and several square inches of medal ribbons; but none of this struck Poumphrey so much as the man's eyes, which were brown, humorous and friendly. I know you, they seemed to say. *I know all about you.*

But, by God! Poumphrey thought, I don't know you. The eyes are familiar but I don't really know you. Just say something to remind me. Give me a hint.

The Colonel waved towards a chair and Poumphrey lowered himself into it, sweating horribly. He must be in a TV studio. The temperature was over 100° F. The technicians crowded round. There was something about their smiling good-humour that promised they wouldn't hesitate to start transmitting the proceedings that followed; if they were interesting enough, that was. They'd put them out to the Syrian Arab Republic and Poumphrey was at a disadvantage because the Colonel knew who he was all right, judging by those brown eyes. But he didn't know who the Colonel was, unless—this was a crazy idea that came to him—he was Collison dressed up.

In spite of Raouf's opening remarks he had been talking to

the Colonel in Arabic for some time before he turned to Poumphrey and said, "Colonel Asraf is the head of my department and I thought it correct to introduce him immediately. He is a most important member of the Government. He knows all that is in my heart."

Or, if not Collison dressed up, something even odder. Poumphrey looked into Asraf's eyes with the idea that behind Collison and behind Asraf was some remoter personality who masqueraded as both. Who? This creature knew who he, Poumphrey, was. *He* didn't know who the being was who stood, in recession, behind Asraf and Collison. *Somebody* was there. Poumphrey understood what Raouf meant when he said Asraf knew all that was in his heart.

Raouf was still talking. "I explained that you came to my house uninvited. I told him this visit was preceded by a telephone call which much upset me. I call on you now to confirm that we had conversation of no significance. It was of no consequence, was it, sir? Now, what I want you to tell Colonel Asraf is why, not invited by me, you nevertheless insisted on calling at my home."

"Because you said you didn't know me."

"You thought this was untrue?"

"I've a feeling Colonel Asraf knows the truth of the matter."

Asraf had all the time in the world. He had been neither surprised, it seemed, to see Raouf burst in with a fattish Englishman in tow, nor was he now impatient to put an end to the interview. The way his mouth kept twitching under his little moustache he might even have been smiling.

He said to Poumphrey in good English, "If you did not know him why did you get in touch with him?"

"I didn't say I didn't know Raouf. Of course I know him. We are old friends. I don't necessarily think he was aware who I was. He said he didn't know me on the telephone. It sort of provoked me. That's all. Do you know who I am?"

The Colonel talked with Raouf in Arabic. He turned to Poumphrey.

"Mr. Omra says he does not know you and you appear to agree. You also say you know him. How can you know him if he doesn't know you?"

"I have an impression that you know me. I do not know you. I had experiences."

"What kind of experiences?"

"They wouldn't interest you."

Colonal Asraf removed his cap and showed he had a lot of curly grey hair. He had a tight little face, too now that it could be seen without the cap, and eyes like currants. The eyes, though, were what held Poumphrey.

"There are a number of possibilities," said Asraf. "Mr. Omra may have forgotten you. He may be lying. He may be suffering in his mind. Who can say? Perhaps you are lying. Perhaps you are suffering in your mind. Would you not like to tell me about the experiences. Mr. Omra says you claim someone has threatened your life."

Poumphrey could not remember having told Raouf this. But a man with those eyes would know. "I wouldn't think you'd be interested," he said.

The TV technicians moved back, more lights were switched on, Poumphrey noticed a red light appear on a camera. By God, they were transmitting. At the very least they were filming.

"I have observed myself from, as it seemed to me, a point outside my own body." This is what Poumphrey eventually said.

The Colonel, quite unsurprised, was writing on a large sheet of paper. A camera was focusing on the paper over his shoulder so presumably whatever he was writing was being transmitted to the entire country. They were taking a hell of a risk. There was nothing to stop him saying whatever came into his head. Such as the Colonel wasn't the Colonel.

"So", said Asraf, "when your friend, as you regard Mr. Omra as being, declared that he didn't know you it was natural for you to think you were once more experiencing some kind of delusion?"

"Yes."

"In fact he was just thinking his telephone was being tapped."

"I see. That hadn't occurred to me."

"As Eliot said, 'Human kind cannot bear very much reality.' Yes, I read poetry. I too am a graduate. We always arrive at explanations that suit our inner needs. Have you a family?"

"I'm married, yes."

"You have a son?"

"What goes on here?" Poumphrey was getting annoyed. Yes, he had a son. But Jinny didn't know. Mrs. Abel didn't know. Mitty knew, but that was the sort of thing he told Mitty and nobody else. The only other person on God's earth to know was the boy's mother. The boy didn't know, even. Now here was this poetic Colonel hinting that he knew, judging by the expression on his face. By now Poumphrey didn't give a damn about Raouf. He was too busy reacting to the aura of conspiratorial friendliness that Asraf was putting out.

Hell! It was as though they'd known each other in some previous incarnation. Not that he believed in that sort of nonsense.

"What goes on?" said Asraf in surprise. "Training."

"What training?"

"TV training."

"Who's being trained?"

"Me. Who else?"

Poumphrey said he'd better be getting back before the Ambassador missed his car but Asraf said that would be all right, they would send a message that he had been detained. "I didn't exactly invite you in, Mr. Poumphrey. Now that you are here, please go ahead. Interview me. Ask me any question you like. It will be good practice. The Jews put their case better in the West because they are better at television. Let us assume you are interviewing me for America or for England."

More powerful lights were switched on, a camera was rolled

forward and then withdrawn, everybody's face shone with sweat, coffee was brought in by one of those girls in uniform, and "Colonel Bogey" could be heard even more strongly in the background. They must have been playing it on a loop tape. Such was the heat, the blaze of light and the clouds of cigarette smoke the building could have caught fire and burned for some time without anyone in that particular room noticing it. A very fair, round-headed man in an ill-fitting suit came up to the table and began speaking in Russian. Poumphrey, who for some time had been addressing Asraf on the history of the Middle East from the Balfour Declaration onwards, stopped and cocked an ear. He knew a bit of Russian.

"He wants me to say something too," Colonel Asraf said when the Russian's remarks had been translated into Arabic for his benefit. "He is my producer."

"O.K. What point has the Syrian Government reached in its negotiations with the Iraq Government and with the Iraq Petroleum Company?"

"No comment," said Asraf.

"You can't duck out like that."

"Please do not shout," said Raouf, coming forward. "Please do not hit the table with your hand. The Colonel does not like it."

"I've had enough of this charade."

Asraf was drinking coffee and listening to what his Russian producer was, through an interpreter, saying to him.

Poumphrey stuck out his hand. "Good-bye, Excellency. I must apologize for my intrusion. Thank you for the courteous way you received me."

Asraf stood up. "I was interested in what you said about assassination. As Hobbes remarks, 'continual fear and danger of violent death; and the life of man, solitary. . .'. But you are not solitary. You have a son."

"Yes."

"So have I," said Asraf, his face lighting up in real pleasure.

Raouf, looking as stricken as ever, remained behind when

Poumphrey left with a soldier on either side. Poumphrey gave him a nod but there was no response. The Rolls had gone when he reached the street and this was not unexpected either, knowing what a fidget Jimmy was. He might well have come out in person to look for his bloody car.

The upshot of all this was that at Rome, where Poumphrey was breaking his journey on the way back, the Chairman rang up and said they were in a high state of excitement at the Foreign Office. Could he come straight to London and give the Board an account of what had happened in Damascus? The Chairman said he appreciated Poumphrey might be tired after all his exertions but Cooper had seemed almost hysterical on the telephone. The Chairman said his experience was that this kind of abscess needed lancing immediately.

"I'm not tired," Poumphrey said, a bit testily. "The only strain has been a murder threat hanging over my head. Absolutely nothing happened. You mustn't take any notice of Cooper. He has these manic phases. I expect it's this silly nonsense about the Ambassador's car. I only borrowed the damn thing. Anybody'd think I'd pawned it. Jimmy's a small-minded fool when you consider what I managed to achieve. Haven't these diplomats any bloody sense of proportion?"

"What do you mean, managed to achieve?"

"The new rate's agreed. The oil starts flowing on the 2nd."

"How much?"

"Ten cents a barrel."

"Christ!"

What a snoring, boring voice the Chairman had. He would be retiring soon and Poumphrey knew precisely what he would say to him at that farewell party. When the speeches were over and they were all filing past the old fool shaking hands Poumphrey would, when his turn came, smile and say, "It's been a great privilege working under you all these years. We've had our disagreements, of course. But I don't bear any animosity and I'm comforted by the thought I was always in the right."

"I wish I understood what was happening," the Chairman

was saying plaintively. "Did you say something about a murder threat?"

"Some nut. The Syrian Government is signing the new tariff agreement with Baghdad towards the end of the week. I fixed it. I saw Asraf."

"Asraf?"

"He's the real power in the Syrian set-up. I talked to him like a Dutch uncle. Don't let me keep you on the phone. Anyway, there's the news, from the horse's mouth."

"Horse?"

"Jimmy's pretty gaga, you know. I pretty well had to pinch his Rolls and drive to the Ministry."

"How much did you say?"

"Ten cents."

"That's highway robbery!" The Chairman put the phone down leaving Poumphrey with the further thought that at that farewell party he would so arrange it that he was last in line to shake the Chairman's hand. He would look into his eyes, holding his hand very tight, even hurting him a bit, and say, "We shall all talk about you a great deal after you've gone. More, indeed, than when you were actually with us. In many ways it will be difficult to do justice to your memory. But I expect, then, we shall be able to see the funny side."

He ought to have phoned Jinny from Rome, but he didn't. He couldn't summon up the nerve. There was no reply when he phoned from Heathrow and when he let himself into the house she was not there. He had a bath and went straight to bed with a lot of whisky inside him. He woke to find Jinny looking down at him. The time was just after two in the morning, as he saw from the bedside clock; so he reckoned she had come home, or had been there all the time.

It wasn't accurate to say he went straight to bed because in addition to the bath and the whisky there was the mail to be gone through. It was in the usual place, the top right-hand drawer of his desk, and although this *might* have indicated

Jinny was home and looking after him in the usual way there was just the chance the daily help had put the letters there. But he really thought Jinny was responsible. He really thought she was back from Sidlesham and out to dinner with friends, the Pughs most likely. He'd give them a ring. It wasn't fair to expect her to be on hand. She didn't know when he was due back. She was a good girl. She stuck by him. He couldn't be quite clear about his behaviour immediately before he went to Damascus but he guessed he must have played up a bit. His recollection was of something that common sense told him could not have happened. This meant Jinny must have suffered. At times like that it must have seemed to her she was married to some sort of drunk. The house seemed to have no air in it and he went about opening windows. He looked at the rooms carefully. No changes. Just as he remembered them.

Among the mail was a blue envelope addressed in a hand he did not recognize. Poumphrey fancied himself as a graphologist. A woman, he thought. That big, rather wobbly hand indicated an emotional and possibly unstable nature. The ink, though, was rather pale. It did not stand out against the blue envelope. What did this mean? It gave off a slight smell of—what? some spice? vanilla? A domestic personality, then. The letter might even have been written in the kitchen. As for the lack of contrast between the colour of the envelope and the colour of the ink, that could only indicate the passionate nature of the writer was something she wanted to be discreet about.

As he had supposed, the letter was from Elaine Grice.

Dear Arthur,

I have this very clever psychiatrist, Fred Generaille, who wrote that marvellous book, *Schizophrenia and Games Theory*, and I told him about you, without mentioning names, of course. Do see him, darling. Let me know and I will arrange it. He's not at all the conventional head shrinker—not that your head wants shrinking, but you know what I mean. He'd be so interested in you *as a person*.

And guess what! Reggie's got to go before a Committee

over his nomination and I've got to go with him so that they can cast an eye over me too. Talk about Susannah and the Elders! Reggie's pretty sick because he thought the nomination was all tied up but apparently there's been some sort of row.

Does that mean that you and Mrs. Poumphrey will be appearing? What fun! They are not terribly permissive in East Dene as I expect you know, so there's not much chance they'd get confused and pick you and me, or Reggie and Mrs. Poumphrey. I mean, they'd probably want to consider us as we are now.

Fred is very interested in insanity and that's what I'm really writing about. He wants to meet you, dear. Please let me arrange it. Give me a ring and if I'm not here Reggie is working at home these days and would take a message.

Love,

Elaine.

When he woke and saw Jinny looking down at him at two in the morning the recollection of this letter, once his mind had cleared sufficiently, came back to him and he put out a hand for Jinny to take and to hold and to steady him.

"I got back," he said hoarsely, sitting up.

"Yes." Her eyes were inflamed, she blew her nose all the time and the stringy muscles in her throat trembled when she held her head still, making her look more like a worried mare than ever. She must have come straight in from the street and was still wearing her musquash over her green dress.

"I went back to the Pughs after a show."

"I'm getting up."

She told him not to be silly but he said he'd just put his dressing-gown on. Maybe she'd make a cup of tea. He'd like to talk. He wanted her to know he was thinking of seeing a psychiatrist.

She went off to make the tea, telling him to stay where he was and she'd be right back. When she did come back, still wearing her musquash and carrying a tray with cups and a pot of tea and the rest she made no comment on his mention of a psychiatrist. He thought she hadn't heard.

"Last time I saw you you were down at that woman's," he said.

Jinny poured out a cup of tea, added milk and handed it to him. "If Mrs. Abel weren't such a Fascist she'd be a really wonderful person. We disagreed about the future of South-West Africa."

"So you didn't stay long?"

"No. Do you know she actually killed a man by not warning him about a rattle-snake in America once."

"What did you do? Did you walk out on her? How did you get up to Town? Did she hit you?"

Still wearing her musquash Jinny was sitting behind the tray with a biscuit in her left hand and a cup in her right. The house was very quiet. No traffic noises came from outside. The night pressed around them, absorbing their whispers, the creaks, the tinkle of a spoon.

"Apparently he was a friend of her second husband and he was making a pass on the very lip of the Grand Canyon. She *saw* this snake and didn't warn him. So when it bit him he fell over."

"I don't believe it."

"It's what she said."

"Anyway, that's not killing a man. And I can prove she's not my mother, either."

"Oh, she's just marvellous," said Jinny. She gazed in front of her with what he thought was a silly smile on her face. "I think she's awfully intelligent. But she's no heart. Her affections are undeveloped."

"Why don't you ask me about Damascus? What's the matter? Aren't you interested in me any more? Don't you love me?"

"Love you?" She blew her nose in the usual melancholy way. "No, I don't love you. In fact I think I've always hated you, rather, ever since I first set eyes on you."

He laughed because he knew she was joking. "Then why did you marry me?"

She was laughing too, in a melancholy sort of way. "You were determined to marry someone."

"Don't deceive yourself. I'd only have had to lift a finger and you'd run. You loved me. And I loved you. Now what are we?"

"What's all this about a psychiatrist?" she asked.

"I loved you," he said. "I would never have married somebody I didn't love. Don't you understand that? Don't you understand the sort of man I am?"

"Yes, I think so."

"I'm having a bad time."

"What's the matter with you?"

"There's nothing the matter with me. I just want to tell this psychiatrist something."

"Tell him what?"

"About my experiences."

"Why?"

"They may be of scientific importance."

Jinny said nothing for some time and did not even blow her nose. She got up and examined one of the curtains as though for signs of wear. He looked at her thin, middle-aged, middle-class face and noted the glint in her eyes that indicated the damped down fires of Liberal optimism. What had it done for black Africa? Nationalism, self-determination and bloody chaos. The trouble was that Jinny had no sense of reality and no imagination. She took a desire for the betterment of everybody and everything as evidence that betterment was possible and, indeed, taking place. But she didn't *look* at the world. She'd have been completely flummoxed by the kind of experiences he had gone through in Damascus. She just didn't know such people existed. She wasn't stupid. She was just an old-fashioned English Liberal. If the dawn came up in the west one morning she'd either not notice it or think the solar system was being improved.

"Are you depressed, or something?" she asked.

He snorted. "No, wrong psychological type. Too extravert. Something much more interesting. I recognize people I don't know. That sort of thing."

"You're all right," she said. "It's just male menopause."

"No, no, Jinny, you're wrong about that. Don't take yourself as the measure of all things. My mind isn't really playing me tricks. There really *is* something queer going on."

"I'm very tired," she said. "I'll go and sleep in the other room so that we don't disturb each other."

She kissed him. When she had gone he fished Elaine Grice's letter out of the pocket of his pyjama jacket and read it again. Generaille didn't sound an ordinary quack. He had written a book. Poumphrey thought that in spite of his view the trouble was out there he might as well see Generaille while the experiences were still fresh in his mind.

The question was, though, whether he ought to see Generaille before or after the appearance before the constituency committee. Another letter in the pile—he didn't come to it until after breakfast some hours later—raised the question sharply. After, on the whole, he thought. He just wanted Generaille to confirm he was normal and that could scarcely be regarded as a matter of any urgency.

On the notepaper of the East Dene Conservative Association, dated May 4th, 1968, he read:

Dear Mr. Poumphrey,

I have been asked by the Association to invite your attendance at one of a number of special interviews the Constituency Committee is holding to decide on the nomination of our parliamentary candidate in the forthcoming by-election brought about by the regretted death of our sitting member, Mr. Frederick Scott, M.B.E. A number of people are seeking the nomination, yourself among them.

We hope you and Mrs. Poumphrey will find it convenient to attend the sitting at 7.45 p.m. on Friday, May 20th, at the Clarence Hotel, West Box, where a room has been reserved.

The Committee very much hope that Mrs. Poumphrey will be able to take part in the deliberations. If the time is not convenient for you and Mrs. Poumphrey we shall naturally be glad to arrange another one, but clearly there must be no delay. The date of the by-election has not been set but it can scarcely be later than the beginning of July.

Should you not wish to be considered for the nomination we should naturally like to hear from you as quickly as possible, but we hope this will not prove to be the case. We are anxious to nominate the strongest possible candidate and although you have had no parliamentary experience you are active in international business. Some people would argue that experience of the latter is more important than the former these days, but anyway the Committee feels it would like to see as many strong runners in the field as possible. Refreshments will be served.

Mrs. Poumphrey's presence is particularly desired. I am sure you will agree Frederick Scott represented the constituency very vigorously and that his wife had a lot to do with this. We want another good husband and wife team, particularly if the wife is ready to take an active part in the social life of the constituency. So we hope Mrs. Poumphrey will not mind the Committee asking questions about her private interests.

I expect you know Mr. Gutteridge has retired as Chairman and that his place has been taken by Mr. Arthur Plaistow.

Yours sincerely,

Dictated by Sean Pretty, *Agent.*

Signed in his absence by Joyce Cook, *Secretary.*

Gutteridge retired? He couldn't swallow that. Gutteridge had been thrown out. He had mucked up the nomination issue. No doubt bringing in young Grice had been entirely his own idea and now that the Committee had looked at him and had time to reflect on the matter they had clearly decided a mistake had been made. Grice wasn't strong enough. They also recognized they had a commitment, in honour, to Poumphrey. This stuff about an appearance (with wives!) before the Committee was to save Gutteridge's face and was exactly the sort of manoeuvre Plaistow, whom he knew of old, would get up to. The nomination was going to him, of that Poumphrey now had not the slightest doubt.

Incidentally, it was characteristic of Pretty that he was too idle to sign his own letters. Poumphrey would have to speak to Plaistow about him. Plaistow was all right. He had some coarsely right wing ideas but practised a certain delicacy in human relations and it was like him to avoid an open humiliation of Gutteridge, much though he may have deserved it. Plaistow had been a soldier, then he had gone into the family haulage business, but he had a rich wife too and that was the main thing about him. What he really wanted was a candidate prepared to send the blacks back to where they came from. The British electorate was not ready for that kind of racialism, not yet anyway, and Plaistow would have to be told so.

"Jinny," said Poumphrey just before leaving for the office, "East Dene have decided to offer me the nomination after all. There's some formality about an interview, with wives and that, so you'll have to come. But you'll keep your mouth shut about Africa, won't you? I don't want you talking politics."

"I'm not appearing before any committee," said Jinny, as soon as she had understood what he was talking about.

"We could always say you were ill, I suppose."

"I wouldn't wish to deceive them."

"Look, Jinny, I can't stop and argue now. You won't let me down, old girl."

"If it's a formality what does it matter if I'm there or not?"

"These games have got to be played according to the rules. It's only a formality *if* you turn up, see. You're still an impressive-looking sort of woman, Jinny. Talk about anything but race relations! Look, there's a bargain!"

"I'm not coming," she said.

"You bloody well will," he shouted as he went out, slamming the door. Frankly, he didn't like this nonsense about wives, being interviewed. It implied the Member would carry on intense socializing in the constituency after he was elected. Perhaps it was not too late to phone Plaistow and talk him out of it.

* * *

And yet, in the Board room, as the rest of them talked, he looked at the Chairman and thought—ambition, striving, life, what does it all amount to? They had been discussing some piece in the business section of *The Times* and copies of the newspaper were scattered over the table. Poumphrey picked up the one in front of him and turned to the announcements of Deaths. Nobody there he knew, he was mildly disappointed to note, not even the Chairman.

When he thought of Sidlesham nowadays it seemed that after some profound rest the world was starting up again. The budding trees, caught in his headlights, actually moved. And when he walked into the house Jinny, in her shiny black suit and Mrs. Abel in her old rose gown looked up from their game, but with extraordinary slowness. He stood there for hours waiting for the heads to lift sufficiently for the two women to see who he was. The playing cards were brilliant in the light of the reading lamp. A tremendous yellow and red fire burned in the grate. A half-consumed log lay on flaring coal, flaring because of the wind. Currents of air flowed through the house, the carpet lifted, the air and the smoke streamed up the chimney; and the two pairs of eyes, the women's eyes, were fixed on him and they showed surprise and annoyance to see him there.

"So that's about the measure of it," said Lowther, looking straight down the table at him. "We're sorry. We're all sorry, every one of us."

All these Board members were looking at him. No, Drew wasn't. He was doodling. That strange-looking man with a lot of white hair was Todd and he, now Poumphrey came to look at him, had his eyes closed like a corpse.

"Sorry, Arthur," said Lowther.

"Subject to a satisfactory financial arrangement," said Pugh, still doodling.

* * *

There were chaps who shut themselves up, or went on long walks when they had decisions to make. That was not his way. He liked company, food, drink and a randy atmosphere when he had to make his mind up.

So he booked a table at the Savoy that evening and told Mitty he would pick her up about seven. He could not bear to be in the same house as Jinny, not after the row they had had that morning, and now there had been this further row in the Board room he could not wait for the lights, the music, the good food and Mitty's thigh, fleetingly, under his hand. To his annoyance she was wearing a trouser suit when she opened the door.

"Christ! They won't let you into the Savoy like that. Go and put something else on."

"Oh, Gogo!" she said, delighted. "You didn't say we were going to the Savoy."

While he waited he smoked a cigar to kill the smell of cooking that always seemed to hang about the place. A man was only really alive when he was happy; that was the moment for making decisions. They might err on the generous side but it was a noble weakness. Christian, in a way. He was not a religious man but he enjoyed thinking he bore himself like a man of faith. After dinner was the best time for sorting things out. A man with an excellent digestion like his could take the long view when he had the right food and the right drink inside him. And Mitty! Hell, she just inflamed him. From the rational point of view she was a silly little bitch, but there was something about her that inflamed him and made him decide. Yes, by God, he'd do such-and-such a thing tomorrow.

She came out with her hair sticking up all over her head in some kind of wet-looking new coiffure. And she had bigger eyes than ever, they were ox-like. She was wearing a furry, silky, brown gown with black flaps that came over the shoulders from the back. Very red lips. The vampire effect made him hold his breath.

"I know what you think of me. I'm just a sexual object," she said in her pegged-nose manner as she half-heartedly defended herself in the back of the taxi. "Anyway, I haven't see you for three weeks. Where have you been?"

In the light from a shop window he could see the tip of her tongue flicker across her teeth. He had never known a small woman with such big tits and the realization made him snort and try to put his free left hand up her gown. It was too long. He couldn't find the end of it. She giggled. "You don't think of me as a real girl with a family background, and that. Say something, Gogo! You really are moody."

"Are you a virgin?"

"How dare you!" she said. "Of course I'm not!"

"I only asked."

"Gogo, you sometimes treat me as if I knew nothing at all."

"How did you lose it? I mean, you had many men?"

"I don't ask questions about you and women."

"You're not jealous, like I am." After he had said it he realized he had spoken the truth. He just hated the thought of Mitty being had. Why the hell was she spoiling his evening by telling him things like this? It wasn't as if he loved her. If he loved her he could have forgiven her. She excited him, she made him feel competitive, and it just hurt to learn someone had beaten him to it. "You didn't love them, did you? Or him. You weren't in love?"

"Of course I was. I wouldn't get physical with anyone I wasn't in love with."

She shocked him so much he allowed his right hand to fall away from her shoulder. *Get physical!* What a prissy way of talking. "I love you. You know that, don't you? And you love me?"

"Yes," she said.

"Well?" At the best he would be second. Or third. Or fourth.

Surprisingly she kissed him on the cheek. "I like you, Gogo. You know that? Don't be angry." He could not understand why she was giggling so much her whole body seemed to be shaking. And it was queer how, even though he did not understand and in his heart thought her a bit silly, she made him feel helpless with lust. She isn't even beautiful, he thought, as the taxi turned into the Savoy cul-de-sac.

"I've been abroad," he said over the drinks. "That's why I haven't been in touch. Then what happens: You negotiate an agreement, the oil flows, and you come back and you find a conspiracy. I had one hell of a Board meeting this afternoon. They turned on me like a lot of wolves. They tried to kick me out."

"Oh, goody! That'll give you lots of free time. I've never been here before, Gogo." She looked around, showing her crossed teeth in a smile of gratification. "It's really lovely and it was sweet of you to bring me here. The last time we had dinner together do you remember what you said? You said you were going to be re-born. I said you needed a mother for that. Remember?"

"Yes. Fancy that now!" He stared at her for some time. "You really did say that, didn't you?"

"Well, I mean, what happened? You *are* reborn, aren't you, sweetie?"

"I don't know what I am."

"You look so young."

"I'm not old, Mitty. I wish you wouldn't talk like that." On an impulse he took his wallet out and extracted a letter. "This is what happened, in a manner of speaking."

The lamp on the table gave such a dim light Mitty had to hold the letter quite close to the bulb to read.

" 'Dear Edward,' " she read. "That's not your name."

"It's my re-birth name."

" 'Dear Edward, When grown men behave like children I

always suspect their upbringing. Childhood is an unfortunate state that should be escaped from as soon as possible. The view that children should be indulged and confirmed in their childishness means very often that the attitudes of the infant are perpetuated in adults who are afraid to shoulder their responsibilities. If only I had been allowed to enjoy the bringing up of my own child he would, from the beginning, have been treated as a little man. It would have been the best way of ensuring that he did not grow up into a big baby.

" 'In certain societies womenfolk are allowed to withdraw from the tribe at certain periods to lick the wounds of their femininity. You trample on us. I am not referring to your boast about the way you would gain ascendancy over your rival for the East Dene nomination, though that is disgraceful enough. I do not wish to bring up once more your terrible involvement in the death of poor Mary Collier.'

"I don't understand, Gogo. What is this all about?"

"Go on reading."

" 'What your wife and I suffer from is what all women suffer from—male hardness, lack of inwardness, greed. We had an intruder the other night. He left the back door open and there were muddy footmarks on the carpet. The signs were unmistakable. Nothing was taken, but we know there was a man in the house. Jinny thinks we may have left the door open ourselves and the footmarks are old ones. But I know we had a visitor, and this is what it is like to be a woman. She feels she has endured a visitor who has left his muddy footmarks and gone, unfeelingly, away. Yours sincerely, Edith Abel.'

"I don't understand all this, Gogo. Who is Edith Abel?"

She had read the letter clearly and well, pronouncing the words with deliberation but with an upward inflection of surprise every three seconds. She was amazed.

"You're not hard and greedy, Gogo."

He took the letter back, studied it for a few moments and then tore it into small pieces which he then placed in the ashtray.

"You say yes to life," he muttered. "And what happens? You get a kick in the pills."

Above the tinkle of glasses and conversation he heard an unmistakable rhythm coming from somewhere on the other side of the hotel. He wanted to dance.

"But who wrote that letter?"

"It's from a diabetic old girl who hit me with her stick. Did you notice that bit about footmarks?" He rapped the table with his knuckles. "That's the interesting and important bit. Have you noticed anything wrong, Mitty?"

"No, what do you mean?"

"The world functions? You haven't noticed anything strange happening?"

"No. What sort of things?"

"The way it all looks, like some sort of film that's cracking up and falling apart. You know?"

"No."

Although Mitty had not finished her drink (one of the irritating things about her was her abstemiousness) he dragged her to her feet. "That's bouzouki music," he said. "Let's see what goes on."

They found a Greek music and dance troupe in one of the rooms off the main restaurant and Poumphrey said, "Let's go in here. Let's sit here. Hey, waiter, bring us some champagne. We'll sit here. No, that's fine. We can see the show fine from here."

There were three musicians and a team of six dancers, young men in black waistcoats and trousers holding hands and kicking their legs out stiffly, like figures in a frieze. Poumphrey was delighted. They ought to have been drinking ouzo, not champagne. He clapped and began shouting at the dancers in the few words of Greek he knew. They waved at him and smiled. Some time later they were prancing through the room with their outstretched arms on each other's shoulders. Poumphrey had taken a couple of glasses by then. It was hot in the room and he was thirsty. He seemed to be sprinkling sweat on everybody.

"Mitty, let's dance."

"I had a very light lunch. This drink is making me dizzy."

"I'll dance by myself then," Poumphrey could smell the aniseed alcohol and see the snow-flecked mountains folded one behind the other northwards into the morning dazzle towards Olympus.

"You're not supposed to be dancing, Gogo. People are staring. I shall go home."

Poumphrey stood up with a glass of champagne in his hand encouraging the dancers in broken Greek. He would have liked to take them all into his confidence. He would have liked to tell them about the row in the Board room and the muddy footprints on the carpet, but only a drunk would have done that and he was not a man to lose control.

As soon as Mitty talked of going home he realized she was frightened and sat down immediately, patting her hand. "We'll go and have something to eat immediately. I'm hungry too."

Was it true she was no more than a sexual object? He could buy a woman any night without having to take her to the Savoy and tell lies about loving her. *That* is what he would have understood as a sexual object. But Mitty was different. He put himself out for her, humiliated himself, confessed to her, told her about his bastard and even now, not more than a few minutes ago, he had told her about his resignation. Mind you, he wouldn't resign. They hadn't the power to force that on him. He'd go to the shareholders. But the point was he'd told Mitty about all this. You didn't talk to a sexual object that way.

"I shouldn't have destroyed that letter," he said. "It contains important information about certain natural phenomena."

He was feeling intolerably hot. There ought to be better ventilation in a place like this. He said they'd have oysters. Or whatever else Mitty wanted. If Elaine were there she'd have loved oysters but Jinny would have taken smoked trout. Mrs. Abel? Vichyssoise. He'd give a dinner for these women one day and observe the way they talked and what they ate.

You could learn a lot about women that way.

Going to the Grill he ran out of breath, stumbled and fell, first to his knees and then toppling sideways. He lay with his cheek to the carpet inspecting shoes, black and glossy, silver, gold, in a vista running away to a smoky horizon. Not like Greece. Mitty screamed, so he rolled over on to his back to get a sight of her.

"I'm all right. I'm just a bit tired."

Mitty was on her knees trying to put an arm under his head but he said, "No, leave me alone. I'll be all right in a minute." He could not for the moment remember where he was. Except for the copious and unpleasant sweating he felt utterly relaxed just as he would have been after a deep sleep. He could not move, nor did he want to. Somebody, not Mitty, a man in a white tie and medals who reeked of after-shave lotion, was trying to undo his shirt front.

"This heat," Poumphrey said. "I'd be all right out of this heat."

Mitty was whining anxiously but he could not make out what she was saying. Where were the other women? They had been there a moment ago. Jinny would have known precisely what to do and it was extraordinary she was not doing it. By now he was beginning to think someone had hit him. Could have been Grice. Then why hadn't Mrs. Abel stopped him? She could have felled him with her walking-stick.

He was picked up by four men who found him so heavy his behind repeatedly struck the floor as he was conveyed into a private room where he was placed on a settee. The rest of the furniture was under drapes. There was even a drape over the chandelier which, as a consequence, gave out a dull, dreamy, wobbly glow.

They had his collar and tie off by now and this man with the medals was listening to his heart. He had his head to Poumphrey's chest.

"Get off, damn you," said Poumphrey. The man's head was intolerably heavy and what was more he had a moustache as big as a loofah. Poumphrey did not like the feel of it against his bare skin. He was so angry he pushed the fellow away and tried to sit up. But the dizziness defeated him.

"Mitty, afraid I'll have to go home. Get a taxi, there's a good girl."

"There'll be an ambulance along in a minute or two," said somebody else. Poumphrey did not want an ambulance. He would be perfectly all right in the fresh air. Had they got the fellow who felled him? Was it Grice?

"Nobody hit you, Gogo." Mitty was on her knees with her cheek to his. "You went terribly white and then very red and all shiny. But you look a lot better now."

"Bit out of condition," said Poumphrey. "I'm terribly sorry to have spoiled your evening."

"Darling Gogo, I'm taking you home."

"You with him?" This man with the moustache was probably some retired Medical Corps man in for a reunion. "Well, he ought to see a doctor when you get him home. Has he had anything like this before? Or wouldn't you know?"

"Somebody hit me, I tell you." Poumphrey could sit up now. He drank some water and sat with his head dropped between his knees.

Two ambulance men with a stretcher came in and wanted him to lie on it. In a moment they had it made up like a bed with a white pillow and scarlet blanket. Poumphrey stood up, with the assistance of Mitty and the Medical Corps man. A bunch of keys and money fell out of his pocket. People scrambled about, picking them up and restoring them to Poumphrey's outstretched hand, while a waiter did his shirt front up. "Sorry you chaps have been brought out on a false alarm. I'm going home now, in a taxi, with this lady."

And this is what he did.

It had been raining. The black road glistened and winked. Mitty had the window half down to let in the cool night air and they might have been floating through polished tar that shattered into crimson, sulphur and sapphire stars; traffic lights, he realized. A watery coolness in the back of the cab made him shiver. Raindrops slid on the windows and he wanted to stop them.

He forgot he was ill. He forgot where he was and said, "Let's go to the Caprice. You always liked the Caprice. I don't know why we went to the Savoy. Look at the river, I suppose."

"I'm taking you home, Gogo."

"I can't see a thing now. Isn't it hot?" It amused him that silly little Mitty was showing so much concern. "I wasn't tight, you know. I'd only had a couple of gins and that champagne. Just a glass or two. I don't think I'm ill." A thought struck him. "You can't come into the house. I mean, my wife'll be there."

"We'll see."

In the event Mitty had to run up to the front door—it had started to rain again—and ring the bell. The driver stayed in his seat until Poumphrey, who had now gained the pavement, showed evidence of staggering away up the path without paying the fare. Then he came out smartly and Poumphrey rested a hand on his shoulder. By this time the front door was open and Jinny was standing there in her burgundy kaftan with gold trimmings.

"There is no need for alarm," said Poumphrey. "I have had either a heart attack or an epileptic fit. However, this young lady——"

He walked firmly up the steps and into the hall. He could tell by the expression on Jinny's face that he must look awful; a blazing, sweating, face no doubt, his shirt burst open at the collar and his tie dangling. Even Julius Caesar had attacks like this. He wouldn't have taken any bloody nonsense from his women. But times had changed.

"Pay the taxi, there's a dear," he said to Jinny. "I passed out in the Savoy. I thought I was dying. This is Mitty, if it's any business of yours. She's not a virgin, in spite of appearances. But *I've* had no success. You'd better call the doctor."

It amused Poumphrey that these two women, who did not know each other, should put him to bed. He was very tired or he would have made more resistance. They actually undressed him, they stripped him pretty well naked, and he didn't resist that either. He sat on the edge of the bed while Jinny, on her knees before him, worked his legs—hairy as a spider's he thought—into his pyjama trousers. Mitty was wiping his face with a flannel dipped in eau-de-Cologne.

Women were queer, weren't they? you wouldn't imagine men, similarly placed, behaving in the same way. If Jinny, for example, had come home with some fellow—but, then, that was unimaginable. Put it like this. It was remarkable Jinny wasn't asking questions. Who is this young woman, etc? And it was odd Mitty hadn't cleared off immediately she had seen him indoors.

Mitty was still there when the doctor, who happened to be Rogers, a personal friend living near, arrived and went over his chest with a stethoscope. He examined Poumphrey's eyes very carefully. He waved his finger about and asked Poumphrey to follow it, first with his right eye and then with his left. Eventually he cleared off, saying he'd be back in the morning.

That left just Mitty and Jinny.

"I nearly died, Jinny." It was not often he gave her any delight. This was the nearest he had got for some time. What a funeral she would have given him! How she would enjoy it! He knew her imagination was racing ahead. What flowers! What a cortège! What a service! What thanks for sympathy!

"Think you'll be able to sleep?"

"No, can't sleep. Somebody, Grice I reckon, clobbered me."

"You know very well that's untrue. Ian Rogers examined your head and there isn't a mark on it."

"I didn't see anybody hit him," said Mitty. She began to cry at last. "I don't want him to die."

"I was nearly gone." Poumphrey thought he really must be ill. He was too far gone even to mind that Jinny was already planning his obsequies. "The four queens came for me."

"What four queens?" Jinny, sceptical as ever, had to pitch her voice above Mitty's whimpering.

"It was just as though I was lying in a dark boat with four queens. I was resting my head in the lap of one of them. She was Morgan le Fay."

"There were only three queens," said Jinny.

"No, four. You, Mitty, Elaine and Mrs. Abel."

"Who is Elaine?"

"Mrs. Grice."

"Quelle galère!"

"There were no other women," said Mitty, "nobody he knew, that is. I didn't see any queens."

"They were wearing crowns, all four of them," said Poumphrey from his bed, "and I could hear lake water lapping by the shore."

The rain had started again and the wind drove it spluttering against the window, Later, Poumphrey heard the two women talking to each other. "Jinny", he said with some difficulty, "I'd like you to know I've been asked to resign from the Board. They're annoyed the way I went ahead without consultation."

She was silent for a while. Then he heard her say, "That really is something of no consequence, isn't it?"

"Don't soothe me. It was a fast moving situation. How could I consult? I'm not dying now. Sorry to disappoint you but I've done my dying for tonight. Jinny! Can you hear me? They criticized my way of negotiating in Damascus. Don't go away. Resigning from the Board *is* of great consequence. I'll not resign."

"I've asked Miss Flavers to stay for the night and she's going to."

"That's nice of you Jinny. Isn't that nice of her, Mitty? She's my wife, you know. Have I introduced you?"

"Mrs. Poumphrey and I have introduced ourselves," Mitty said, having pulled herself together and sounding ten years older. "Do you want me to stay with you, Gogo?"

"I want to see Mrs. Abel."

He thought he heard Jinny promise to send for her.

5

At first Mrs. Abel would not come, and when she did come—bringing some elegant purple leather luggage—she was given the big first floor bedroom, *their* bedroom, because with her leg she couldn't climb any higher. The only other room of any consequence on that floor was a sitting-room and it was convenient for her to have the use of that too. Jinny went up to one of the small bedrooms on the second floor and Poumphrey—when he came out of the London Clinic—installed himself in the attic studio. Even when Poumphrey was well enough he could not have left the house without Mrs. Abel knowing. And neither could anybody visit him without her knowing. She had her bedroom door open even when she was in bed. And she asked for the light on the landing to be left on. She was nervous, she said, in a strange house. She couldn't understand why Edward should want her about the place and that made her nervous too.

The tests carried out on Poumphrey at the London Clinic were mainly negative, and this did not surprise her. He was thirty pounds overweight but, as she pointed out, you didn't need a clinic to tell you that. A bit of blood-pressure, but that she had taken for granted too. A salt-free diet was prescribed, gentle exercise, cut out all starchy foods, no drink, that sort of thing. This amused Mrs. Abel because she prided herself on her medical knowledge and nobody could tell her this regime was the best the twentieth century could offer. She wanted him to go to the States for a real check up. The inability of Rogers and some specialist he had called in to find anything radically wrong made her contemptuous.

Rogers said perhaps he had been working too hard. He showed marked signs of stress. At one time it might have been said he was having a break-down.

"Break-down," said Mrs. Abel who sat in on all the consultations and was now called Mother by Poumphrey. "I don't believe in anything so vague as a break-down, Dr. Rogers. There is something physically wrong and if you were a little cleverer you would discover what it is."

She also took the line that Poumphrey was on no account to resign from the Board because she had private information (the source of which she could not disclose) that Poumphrey was the victim of a conspiracy involving not only directors of his own company, but the directors of another big oil company and one of the most respected merchant banks in the City. If his health was ever restored he must investigate this very seriously. But of one thing she would not hear, and that was going on with this attempt to get the East Dene nomination. Parliamentary democracy was a sham. It was quite wrong to go on using up nervous energy pretending otherwise, particularly when in all probability he had some serious organic defect. (Had the Clinic thought to examine his pancreas? It was often overlooked!)

Mitty had already left the house before Mrs. Abel arrived but whenever she rang up to ask how Poumphrey was it seemed to be the case that Mrs. Abel always answered the phone, and what she usually received was a rebuke. "If it hadn't been for you the boy would never have been disporting himself in that absurd way." Mitty giggled to hear Gogo spoken of as "the boy". She was very good-humoured about Mrs. Abel. She had the idea she was Gogo's very rich and religious aunt, though she wouldn't have known quite why she thought this. Anyway, the old girl would naturally be annoyed at the part Mitty played in Gogo's life and it was perfectly in order for her to show it. Jinny was sweet. She wasn't jealous even though she'd been unable to have any kids.

Mrs. Abel liked the house. It had once been lived in by a

Victorian artist called Pennyquick and it was he who had turned the attic into a studio. Poumphrey had stereo equipment up there, a bed, a wardrobe, a chest of drawers, and very little else. Leading off the studio was a bathroom. Except for food, which Jinny brought up on a tray, he was self-sufficient. He could lock the door if he wished. At the foot of the flight of stairs, on the floor below, was another door and he could lock that too. So he mostly did not leave the attic. Rogers put him on sedatives.

He liked the way Mrs. Abel seemed to have taken over the running of the house. He didn't resent her any more and he was pleased that Jinny, too, accepted the ascendancy Mrs. Abel had established. In spite of what he called their philosophical differences they got on very well and the more Poumphrey thought about it the easier it was for him to regard her as though she really was his mother. The knowledge that she was there brought reassurance. He was not normally the man to need reassurance. Perhaps it was because he couldn't be aggressive when he was ill and she was aggressive on his behalf.

He told her the thought had occurred to him he might have a tumour on the brain and she laughed until the tears actually trickled down her puffy cheeks. Poumphrey, watching her carefully, had given short barks of delight.

"Oh dear! the human body," she said. "It's grotesque. Look at me and think what my pancreas is doing. We're the victims of our bodies. It's so absurd what our bodies do to us you've just got to laugh. You haven't a tumour, of course. Even Rogers would know that."

"If it weren't for insulin I suppose you'd be dead."

"Yes." That made them laugh once more. "Reggie Grice telephoned and said he wanted to come and see you. I said he might. I don't encourage visitors but if Mr. Grice can talk you out of attending this absurd interview with Jinny I'm in favour of him."

He loved to sit in his black leather armchair with his head back gazing through the northern light. Pennyquick must have made money too. He had removed most of the roof to have this great window constructed. Poumphrey looked up at the sky listening to his radio or L.P.s with the volume up: Wagner, Brahms, Strauss. He lay with his feet up, watching the clouds and listening to the music belt out, thinking that any moment now he would understand everything—life, death, suffering, love, God, the lot! As he listened to Siegfried's Funeral Music it occurred to him he had reserves of generous feeling still to be drawn upon. Why was he not more often seen with these tears of compassion in his eyes?

"Reggie Grice?" he said. "Wonder what he wants. I'd like you to be on hand when he calls."

She was usually present when the few visitors she permitted had climbed the attic stairs. She herself took two or three minutes for the ascent, pulling on the handrail and giggling at the way she had to drag her right leg after her. The stairs were too narrow for either Poumphrey or Jinny to give much assistance.

"I should like to speak to you privately," Grice said when eventually he came some days later. He looked at Mrs. Abel who was sitting in the armchair while Poumphrey paced about restlessly. "It is a bit embarrassing."

"Come off it," said Poumphrey. "Mrs. Abel can't go clambering about the place."

"It's about your wife, I expect," remarked Mrs. Abel unexpectedly.

Grice looked startled. "Yes, it's about Elaine. I just called to say it didn't mean anything."

He was younger than his wife, just a lad of thirty, clear eyed, clear skinned, and clean. He still had his narrow-brimmed grey hat in his hand and he wanted somewhere to put it. Lacking any guidance from Poumphrey he found a chair and sat down, hitching up his striped trousers and looking around with a nervous, almost quivering smile on his face. He had dark brown hair with a touch of red in it (like Elaine's) and a slightly cracked baritone voice, not properly under control. He really was Grice. He had the brown eyes but they were spaced wider apart than Collison's or Asraf's; and they hadn't the same knowingness. Anyway, there was no evidence anyone but Grice was present and looking out of that skull.

"I heard you were ill so I thought I'd call round and say, about Elaine, that whatever you might think, there was nothing in it." He had a habit of running his forefinger across his mouth and he even talked when he was doing it. "Elaine told me you were ill."

"What doesn't mean anything?" Mrs. Abel was always impatient with vague statements.

"Well, I love her, you see," said Grice still smiling uncertainly in the way, no doubt, he would have smiled on the scaffold.

"Politically that is very astute of you." Even Poumphrey thought this remark of Mrs. Abel's a bit unfair but Grice ignored it.

He just went on smiling, and said, "It's about my wife, really, and bed, and all that, and not wanting to attach too much importance to it."

"Bed?" said Poumphrey.

"Sexual intercourse," said Grice after a struggle.

Poumphrey stared at him. "You can't frighten me with legal jargon. What's this got to do with me?"

"Elaine sleeping here when your wife was away."

"What gives you this idea?"

"She told me. Oh, please don't get upset. She always tells me. She's very sweet and honest about it all. It doesn't really matter, that side of it. What I'm really trying to say is this. Has it not occurred to you that it might be seriously disadvantageous to both of us. If Plaistow got to know, I mean." He looked at Mrs. Abel. "Please excuse me. Mr. Poumphrey and I are competing for the nomination at East Dene. Tory," he added as an afterthought.

"I have advised him not to go on with this nonsense. What with one thing and another. Do you mean your wife's a whore?"

"No, I don't mean that," said Grice, not smiling now and talking quietly.

Poumphrey broke in. "But you said she always tells you. What does that mean?"

"I can assure you", said Grice, "that so far as I am concerned there is every reason for observing considerable discretion. If you are still seeking the nomination you have cause, in your own interest, to see there is no scandal. And if you are not seeking the nomination you would presumably have no motive for doing anything that would affect my chances."

"He is not seeking the nomination," said Mrs. Abel.

"I *am* seeking the nomination," said Poumphrey. "You've got to admit, Grice, that if this business came out it would be more to your disadvantage than it would be to mine."

Mrs. Abel said, "Excuse me, I've just noticed the time," and drew a syringe from her handbag, made various adjustments to it, lifted her skirt, rolled down her stocking and gave herself an injection. She did not stop talking. "I prefer to take my daily dose at this time rather than any other. You must both beware of being led into excited remarks you will later regret. Edward is withdrawing from this election business and it was very wrong of him to be manoeuvred into any claim to the contrary." She put the syringe away.

Grice had averted his eyes from all this. "Perhaps the state of your health will put a different complexion on the matter, Mr. Poumphrey."

"I'm all right."

"I suppose", said Mrs. Abel, "that what sharpens the issue is the way the constituency takes an interest in the wives of the prospective candidates."

"Constituency committees are always interested in a candidate's domestic set-up. And on the whole I'd say they'd rather have a Member who does it than a Member who has a wife to whom it's done." Poumphrey rattled this off as thought it was ancient doctrine.

"But neither would be very satisfactory, would it, Mr. Grice?

Would you like a cup of tea? I'm afraid you'd have to go down to the kitchen and make it yourself."

"There's some coffee in that flask, actually," said Poumphrey.

"I'm all right, thank you. What you say might have some relevance if there were only two candidates for the nomination. But there are others. My point is that a scandal would probably exclude the both of us from further consideration."

"Did Gutteridge's resignation have anything to do with the Association changing its mind about you? My information was you'd got it."

"Plaistow said there'd been a shake-up."

"Certainly! They realized they'd made a mistake. They wouldn't give you the nomination now whatever view of your wife they took. So far as your wife's conduct has any bearing on the Committee's decision it affects my chances, not yours. You're out of the running."

"Naturally I do not take this view." Grice had started smiling and drawing his forefinger across his mouth again.

"I haven't the pleasure of knowing your wife, Mr. Grice, but she obviously wouldn't wish to be talked about behind her back in this way. Probably you treat her badly. Edward treats his wife shockingly. Most men treat their wives shockingly. Your accusation about her behaviour might be entirely unfounded. It is unfounded, Edward?"

Poumphrey wanted to give an honest answer to this but when he recalled the events of that particular day and night they presented themselves first in this form and now in another. To begin with, for example, he remembered Mrs. Abel and Jinny standing quite motionless in the Sidlesham sitting-room. Then, when he thought of the visit again, it seemed that the two women had started to move. There was even some doubt in his own mind, now, whether he had actually entered the room or had just looked in through the window from the garden. The night with Elaine was a bit clearer but he could not swear to what had happened.

"You have no right to ask that question," Poumphrey replied.

"I have but I don't need to ask it," said Grice.

"She's probably teasing you, Mr. Grice, and if you ask me it is absolutely what you deserve. If you really believed her—but perhaps you're a Catholic?"

"Madame," said Grice after a silence of perhaps half a minute while he wiped his face with a handkerchief and then used it to polish the toes of his shoes. "We haven't been introduced and I feel at a disadvantage."

"Mrs. Abel is possibly my mother," said Poumphrey shortly.

"You don't know for sure?"

"We haven't had time to discuss the matter in any detail."

Mrs. Abel opened her handbag, saying she had letters and photographs—but no, they were not there after all. She would find them. The truth could be established quite quickly. There were certainly some remarkable coincidences. So much had emerged from earlier conversations. No doubt they would get down to comparing notes in a more businesslike way when Edward recovered, if he ever did. Sometimes it was pleasanter not to establish the truth of a situation. A satisfactory relationship always had an element of ambiguity in it.

"To a lawyer this is incomprehensible." Grice looked from the one to the other of them with a kind of alert blankness on his face. He thought they were laughing at him. "Since you ask me, I am not a Catholic. But I have no intention of divorcing Elaine. She is well aware of this. You see, with her sex doesn't go very deep. I didn't want Poumphrey, here, to think he was anyone special so far as she was concerned."

"All balls!" Poumphrey exploded.

Mrs. Abel sighed. "So you *are* telling us your wife is promiscuous, Mr. Grice."

"She can't help it, poor dear."

"Now that, Mr. Grice, is very insulting to her and I can't allow you to speak in that way."

"It's bloody insulting to me, too," said Poumphrey, "I hope everybody realizes that."

"I don't want to upset you", said Grice, "but you really must understand there is no future in this for you. She's had hormone treatment, she's had analysis, but nothing steadies her. You mean absolutely nothing to her. The relationship, from her point of view, is totally without significance."

"This is not the way I see the relationship, nor myself, for that matter."

"It's the truth." Grice stood up, ready to leave. "Stay away from her, will you. Face reality."

"Reality? Me?" Poumphrey was outraged at the suggestion that he, rather than Grice, had his head in the sand. "I'm having an affair with Elaine. I like her. She likes me. How dare you vilify the relationship!"

"Elaine and I love each other very much, you see," said Grice with dignity. "Nothing is going to affect that. Nothing is going to come between us."

"What a dreadful man," said Mrs. Abel when he had gone. "He is prepared to blacken his wife's reputation for political expediency."

Poumphrey, too, had been shocked by Grice's behaviour but he wanted to be charitable. "I don't know that it's deliberate cunning. Self-deception, more like, I'd say."

"You mean he can't help it?"

"He's living in a dream world."

"All self-deception is deliberate, Edward. You and I, at least, should know that."

* * *

At about this time Jinny was busy trying to help her African friends raise money for a trip to Addis Ababa where a Cultural Congress was to be held the following autumn. Taxi loads of blacks were always rolling up to take over the ground-floor dining-room where they drank gin and talked in low, deep, tones while they wrote endlessly in huge notebooks. Jinny was all the time running upstairs to see if Mrs. Abel was all right when these parties took place. Mrs. Abel was usually watching television with the volume right up. Poumphrey, in his attic, would also be playing records as loud as he could. The Africans complained about the noise and tried to get Jinny to stop it; and when she didn't succeed they took to singing and guitar playing.

It was during one of these evening sessions that Fred Generaille arrived for the first time and was sent away by a tall Senegalese intellectual who opened the front door to him and did not believe his story. There was no Mr. Poumphrey living in that house, only a Mrs. Poumphrey who was too busy to see him at that moment. In fairness, Generaille looked rather scruffy. He was about fifty, wore jeans, had a mop of grey hair and wore a shabby suede jacket over a string vest. When Jinny discovered what had happened she sent the Senegalese up to Poumphrey, to apologize and to learn that his hostess did indeed have a husband.

Jinny had the theory that if only she could get poor Arthur away to Ethiopia she could go to the Cultural Congress, while he travelled about the country and be all the better for it. Mrs. Abel thought it would certainly achieve more than a course of instruction from Fred Generaille, whom she had observed arriving and departing from her sitting-room window. But she didn't want to press her views. She was too frightened by the presence in the house of all these black men and women to be able to think clearly. So Jinny hired a room behind the local Congregational chapel.

* * *

"What would you say if I told you I had a tumour in the pancreas?" Poumphrey asked Generaille when eventually he called.

"You haven't."

"Or cerebral syphilis?"

"That's a possibility," Generaille agreed. "But it would be

kid's stuff. You wouldn't need me for that. I take it you're virile?"

Ever since his collapse Poumphrey had been worried by just this. Nothing could make him randy.

"Strong and easily held erections are the essential male characteristic," said Generaille. "A good jet when you pass water? Excellent. That's all right then. That seems very satisfactory." He walked round Poumphrey inspecting him from every angle. "You known Mrs. Grice long? Mrs. Grice is my patient. Frankly, I am not seeing you in your own right, so to speak, only as part of the evidence concerning Mrs. Grice."

"What's her trouble then?"

"Excuse me, that is a matter between patient and physician."

Generaille had refused to allow Mrs. Abel to remain in the room while he talked to Poumphrey. He said he would leave immediately unless she did. There had been a freak snow shower in the night and the snow was thawing off the roofs and gutterings, dripping from the trees in the garden outside. But you could not be sure what was snow and what was blossom. Thin vapour rose from the sodden white lilacs. House martins flashed about. The sky was blue.

"Make yourself comfortable," Poumphrey remembered saying to Generaille, even as he was thinking there was Chinese blood in this man. He had the eyes and sulphurous complexion. "You've never worked, I imagine, as a telephone switchboard operator in the British Embassy in Damascus?"

"No." Generaille said he normally did not visit patients in their own homes and he would not have done so in this instance but for Mrs. Grice. His relationship to her might have been adversely affected by a refusal to do as she wished. He had discussed the case with Dr. Rogers who had raised no objection. They agreed the visit would have no effect, one way or the other, on Poumphrey himself, but it might have favourable consequences for Mrs. Grice.

This time Generaille was wearing a boldly flowered cravat

and a baggy tweed suit. "What seems to be the trouble, as they humorously say."

"Nothing very much," said Poumphrey, "but I've been seeing the same individual turn up in a variety of guises. The last time he was a Syrian general."

"What's wrong with that? Maybe the same person *is* turning up in a variety of guises. Elaine said you'd been flying through the air."

"How the hell could I fly through the air?" He told Generaille about his trip down to Sidlesham and how it had ended up when he found himself in bed with Elaine.

"How did you get on with your father?" When Generaille smiled he showed red gums and black teeth. "I want to know about your family background. Is there anything unusual about your relationship to your mother? Can you remember any striking incident involving a sibling? That sort of thing. Forgive the old routine, but it *is* rather important, don't you know?"

"This Mrs. Abel", Generaille remarked when Poumphrey had told him something of the background, "quite possibly holds the key to the whole strange experience. Is she your mother or is she not? The answer to that question is, of course, of less importance than the fact that you were separated from your mother at an early age. All your life you have had this unacknowledged sense of loss." He was seated at Poumphrey's side making notes on a piece of blotting-paper. "Your father had a beard, you say. Did he grow the beard before or after your mother had left him?"

"I don't believe in this approach," said Poumphrey.

"I'm sorry, it's the only one I know. Have you had any delusions that involved Mrs. Grice?"

"Only this one about coming back from Sussex and seeing a chap go upstairs with her and the next thing I knew we were in bed."

"The three of you?"

"No, Mrs. Grice and me. I *was* this chap."

"Oh, Gawd!" Generaille moaned. "That makes it difficult. I'm not actually saying you're lying, of course, but it does make the whole thing difficult. Shall we get back to Mrs. Abel? On reflection I suppose it doesn't matter whether she is your mother or not provided you both believe she is."

All the time Generaille had been talking Poumphrey stared at a decanter with a couple of inches of whisky in it. He concentrated on the regular pattern of glass lozenges into which the sides of the decanter were cut, and thought, "Am I really looking at a glass decanter with a couple of inches of whisky in it?" At the very moment he was pitching into some abyss of self-awareness he also knew that he was being accompanied there. Or watched. Not by Generaille. He was still writing on the blotting-paper with a yellow pencil and seemed to be on a different plane of reality.

Poumphrey had been losing himself in the coruscations of light patterned by the decanter and the more he was lost, or fell, the stronger grew this sense of someone else being present. He thought of his father and his father's bad breath. He remembered sitting on his knee while his father drew an orchid on a sketching-block. He remembered the angle of his father's jaw under the thin beard and the bad breath. He could smell it again, as he went falling. Now he knew exactly what the experience was. He was on the Big Dipper with his father. He was screaming with fear while his father laughed, with his arm around him, spraying this stinking breath over him. It was a treat, for Christ's sake!

"Frankly", he heard Generaille saying, "I don't think there's anything the matter with you at all. You seem quite normal to me. Pity Elaine's got this frigidity thing."

"Frigidity?"

"Oh, Lord. Did I say frigidity? Well, yes, that's part of it, don't you know. What's that thumping? There's somebody coming up the stairs."

Mrs. Abel pushed open the door and came into the studio carrying her stick with the rubber ferrule. She was wearing a blue linen suit with a cameo brooch in her left lapel. And she stood there in the doorway with that Cheshire cat smile on her face, saying, "I've read your book, Mr. Generaille, and I don't believe a word of it."

"So you *are* the Mother Goddess," said Generaille when Poumphrey had introduced them for the second time that afternoon. "*Very remarkable!*" He walked all round her as she stood leaning on her stick, inspecting her rather as he had inspected Poumphrey earlier. "Of course she only begins as a fertility figure. As she matures she becomes a symbol of death."

"I don't know what you are talking about."

"Oh yes, you do," said Generaille coolly. "You can't fool me."

"Edward, what have you been telling this man?"

"Not very much, so far as it concerns you, I mean."

"You must have done. I know when I am not wanted." She would have left but Poumphrey caught her by the elbow.

Generaille shrugged. "You ought to let her go, old man," he said. "There are more ways of being killed than by suction back into the womb." Having picked up his coat and the blotting-paper he was himself on the way out. "Toodle-oo, old horse! We all wriggle but we never quite escape. We all want to be unborn."

The conversation with Generaille left a confusing back-wash and as a result Poumphrey made a mistake. He thought he was locked in. He wasn't but that was the way it seemed to him when he rattled the door and tried to open it. The lock was a big, old-fashioned sort you might find on a shed door. The key was huge but it was just not there. It was not lying on the floor. The door was an inch thick and on the other side was a cork backing covered with green baize. Strange about the key. The wood must have warped or swollen and that was why the door stuck. To Poumphrey, though, it did not seem it had stuck. He was locked in and somebody had made off with the key. Even if he shouted they wouldn't hear him downstairs with all that sound proofing. He had no extension phone in the studio. What the hell went on? What if the house caught fire?

He had no immediate wish to leave the studio but the thought he was trapped there made him want to get out as soon as possible. Who had made him a prisoner? Mrs. Abel? Jinny? Serve them right if he climbed out of the skylight and killed himself.

By putting a chair on a table he could in fact climb up to the skylight. It was on a swivel and by pulling a rope he could open the window wide enough to escape through, once he had climbed so high. He stood, one foot on the chair, the other foot reaching up to the window frame while he grasped an iron bar which ran the whole length of these lights and about nine inches away from them. There was another one, parallel to it and about a yard away. Pennyquick must have used them for supporting drapes to control the light. Anyway, the one Poumphrey hung on to gave him enough leverage to swing his legs through the open window. He sat on the frame, after a struggle, with his heels on the slates, looking down into the road eighty feet or so below and across to the row of houses opposite. The air was cool and sweet, just what you would expect on a May evening, moist, a slight reek of blocked gutterings and warm tar.

Poumphrey laughed to himself a bit because if he slipped he was a dead man and the pills left him so confused he did not know whether he was sitting or floating. What other member of the Board would have the guts to do what he was doing now—climb out of a skylight, roll over, grip the window frame and extend his legs delicately downwards until he could feel his stockinged toes in the wet guttering? He was wobbling a lot of flesh. Sweating heavily. What if he passed out? The sun had set. The sky was red.

Getting out of this predicament was not so difficult as might be supposed because once he had worked his way along to the end of his own skylight he could pull himself up to the roof ridge, sit astride, and look straight ahead, through a window of the house next door which had been built up a storey higher than his own house, and where a man in white overalls in a brilliantly lit but nakedly empty room was slapping pink paint on the wall and smoking a cheroot. He turned and saw Poumphrey.

From up there on the roof ridge there was a marvellous view. The evening was pink and soft. The tops of the trees, down below, stirred and puckered in the wind. He could see the Heath right down to the Vale of Health and lights swinging up out of the gathering darkness of the valley. He could see across London to the lights of Surrey.

"You all right?" said the man with the cigar, having come to his window.

"I live here," said Poumphrey. "My name is Poumphrey." He had lost weight since getting out of the window.

"I live here," said the man. "I do my own decorating these days."

"It's always safer", said Poumphrey, "to go climbing in stockinged feet. I've known bad accidents result from men insisting on shoes."

"I often wondered where all that music was coming from," said French. "You have it on real loud, don't you?"

"I got locked in," said Poumphrey, as French helped him into the room, and they stood inspecting each other. "I couldn't attract my wife's attention. Nasty, if there'd been a fire."

French was in his forties, with one of those new handlebar moustaches, so closely cropped they looked as though they were painted on. "My wife's expecting. This is the nursery. Pink for a girl. Be a sod if it's a boy."

French took him down through the house. He wanted to lend him some gardening boots but Poumphrey said he liked walking about in wet socks. A really ancient man with a stoop came out of the bathroom as they passed. French introduced him.

He also introduced the *au pair* girl who was watching TV in the first-floor sitting-room. And Mrs. French who was peeling potatoes in the kitchen.

"Mr. Poumphrey came in over the roof. He got locked in his attic."

They were all amazed. Noting this, Poumphrey became amazed too and when he arrived at his own front door, which he found standing open, he wanted to find someone and say to them, "I've had the most amazing experience." But there seemed to be nobody about. He looked in the kitchen. He went up the stairs. Mrs. Abel was in neither her bedroom nor her sitting-room. He called Jinny. The house was deserted. He was still so astonished by his escapade that he had no room for rage. He staggered a bit as he climbed the stairs. What did it mean? Why should anyone want to lock him in his room and then go away?

The door at the foot of the stairs leading to the studio was certainly unlocked because it opened immediately. He was not too put out by this but when he had climbed up to the door of the studio itself and he was able to open that without having to unlock it he bounced into the studio. There the table was and the chair on top of it under the open skylight and the purple evening sky.

But there, sitting in his own black leather chair, was a man he did not know. Opposite him on the straight back chair with her stick across her knees was Mrs. Abel. A spot light lit up the wall behind them.

The suit did not look like one of his but Poumphrey did not doubt he was to repeat the experience of seeing himself from the outside—as he had seen himself talking with Elaine and going up the stairs with her. There he now was in the black chair! And here he also stood, just inside the door! This time he was going to watch what followed with close scientific attention.

"Mr. Todd called to see how you were," said Mrs. Abel. "I brought him up. Where have you been to?"

"Lo there, skipping about, eh?" said Todd, waving a big bunch of fingers.

Poumphrey was certain the man in the black chair was himself. He was standing way back *here* in the doorway looking at himself *there*. He was over *there* in the chair, looking towards the door and talking to—well, who? The relationship between speaker and listener was so uncertain it was not easy to know what to do next. Ordinary conversation was difficult.

The man—or whoever it was, he himself, maybe—stood up. "Not the normal way to meet a colleague for the first time. We were talking about you at a Board meeting this morning and I thought I'd call and introduce myself. We seem to miss each other at meetings. I'm a new boy."

Poumphrey began looking at the man hard now. He was not tall but he was solid. Under that dark business suit was a lot of meat. If he trod on your foot you would know it. Rugger full-back in his youth. He had dark eyes and a moustache of the old-fashioned sort you saw on pictures of Edwardian soldiers, full but ending with the corner of the mouth. High cheek bones, big, white, banana-like fingers.

Poumphrey thought, "He's not me! He's definitely not me."

The eyes were brown, though.

Asraf? He wondered. Collison? Who stood behind all these men? Whose were the eyes? The bastard knew everything. He talked and it was clear he knew about the ten cents a barrel, he knew about Raouf, he knew about the Foreign Office being bloody annoyed, he knew about the call for Poumphrey's resignation.

Poumphrey accepted he would never have spoken to himself in this way. This really was some other guy. If Mrs. Abel said he was Todd, well, that was as good a theory as any.

Todd went on talking. They were standing in the middle of the studio looking at each other from a distance of about four feet, with Mrs. Abel sitting in her chair, her stick across her knees. She was studying his feet and stained clothes.

Todd said how pleased he was to see Poumphrey up and

about. They were all keen to know how he was. Could the Board do anything? What about a trip for Mrs. Poumphrey and himself? Somewhere warm and sunny—Bermuda, say.

Poumphrey looked at Mrs. Abel. "The door was locked. Where's the key?"

"You've got wet feet. What *is* the matter with you, Edward?"

"I was locked in."

"Locked in?"

"I climbed out through the skylight."

"But the door wasn't locked. We came straight in."

"Then where's the key?"

"Why didn't you bang on the floor?"

"Do you think I'd be crazy enough to climb out of the window and over the roof if there'd been any other way out?"

"Out of this window?" asked Todd, looking up.

Mrs. Abel remarked coolly that it was a well-known fantasy experience certain people went through, locking themselves up, in boxes and things.

"I didn't lock myself in," said Poumphrey.

"Some people actually go so far as to tie themselves up," said Mrs. Abel, "and conceal themselves in small cupboards." She turned to Todd. "My second husband once got himself locked in an earth closet in Arizona. He panicked, just as Edward panicked. The door had warped. The door really had been stuck."

Todd mentioned a scheme the Board had for postponing Poumphrey's resignation so that his pension would be bigger. Poumphrey's mind was on other matters but he said he was going to fight the Board all the way. He was going to circularize the shareholders. Lowther would certainly know he had been in a fight.

"Let's not talk about it now." Todd was preparing to leave. "I must apologize for mentioning the matter in your present state of convalescence. But I'm really glad to hear you talk like that. It's what I'd hoped for."

Poumphrey came back from the bathroom where he had

been changing his socks and drying his feet. "That door was locked. I know what goes on. Do you think I'd climb out of the window and over the roof just for a lark?"

"The supposition that anyone would deliberately lock you in is morbid," said Mrs. Abel.

"I'm not morbid. I know what goes on. Let me tell you this, Todd. If you were sent round to soften me up I'm not your man."

"Who is really behind this move to get Edward out?" asked Mrs. Abel.

The talk about the way he had behaved in Damascus was a blind. The truth was they were frightened of the way he kept advocating a merger with Parthian. Bigger men on the Board would have seen it was an inevitable piece of rationalization. But look at the quality of these men! It amazed him that people like Wainwright or Peel could sit where they did. He honestly thought if you picked up the first two men you met in Leadenhall Street and put them on the Board you could scarcely have done worse. Now that he was sure Todd was Todd and the figure in the dark suit was not one he would find himself inhabiting Poumphrey shot all these words in that direction.

Lowther was a mouthpiece. He was incapable of formulating any ideas of his own. Drew was direct. If Drew had been behind the opposition Poumphrey would have known how to deal with him. He was open and direct. Might go and talk things over with Drew. Nightingale? Too worried about himself to get tough with other people. That left Todd. What about Todd?

"Mr. Todd is your friend," said Mrs. Abel.

Poumphrey felt tired. "I have no friends. I'm not finished. I'm not quitting Murex. The shareholders will vote for me. And I'm getting the East Dene nomination. Did you know that, Todd?"

"I'd like you to know you and I might see eye to eye about Parthian." Todd really was going now.

"I'm not afraid of anybody on the Board. If anyone tries to fence me in I break out."

"That door, I repeat, was not locked," said Mrs. Abel.

Poumphrey was so relieved he hadn't turned out to be the man in the chair he was really elated. Brown eyes? That was nothing. He could live with brown eyes. He was confident success was his for the taking.

Todd waved his big wrinkled fingers at the head of the stairs. "Good to meet you at last, Poumphrey. I've an idea you and I are going to get on fine."

"Nice to know somebody else has a few heretical thoughts."

"It's what the Company needs," said Todd.

A few days later Poumphrey learned there were five men and one woman on the short list for the East Dene nomination but what he did not know was that the new Chairman had it all fixed for an insurance broker called Partridge. Even if Gutteridge had stayed as Chairman it was unlikely Poumphrey would have got the nomination. Gutteridge thought he drank too much and, what was almost as bad, lacked high-mindedness. He said he was one of those money-minded Tories who got the Conservative Party a name for self-interest. Admittedly it had taken Gutteridge some time to tumble to all this, but when he did there was Grice, a young lawyer who was son of a landowner in Herefordshire. This was the tradition Gutteridge believed in—property and the due observance of contracts. So Grice was Gutteridge's man.

The rest of the Committee thought this estate agency view of politics a bit out of date. Even so Gutteridge might have hung on if he hadn't been such an anti-drink fanatic. Meetings always took place in his house and the only refreshment was tea or coffee. He himself drank a malted milk preparation and as time went by he became more and more insistent the others should drink malted milk too.

So when Gutteridge caught flu and the meeting was switched to the Clarence everybody had a gin and tonic in the bar first before going up to the committee room. Here a revolution took place. They did not discuss any of the Gutteridge subjects.

They spoke about trade union legislation, the level of taxation, and a new ring motorway the Ministry were going to drive through the constituency. Plaistow had three bottles of Scotch and some Malvern water sent up. At the end of the evening it had been fixed he should take over the chairmanship; and Plaistow had let it be known he favoured a man called Partridge as their new candidate.

Partridge was an insurance broker who also happened to be son-in-law of a leading member of the Shadow Cabinet. Plaistow had ideas, which he kept to himself, about the way a Member with family connections could shift the ring motorway out of Plaistow's front garden to a point two or three miles safely to the south. The motorway would not be built for at least four years. A General Election was due within the next eighteen months. And after *that*—well, the son-in-law of a Minister might be in a position to get the bloody ring-road out of the constituency altogether. What had Grice to offer in comparison with that? Or Poumphrey? All Plaistow said to the Committee was that Partridge was a future Minister, like his father-in-law. He had ability and he knew how to sell it.

To show that everything was fair and above board Plaistow was in favour of the Committee interviewing a short list of candidates and their wives. He'd like Poumphrey on this list. It had always been on his conscience they might have treated Poumphrey badly. The fellow had been led to suppose he was the next Member only to be disabused at Fred Scott's funeral. The chap had been humiliated. No criticism of Mr. Gutteridge was intended, but there should have been other ways of communicating the Committee's views to a man who had been nourishing false hopes. Plaistow spoke like that, and he had a watch chain. He wanted to be humane. He was even ready to wait until Gutteridge was better in order to tell him he was no longer chairman.

It would be a good idea to see not only the candidates in a formal interview but their wives too. Mrs. Partridge was a pleasant, sensible, girl—as Plaistow was sure the Committee would be quick to see for themselves—and she was, of course, the daughter of a Shadow Minister, no less.

So the reason for Poumphrey's not getting the nomination had nothing to do with his illness, or any scandal concerning his private life, nor yet even his political views. And Grice was out on his ear not because he represented the old romantic wing of High Toryism (however inadequately) or because he had a doubtful wife; but because the constituency committee finally jibbed at malted milk and the new chairman thought he saw a way of keeping the new motorway off his land. Neither Poumphrey nor Grice could have known this.

It would have annoyed Poumphrey to learn that the situation was not of his own making. He assumed that it was—and his life changed.

"Sorry to hear about your illness. Hope you're quite recovered."

"Kind of you." He could not quite make out the chap's face. This was not because Plaistow was sitting in a bad light. It was a sunny afternoon and this large upstairs room at the Clarence faced south. Light flooded in through the huge eighteenth-century sash windows. Poumphrey could not quite focus on the Chairman's face. Everyone else he saw quite clearly. He knew them and nodded. Wanting to show he was friendly and at ease, he smiled at them individually. They were sitting about, quite informally, in arm-chairs and a couple of settees in one of the lounges which had been hired for the afternoon complete with a man outside the door to stop hotel guests wandering in.

It wasn't quite true to say he could not see Plaistow. He could see him now. He was looking at his face. But the moment Poumphrey looked away the face became totally unmemorable.

"It is a great pleasure to have you here, Mrs. Poumphrey. We're very conscious of the important part a wife can——"

"That's all right," said Jinny shortly. One of the women on the Committee was handing her a cup of tea.

"We just want a relaxed exchange of views. This is not an interview, you know. Or, put it like this. You are interviewing the Committee as much as the Committee is interviewing you. Just as there's a partnership between man and wife there is a partnership between the Member and his constituency party. Or perhaps you don't see it that way, Mr. Poumphrey? Once at Westminster you'd keep us in our place, eh? You're a man, if I may say so, who plays second fiddle to no one. You've confidence. Too much perhaps."

"I am what I am." Poumphrey was surprised by this approach. He would have been annoyed if he weren't so taken up with Plaistow's failure to reveal a proper face. There it was. He was looking straight at it but without any understanding except, perhaps, that he was being invited to recognize some unwelcome truth.

"You are what you are," said Plaistow. "What is that?"

Bloody cheek! Poumphrey refused tea and biscuits. He leaned forward in his chair and drew a handkerchief from his breast pocket. There was some half-formed notion in his mind that if he could get sufficiently near Plaistow he could rub this handkerchief across his face, as he might across a steamed-up bathroom mirror, and the face would come up clear and bright. The windows were closed. It was very hot. Poumphrey had lost weight but he still sweated easily and now he dabbed at the beads of sweat on his forehead and upper lip.

"What am I?" he said. "Well, you all know me. We're old friends. You probably know me better than I know myself. Could tell me a few home truths, no doubt." He laughed. "No, I'm not as headstrong as you made out. I can't say what I am, like a psychologist could, which I take it is what you are asking. I just know what I want to do."

"What's that?"

"Be your M.P. And I'd be a good one."

"If you don't wish to describe your personality as you see it," said Plaistow with a flourish of geniality, "and I quite agree it was wrong of me to try and lead you in that direction—but I couldn't *not* respond when you said, 'I am what I am'—what is there you would like to say that isn't too introspective?"

Everyone laughed. Jinny said, "Oh, I could give you a better account than he could."

"Proceed!" said Plaistow, spreading his hands in comic exaggeration as though to catch the rain of information.

Before Jinny could speak, Poumphrey said, "I'm a rich man. You know that. This is fact. It has a bearing on conduct. I can be quite independent. I would resign from my full-time job, though I'd continue part time because I don't believe in M.P.s cutting themselves off from first-hand industrial experience. I'm right of centre. I believe in the inequality of man."

Plaistow was sitting immediately opposite him in a high-backed wooden chair with upholstered arms. Impossible to lounge in this chair. He sat erect, smiling—Poumphrey could see that he was smiling—his fingers drumming silently on the arms. His suit was dark grey with a fine red stripe in it. He wore black socks. His shoes were highly polished.

"I simply mean", Poumphrey went on, "that people are different. And, if I can say so without causing offence, I even believe that women are different from men."

"What does that mean politically?" asked a man from the back of the room.

"Freedom."

"Yes, but what does that mean in practice?"

"The kind of enlightened self-interest that comes from the belief that no one is more responsible for an individual's welfare than that individual himself."

"But in *practice*——" the man went on.

"What do you mean, a rich man?" Plaistow asked. "If required, could a bank give a bond or guarantee that you are worth at least £100,000?"

If Poumphrey had absent-mindedly leaned forward and wiped his handkerchief across Plaistow's face what would have happened? Everybody would think it pretty odd. Plaistow would draw his head back. The Committee would decide, and smartly, they did not want a Member who went about rubbing people's faces with his handkerchief to make them come up clean and bright. That would be an end of his chances, even though he was quite convinced the Committee firmly intended from the beginning to choose him; they were, he supposed, only going through this interviewing routine to preserve appearances. Gutteridge had made a balls-up. They were all set to put it right with a great show of circumspection. You could not be more circumspect, choosing a candidate, than interviewing a short list and its wife.

But if you did wipe a misted mirror whose face would look back at you? Poumphrey hesitated. He moved his own head to see if the head opposite moved similarly; and when it did he was able to look through the mist at the candidate in front of him, and the candidate's wife with a box of paper tissues on her lap dabbing at her reddened nose, and the flowered wallpaper and sporting prints, all trapped in the heat and light of the late spring afternoon, dusty with sunlight behind these closed windows. Poumphrey saw this. He looked out of his haze or ball of lightning and found himself reacting with some hostility to a candidate who could say, with as much smugness as this one did, "I am what I am."

"You are what you are," he said sharply to the man in front of him, the man who wanted to be their candidate. "What is that?"

From the Chairman's vantage point he could see in all its detail the face he had shaved for thirty years. He would never be bald. He was proud of his head of wiry grey hair and washed it twice a week. The hair grew vigorously from his ears and nostrils but the barber kept it under control. The barber snipped it away with the points of his scissors, as he said, flatteringly, "You've very thick hair, sir. You'll never be bald," and he got a big tip for this. Snipping the hair in his ears and nostrils was an intimacy you had to reward. Eyebrows too. Three or four times a year he thinned out the eyebrows. It was a good face. The nose might be smaller and firmer, but it was a good nose, on the whole. Ears too big. That was why he liked to grow his hair long at the back, so that it curled round and made the ears less noticeable. But the cheeks sagged, undeniably. What do you expect? He was getting on for fifty. Bags under the eyes. A full, sagging, moist underlip. That showed his sensual nature. It looked to him the face of a minor Roman Emperor who, when checked up on, did something noble like not poisoning his mother.

There he sat, in a thornproof grey worsted, wearing dark blue socks and a blue knitted tie, looking so sure of himself it was incredible. On his right sat his wife, breathing with such deliberation, lips a firm line, that her nostrils could be seen slightly to open and close. And behind the pair of them were two other women, one really rather old with a puffed-out pussy-cat face and a little black straw hat perched on top of her white hair. The other was just a girl. She was in her twenties. She had golden hair and a lot of pink in her face; to such effect that one thought what a creased and raddled old woman she'll make! How she'll run to seed!

A candidate's wife was one thing; for him to bring along his mother and his mistress amounted to effrontery. This implied a more extreme position than right of centre. It was downright contempt for the processes of parliamentary democracy.

Given a lever long enough and the immoveable fulcrum and I would move the world. Given a change of viewpoint I'd see a little of what God sees.

The ordinariness of these people! Knowing as much about them as he did he was amazed to see them looking so ordinary. They smiled, talked, moved their hands. The pussy-faced woman had her eyes half-closed. She thought she was looking humorously shrewd but in fact she knew nothing at all, she did not suspect that the whole business of interviewing candidates was completely phoney and that in eighteen months time something—well, something disastrous would happen to her. Not knowing what. But something disastrous was bound to happen to a woman that age and here she was, showing no awareness of it, but just playing the sphinx in the most girlish and embarrassing way imaginable. She did not know about herself. Nobody knew about themselves. Even the candidate's wife, who looked intelligent, and ought to have been apprehensive, looked indescribably smug behind the beaklike nose, the smugness of a hen comfortably supported on a clutch of warm eggs. She ought to have been bloody angry.

So much for appearances. She *was* bloody angry, as he well knew. And Mrs. Abel was far from being as self-sufficient as she looked. Mitty, for all her pink flush and fluttering eyes, pretending an interest she did not feel, was scarcely restraining herself from rushing out of the room in tears. They gave nothing of all this away. Nobody gave anything away. They were talking quietly, drinking tea and eating biscuits, looking—most of them in that room—quite jolly. You only needed a shift of perspective to see they were haunted and desperate. That was all there was any certainty of. Everybody was frightened. The extraordinary thing was that nobody showed this fright. They had grown used to it, or if they had not grown used to it they were pretending; and if there were moments when they were neither inured nor capable of pretence they were able to carry on out of unreflecting habit.

The candidate Poumphrey would have denied all this. These people were actually as they seemed. But Poumphrey was a fool. Only a fool could suppose he had a chance in hell of getting the nomination after being ill the way he'd been and the scandal over Mrs. Grice, and now turning up for the interview with another girl friend in tow. Perhaps he even knew he was a fool and had decided to play the part with some magnificence. No, he was a bigger fool than that.

He knew perfectly well they were a puritanical lot in East Dene. In a gesture of baroque splendour he went to bed with the rival candidate's wife. They were so puritanical this probably ruled out the rival candidate as well. Being the creature he was, he needed to assume total responsibility. There were moments when he would have accepted responsibility for the rate at which the universe was expanding, or the Fall of Man. That was why he was the biggest fool in the room. The disaster was entirely of his making and he was going to allow nobody else to take credit for it.

"Tell the Committee what all these women were doing in your house," he said. "I'm sure they will be fascinated."

To begin at the beginning.

He was conceived and, nine months later, ejected by a muscular spasm into a harsh and hostile climate where no doubt he yelled and drew some of this filthy atmosphere into his lungs which immediately frilled up and expanded from the wet flaps they'd been; and since that time nothing had been the same. The umbilical had already been cut and tucked away. No good saying this was absurdly far back to go in answer to a simple question. Any question involving women brought up the manner in which you were born and who you were born to. Whose flesh were you?

"We could pretend a little," she said. "I just love the theatre. I should have been an actress. May I call you Edward?"

"Yes, all right," he said, and kissed her on the cheek.

"If my son *really* came it would finish me off."

"Good-bye, Mother."

"Good-bye, my dear."

Turn the really great and puzzling questions on their heads and you usually see the truth of the matter—and where did that get you?

"If my son *really* came", she said, "I would finish *him* off."

"Is that why all these women were in the house?" he demanded through the steamed-up mirror.

After some hesitation Poumphrey said, "Mitty was trying to save me, I guess."

* * *

The yard, he remembered, reeked curiously. A sweetness of

flowers, wallflowers probably, and an animal sourness; as it might be, ancient cat piss dried in the sun and blown over by salty breathings from the muddy tide caught up in the reeds out there in the blackness. An electric bulb burned in a carriage lamp over the kitchen door. There was a light in the kitchen, and the door stood wide open. The night was clammy with salt.

From the kitchen he heard voices. The two women were in the sitting-room. From what he could hear they were playing some game.

"I just can't remember what my first husband looked like," he heard Mrs. Abel say. The house was so quiet he could hear a playing card being put down on the table. There was chat about the game and the scoring. Canasta. Two women playing Canasta on a mild spring evening with all the doors open, that wasn't what he had expected. You'd think they were in the tropics.

"I remember the way he used to talk, but his actual appearance and his smell, and his *feel*—I just wouldn't recognize him, and that's an extraordinary state of affairs. I was married to him. I bore him a son. He's not in my mind's eye any more. If you showed me his photograph together with photographs of a lot of other men his age, I just wouldn't——" She laughed.

Jinny had a smaller voice. Nevertheless he could make out what she said very clearly. After more chat about the game he could hear her remark, "I've got a good memory for faces. Edward's father was a big man with a beard."

A glass was picked up and put down. "Some people you remember, others you don't."

"He never seemed to listen to what you said," Jinny went on. "He'd a white scar above his right eyebrow from a climbing accident."

After a silence Mrs. Abel said, "The funny thing is I can remember everybody else perfectly well."

"Edward's father had very bushy eyebrows. He'd never get them trimmed."

"What colour eyes did he have?"

"Very brown."

"Of course," said Mrs. Abel as though to excuse herself. "All men look much the same, I always think."

"I hadn't noticed."

"Yes, really. There are big men and little men, I agree. Otherwise——" she shrugged. "Perhaps I didn't think so when I was young. I liked men as much as anybody did. But it was when I was young, you see. I had all the common illusions. Now all I know is men have the ability to inflict pain and humiliation. Women can give pleasure. On these facts the relationship between the sexes is based."

"I don't believe you've put up with much pain and humiliation," said Jinny.

"I looked after myself."

He went out into the yard with the idea of walking round to the other side of the house where he could look into the sitting-room through the big window. He took off his shoes and carried them in his right hand, using his left to push back the lilac that grew where the terrace began, releasing a spatter of rain drops. It was extraordinary, this removing of his shoes, because he could have walked quite silently on the grass. Grass, in fact, grew right up to the picture window and when he arrived outside it his stockinged feet were soaked and cold.

His father had a beard. Except for that Poumphrey looked very like him; and the beard was close and neat. Were the two men to stand side by side in the darkness looking through a window into a lighted room they might have seemed very alike indeed to those who sat inside, looking out.

The two women played by the light of a reading lamp and a wall lamp. Jinny had her back to the window. The comb he had brought from Bahrein, studded with seed pearls, glinted as she moved her head; she gathered her hair up at the back with this comb. It was about all he could see of Jinny. But Mrs. Abel, in a dark green dress and with a white stole over her shoulders, was sitting with the two lights above and behind her, facing the window.

She looked up and saw him. With a card in her right hand, she looked up and saw him. She hesitated. She did not look surprised or alarmed. Indeed, her expression seemed to change in no way at all. She was smiling. Her lips were parted enough for him to see her teeth. Perhaps she had not seen him. Perhaps, from inside the room, the window was an opaque, black panel, and Mrs. Abel had seen nothing. She hesitated only because she was thinking, or remembering. But he felt sure she *had* seen him because when she put the card down she went on looking at him. In a moment Jinny would notice and turn round to see what she was looking at.

The two women were talking. Now that he was outside the house it was harder to make out what they were saying, particularly as on this side there was a breeze. The elm trees at the end of the garden strained in the sea wind. The salt air moved about the garden, hissing enough to make it hard to catch what the two women, on the other side of the double-glazing, were saying. But some words came through. There were snatches of words.

"I can't remember," he heard Mrs. Abel say, as she still watched his face. Perhaps there was an open window he couldn't see and the sounds were coming through that. They came without resonance but from quite close. Someone might have been breathing them into his ear. He even turned to see if anyone was there.

If she could see him could she see this other figure at his side? They stood in the dark, the one bearded, looking in through the window.

"If I met him I wouldn't know him."

"You didn't keep any photographs?"

"I've lots of Edgar's photographs, but none of *his*. I would have *liked* to remember, Jinny. It's pathetic. It would have been wrong to depend on photographs. The holiness of the heart's affections is much exaggerated, I think. Photographs are its little shrines. I wouldn't mind not being remembered myself. It's a sort of responsibility, being remembered. It's one he hasn't got, not so far as I'm concerned. Poor man. I expect he's dead. He loved me."

Poumphrey and this other man stood very close to the window.

"She's just a bitch," Poumphrey said to the man at his side. "Don't take any notice. She wouldn't talk like that if she didn't know we were here."

There was gravel under the grass, cutting into his feet. His father seemed to be calmer, more relaxed, even genial. Perhaps he was drunk. He was usually a bit high this hour of night. He was not so good-natured at other times.

Jinny went and fetched Mrs. Abel another drink. If Jinny had seen him she'd certainly have screamed. Jinny looking and not screaming would have meant he was invisible. She didn't look and he still could not be sure. But he was sure.

He knew damn well Mrs. Abel had seen him. She might have seen this other man too but at the very least she must have seen *him*. He was so close to the glass now he was almost touching it with his forehead. His face must be catching the light and hanging in the black window like a lantern. It didn't matter whether she saw the both of them. One would be enough. See one, see both.

A bowl of late daffodils stood on a side table. They looked plastic in that light and if he had been right there in the room with these two women he would have taken one of those daffodils out of the bowl just to see if it was real.

Mrs. Abel stood up and he thought she might have been coming over to the window to draw the curtain, but instead she went out of the room. When she came back she had what looked like an album of photographs.

"I don't remember this poor man. I just remember some of the things he said. He was always making loving gestures and remarks. He surrounded me with affection. The atmosphere was what I would describe as hothouse. I didn't like it because I didn't want to be loved. I didn't need it. Neither do you. You don't love Edward, do you? These are all my family. That's mother. That's my father. My brother is in the sailor suit. He's dead too."

Poumphrey actually looked round in the blackness to see where his father had gone to and when he turned to the window again there was Jinny standing squarely in front of it and looking out. He drew back and to one side. The strangeness of her long, hanging, Anglo-Saxon face struck him as it had never struck him before. She had a great long nose, great teeth, and a clumsy jaw.

"That's the reason I'm here," she was saying to Mrs. Abel. "I don't like him at all. I don't approve of what he does. But I love him."

Poumphrey looked at her in amazement. This was his reward for eavesdropping. He had driven sixty miles through the night to be jeered at by this woman. He'd scare the hell out of her. He'd put his face close up to hers.

"I love him," she was saying.

Poumphrey was so angry by this time he might have started to hammer on the window. They were playing him up. They knew damn well he was there. They'd been expecting him. The moment they heard his car drive into the yard they had started this play acting. But they couldn't manipulate him.

The knowledge the old man was there stopped him from hammering on the window. The old man would not like that. It was too crude. Take it easy, he was saying. Don't let those cows manipulate you.

Poumphrey prepared to walk back round the house to the kitchen. He was going to knock on the table or ring a bell, or something, and pretend that he had just arrived. But it was black hell in the garden and he got lost in a shrubbery. Every time he moved he shook a branch and the water came down remorselessly. For a warm evening it was icy. Come on out this way! The old man was beckoning. He was laughing, too, the old soak! Come on out, son!

Underfoot there were sharp-edged stones in the shrubbery. His clothes had mopped up so much water he could feel cold patches creeping over his back and belly. By the time he reached the yard he knew he couldn't possibly go into the house.

What could he say? There was always the truth. But his instinct was always against too much of that. To lie was humiliating, particularly if he could not lie well. Dignity required him to clear out silently.

He had to leave silently because if they heard him start the car and rushed out in time to stop him making a getaway they would have him in the house taking a bath and drying his clothes. He could imagine all that. But say they didn't manage to stop him. Say they came out only in time to see the car drive off up the lane.

The truth was he couldn't be sure they'd actually know he was there. He disagreed with the old man on this point. There was a real chance everything was as it appeared to be, and if that was the case he ought to be away, taking stock. He had come down with some idea of making Jinny return home. Did he really want that now? If it was true she loved him the way she said, might it not be more wounding to leave her where she was?

If Poumphrey could have put an arm round his father he would have done so. Nobody forgets anything, Poumphrey would have told him. She's got a constipated soul. Any analyst would treat her free, just for the pleasure of pulling the handle, listening to the whirr and see her psychic jackpot spill out. So don't upset yourself, he said to the old man. You ought to feel sorry for her and forgive her for the way she has driven you to all this drinking. Maybe it's true she doesn't remember you, but it's only forgetting the really big things you have to work at. She's worked at it all right.

He had to put his shoes on over his wet socks. The shoes were too tight to lace up. He didn't get into the car. He released the handbrake and allowed the car to run gently back out of the yard. On the other side of the lane was a three-foot ditch so he had to take his time over this manoeuvre. The lane didn't climb much. He did not care which way he went, up or down, provided he could get far enough away from the house before starting the engine. The car was, however, pointing towards the village, so he thought this was the way to go. After he had been pushing for some minutes it was clear he had underestimated the gradient. He could not let the car run backwards because although he had switched the lights on the reversing light simply wasn't strong enough. He couldn't steer the car, in that blackness and in that narrow lane, any way except forward. After some minutes he thought the effort would kill him.

He wanted his father to get in as well. They would drive back to London, exchanging a few thoughts. But when Poumphrey, quite exhausted, found himself in the driving seat, there really was nobody else about. He was quite alone. Nobody wanted to cheer him up, nobody wanted any consolation from him, just a remote, dry tang of whisky which might have been complete illusion, or Poumphrey's own sweat drying as the car heater pushed the temperature up, or some mixture of smells brought about by the clear, clean, breeze from the Channel playing through dead and rotting Brussels sprouts.

* * *

This other woman was in the house for quite different reasons.

She arrived very soon after telephoning, so soon he had no time to take a bath and change. All the way up from Sidlesham he had been promising himself a bath. Good job he was fit. Good job he could do without sleep. Good job he knew when to take the initiative and when to play a waiting game.

In the upstairs room at the Clarence the Committee sat in silence. The sun was so strong the curtains over one of the windows had been drawn. What were they all waiting for? Why did no one speak? The answer was that everything depended on him. No one knew as much of the candidate. Or the chairman, for that matter. He wasn't sure which role he was playing. One moment he was the candidate, the next he was asking all the questions. He took stock of what was going on from some point where it didn't matter, frankly, whether he was one or the other. The point was remote, transcendent, and yet at the same time very close. A bloody queer way of approaching Westminster, he was thinking. A door opened and a man in a brown suit appeared, only to be retrieved by someone in the corridor outside. He looked bewildered, too.

* * *

So he had driven down to Sidlesham, been worked over by a couple of bitches, driven back again, only to be pounced on by Mrs. Grice. It must have been one or two in the morning. Turning up at such a time was odd in itself, and odder that she should have started talking and behaving as though they were alone in the house. What could have led her to the making of such an assumption? Poumphrey remembered that he was not so much perplexed as rushed off his feet. She spoke of herself as a lady. It was such an old-fashioned term. She used the word 'honour'. That, again, was questionable. Language like that should have alerted him. A man of his experience ought to have known, without being told by her husband, that any woman who laughed the way she did and talked about trust and respect was a bit vulgar.

She broke off in the middle of what she was saying and looked at him. "You're in a bit of a mess, aren't you? What have you been doing?"

He could see no reason why he should tell her.

"Look, your trousers are wet. Your coat's wet. Where are your shoes?" Under the chair, as it happened, but once again he saw no reason to be informative and padded up and down on the parquet flooring leaving damp marks. "You'd better get those socks off. You've got scratches on your face. Your shirt's wet. You must take all these things off and have a bath. Look!"

Mrs. Grice, who was still wearing the expensive-looking fur coat she had walked in with, began unknotting his tie. She pushed him down into a chair and tugged at his wet socks. He did not resist.

"I'm perfectly all right," he said. "What's going on? I mean, it's late. Can I give you a drink?"

She had the coat off him, and the tie, and the socks and she would have dragged the shirt over his head if he hadn't taken her head between his two hands and kissed her firmly on the lips. He laughed at the amazed expression she'd put on like a mask and went over to the sideboard. She said she would like a straight gin with just a dash of lime. When he returned she had removed her coat and was looking round for a light for her cigarette. "Where's your wife, then? In bed?"

The truth was that he'd been taken in and shouldn't have been. The experience was as bogus as the colour of her reddish hair. He ought to have known he wasn't a real person so far as she was concerned. He was just another man. He was an experience. He ought to have known it because of the way she behaved but he had to admit now that at the time he was too flattered and delighted. She was undeniably attractive. It had little to do with that foxy little face of hers, or the laugh, or the boldness. She conveyed eagerness and vitality. The way she moved her legs roused him.

At the time he was dazed by the way she moved her legs and body, and the way she looked at him, laughing and showing her teeth like the vixen she was. If she'd had a brush she'd have waved it with extraordinary sexual provocativeness. He wasn't sure, in his excitement, that she hadn't one. He could see this narrow mask showing up, in moonlight, among leaves and wild flowers.

"I just had to rush out. I wasn't going to stay there any longer and be questioned."

"You've had a row with your husband?"

"Well, what do you expect. Apparently there's some story about you and me. Quite untrue, of course, but Reggie wanted to know what the truth was. Now, I may be a bit Victorian but I don't answer questions touching my honour."

She eased her shoes off for comfort and wiggled her stockinged feet. Her dress was a natural green with touches of white and yellow, so perhaps that was why he thought of leaves and wild flowers. She had a way of pouting out her lips to receive a cigarette.

"It's only natural." Poumphrey sat drinking his whisky, watching her right knee and wondering how genuine her anger with Grice was. Did women get angry when asked questions like that? He guessed they usually did, though he could never see the justification. The question seemed quite a natural one in certain circumstances. He thought Mrs. Grice was putting on an act. The word "honour" was a give-away. He had been cute enough to spot this at the time, so he wasn't so stupid.

"I told him if he wanted to believe it he could. What he believed was his affair. I wouldn't help him."

Poumphrey could see she was annoyed because of the way he seemed to be sticking up for her husband. "You only had to say it wasn't true."

"Why should I? No self-respecting woman would answer questions of that kind. A man who asks questions about his wife's sexual behaviour can't possibly have any respect for her. Or for himself, for that matter. What sort of a woman does he think I am? The least I can expect is absolute trust and confidence. What's so excessive about that? I just wouldn't be insulted. So I walked out."

"He was only asking." Poumphrey was not thinking of what he said. He was just thinking of taking hold of her. He was no longer the defeated man in the Sidlesham garden. He was stiffening up for the pounce and so delighted with the vigour of his bodily functioning he did not notice how cross she had become and was taken aback when she said, "No gentleman could possibly question his wife."

Gentleman! What a vocabulary! She was still on the boring topic.

"I still don't see why a woman shouldn't give a straight answer to a straight question." He was really puzzled.

"You are determined to tease me, my dear." Mrs. Grice leaned forward to kiss him, first on his cheek, then on his ear, and finally, having turned his face towards hers with the tip of a finger, on the lips. "Now, go and have that bath. Your clothes are so wet they're giving off a smell."

"Within the limits of what is humanly possible", he remembered saying, "I try not to refuse a challenge or a relationship."

"Sounds a bit twentyish to me," said Mrs. Grice as they moved towards the stairs. "I like to be a bit more discriminating."

"As long as you realize my motive is not political."

She sat on the cork-topped stool in the bathroom, smoking, watching him soak. He was not the slightest bit self-conscious or embarrassed. He was a big man. Maybe he had run to fat a little. But he was not what you could call flabby; he hadn't a real paunch like some men. Once he realized she wasn't particularly excited at the sight of a naked man he began thinking he wasn't such a bad figure. He had never taken his clothes off and climbed into a hot bath with a woman watching before. Odd how natural it all seemed. No, not odd. Sensible. A hot bath was just what he needed. He soaped his chest and shoulders, then wallowed.

"You're right about your husband," he said. "He shouldn't ask questions like that."

"I could do with a bath myself," she said. She stubbed out her cigarette and began taking off her clothes. "That's a nice big bath you've got there. It would be a shame to waste all that hot water. Doesn't your wife use bath salts?" With surprising rapidity she had stripped and was pouring green pine essence into the water.

"Reggie would be furious." She lowered herself into the other end and began soaping her breasts, stretching her long arms and gazing at her finger-nails. He found her surprisingly white, wobbly and unappetising. It was quite absurd. The bath was big but it wasn't as big as all that. She could not stretch her legs out, he could not stretch his legs out, at least not to begin with; and then they found they could sit more or less side by side, facing in opposite directions as in one of those eighteenth-century conversation chairs. She shrieked and started splashing.

They had to take a grip of each other as a means of maintaining the sitting position. This was both uncomfortable and unerotic. There was so much water in the bath it flooded over the side and Poumphrey could not help remembering the last time this had happened the water had eventually found its way through the dining-room ceiling.

He told her about this.

"Do you always have a woman in your bath?"

"Not at all. I was standing up and slipped on some soap. I fell heavily. The water just went over the side in a wave."

She shrieked again. "What would you tell your wife if she came in?"

"Hell," he said. "I don't know. You could be demonstrating something." He was so taken out of himself by sharing a bath with this woman he scarcely knew what he was saying; he was in a kind of delirium. "Your husband wasn't right to ask you those questions. I agree with you, I've come round. He doesn't love you."

"He loves me all right."

"A bloody hypocrite!"

"An M.P.," she said. "Fancy wanting to be an M.P." She gurgled. "But you do too. I was forgetting. You *are* a pair!"

"He doesn't love you. If you didn't go back to him, do you know what? A year afterwards he wouldn't even remember what you looked like."

"Oh, that's all shit," she said.

"If he were to meet you in the street in a year's time, or say two years, and you hadn't gone back, do you know what? He'd pass you by. He'd not know who you were."

"Shit!"

"That's what people are like," he said. "They forget."

"I don't think Reggie should ask me such intimate questions, whatever you say. You're on his side. I can see that. Men stick together. He shouldn't have such a low mind."

Eventually they climbed out of the bath, dried in the big, furry towels that had been draped over the hot rail and took it in turns to puff lily of the valley talcum powder over each other out of a plastic flask.

"As a matter of fact, I've never had a bath with a woman before," he said very seriously, as though he had been initiated into some privileged cult. "I hope the water hasn't gone through. We ought to mop it up."

"You poor bloody deprived Englishman," she said. "Life's for the living. Let's get to bed."

He couldn't do it. He was either too tired or the hot bath *à deux* had served some unexpectedly lustral purpose but he was impotent once they slid between the sheets and she had to make consoling and humiliating remarks to him, like, "Relax now, and don't worry about it. Just go to sleep like a good boy and see what the morning brings."

The morning, when it came, was no better and he could tell by her manner she thought badly of it. Insanity was more dignified than impotence, so he asked whether she had noticed anyone else in the house when she arrived last night. No, she said, sitting up and stroking her breasts, she thought they had been alone, unless his wife had been about the place, that is to say.

No, she had not been there, said Poumphrey. She was on a visit to the country.

"Then what are you talking about?" She was quite distant with him.

"I had a feeling somebody else was here. Watching."

"You're crazy."

"I'm tired. I've had very strange experiences. You wouldn't believe what experiences I've had. I've never let a woman down in this way before."

"It would just have to be my luck, wouldn't it?" She giggled at the way she made her nipples wobble.

"Sometimes I think I'm just losing my grip."

"That's silly. There's a drug for everything nowadays. Wouldn't you like to try again. I feel terribly disparaged you know. I don't mind telling you the experience is a new one on me. Frankly, I didn't know the system was so fallible."

"I wouldn't take any drugs."

"Maybe you've got a brain tumour?"

"You shouldn't joke about such things."

"If our present situation is not something to joke about I don't know what is."

"Cancer isn't a joke."

"I said tumour."

He said he was going to have a look round the house to make sure there was no one else on the premises. Then he'd have another bath, a cold one.

She sat up in bed, her hair, which must have got wet in the bath, hanging down in rats' tails. "You don't really think Reggie would forget me, do you? That would be awful."

He came back after his cold shower and tried again but it was still no good. He felt more humiliated than ever and went on pleading insanity.

"I simply don't believe people forget each other as easily as all that," she said. "Or abandon each other."

The most crushing remark was the one she made after they had breakfasted on grapefruit juice, toast and coffee. "I think I know just the man to help you."

* * *

Poumphrey was all for being completely honest and frank. He knew precisely how the candidate had been conducting his private life but the committee should know too. There was no simple account to be given of the sort of man who stood before them, or sat rather. But we must try. We have to know all about each other in order to talk to each other. We cannot afford mysteries or reticences. They only lead to people being thought inscrutable. Who wants an inscrutable Member of Parliament?

It was to the candidate's advantage that he was married. A

bachelor was always a risk. He might marry somebody who hated politics.

On the other hand, he works for a petroleum company and might be off to Borneo, here today, gone tomorrow, and not playing a proper role in parliamentary life. Was a political career of such importance to him he was prepared to resign. Or, more exactly, having been asked to resign would he? Or would he fight the Board? Would he be as good as his word and force a few other resignations instead? Why had the Board asked him to resign anyway?

"Why on earth should they do that?" poor Mitty had said between her irritatingly tiny sips. Champagne was a healthy drink. He liked to see women take a good swig at it. "Go on! Drink up!" he shouted at her. He was all in favour of complete candour about the sort of difficulties he had to put up with.

* * *

Death. He really had died in that taxi. The event had taken place in the taxi and not, as he told Jinny, in the Savoy Hotel. Why he should have misled her on this trivial point (trivial, that is to say, as between the Savoy and the taxi as the place of his passing when the Queens appeared) he could not imagine. Mitty had been deceived too. Perhaps the explanation was that when you are anxious to get at the really large truths you slip in a few trivial lies to propitiate God; He doesn't want, or is over-anxious about, the *absolute* truth.

"Please don't die, Gogo."

But, of course, he had to.

He didn't quite know what to think about death. He was always sorry when it happened to people he loved. Sometimes he didn't know he loved them until they *were* dead but maybe that was only another way of saying that when they were dead he no longer envied them. Death was for the women. At the moment of dying there were women everywhere.

"Gogo, if you die on me I'll never forgive you."

How little that particular consideration weighed with him she would never know. He was too far gone. He was incapable of speech. He could not have blinked his eyelids.

"If only you'll live I promise not to see or worry you again."

She was taking too much on herself. His dying had nothing to do with her. He had these other women in the boat. His mother gave birth. Then he died. That was all. Mitty didn't come into the calculation anywhere. She went on, though, as though it was all her fault. He had not realized she had this depth of character. He would have liked to take her hand and say, "You're not just a cock teaser. You're a real woman. That's fine. But don't take on so. It really doesn't matter."

He could neither move nor utter. The river was not wide as he had expected, but confined within quite narrow banks and the women had to put out hands from time to time in the gathering darkness and fend off branches and push away from rocks.

You could die with your eyes open and without pain. Poor Mitty thought this was cheating. For her there had to be agony and a sudden total illumination. You advanced through a cloudy door of pain into a brilliant cataract of knowledge.

"Mitty", he would have said if he could, "who are all these women? My wife would naturally insist on being present. And there's Mrs. Abel. Of course, you haven't met Mrs. Abel. Mrs. Abel, I should like to introduce a young friend of mine. This is Mitty. Well, that accounts for three of you. But who the hell is that woman up at the front?"

There simply was no illumination. He would have liked to point this out to poor Mitty. At the moment of light and darkness there was this falling away and resting but also the knowledge that the last question of all was about the identity of the fourth woman. Jinny said there were only three. They were Morgan le Fay and two others, of whom she was one and Mrs. Abel was the other. No, dear Mitty! You are there! By Christ you are! There are four queens!

"Don't die, please, Gogo," said Mitty from the front of the

barque. "I don't know what you mean about this last battle. You haven't been fighting any battle. I just love you. There are other battles, if that's what you want."

She came across, kissed him and cried. Her face was wooden. The tears ran over it like rain over a cask. The experience was enough to make his spirit rise in the air and turn upwards; so that instead of the brown earth he looked into the empty blue.

"You can't come into the house," he said. "My wife will be there."

"If you die, Gogo, I shall hate you and hate you."

Even this was not enough to keep him going. He died into the light that unfolded before him, abandoned by everyone, it seemed, this queen and that queen; they threw down their crowns and faded as the light grew stronger. Mitty stayed on, though.

Which was the very moment Poumphrey found he could speak and move. "I'm all right," he said to Jinny. "I've had either a heart attack or an epileptic fit. I've seen myself."

"You've had too much to drink," said Jinny. "That's what you mean. Who are you?" she demanded, looking at Mitty.

"It is clear", Poumphrey said severely, "that I have made a miscalculation. And now I don't suppose Grice will get the nomination either."

* * *

The Clarence had gardens and a terrace overlooking the river and when the interview was over the Poumphrey party went there to look at the water and cool off. Quite a lot of people were taking tea under Cinzano umbrellas. Children were feeding swans from a moored punt. Seen through the arches of the stone bridge the sunlit water was insubstantial, an uneasy great hole in the May afternoon.

"Gogo, you were marvellous," said Mitty. "They'll have to choose you."

"Yes, good show, Arthur." Jinny had never been known to talk like this before. She seemed a bit embarrassed. The implication was she had expected him to make an ass of himself.

Instead of sitting they were walking slowly along the terrace, Poumphrey slightly in the lead, followed by Mitty, and then behind her, Mrs. Abel holding on to Jinny's arm, saying that, all things considered, she had never seen a more degrading spectacle. "It had all the atmosphere of the slave market with none of its professionalism. I was glad to have seen it."

The women, glad to get away from the restraints of the committee room, fizzed away, Mitty in particular. "Oh, but they were such silly, ordinary people, like me. They didn't know *anything*. They were just—oh, nothing!" She clutched her black, shiny handbag with her left hand and gestured enthusiastically with her right. "You were right to let them do so much of the talking, Gogo."

"When you did answer a question I must say I thought you did it very effectively." Jinny's pleasure was obviously more than the one of escaping into the fresh air. "I didn't know you had it in you, this lapidary style, I mean."

Poumphrey was looking about sharply to see who was in hearing distance. He turned back to say to Jinny, "Must say I was grateful for the way you kept your mouth shut."

"They didn't seem very interested in me, did they?"

"You could easily have said something about Africa. And it won't do, Jinny. It won't do."

Mrs. Abel had stopped and was leaning on her stick. "As you know, my views are different but the way you answered those questions about the Indian Ocean plainly impressed. No doubt you were helped by having seen the Indian Ocean."

"It's the sort of defence issue that can be understood by looking at a map," said Poumphrey.

"I am easily confused by coloured maps. This is true of more people than you suspect, Edward. In this respect I felt myself more like the members of the Committee. We didn't believe the Russians were interested in such a great piece of water."

"Nor are they," said Jinny.

"Well, Edward was impressive on this, wasn't he? Edward

persuaded me the Russians *were* interested. He did it in about two minutes flat. It sounded plausible. But are you sure?"

"Jinny thinks it ought to be called the African Ocean."

"And now I'm off," said Mitty suddenly.

They all looked at her. "Now that Gogo is going to be an M.P. I don't feel he needs me any longer."

Jinny looked carefully into the girl's eyes without the slightest desire to be bitchy. "I can't see the House of Commons making good that sort of deficiency. Anyway, you've helped my husband a lot. He's been through a patch and it's important you were there."

"What d'you mean, you're off?" Poumphrey demanded.

"I'm not going to see you any more."

Mrs. Abel sighed and nodded her head. "You detect ambiguity in the relationship and you think public opinion will seize on the wrong aspect. You are wrong. I can see by your happy manner that you believe you are sacrificing yourself for someone else's well being. You are deceiving yourself. I should have had more respect for your decision if it had been presented as sheer self-interest, which is what it is. How old are you? Twenty-eight? For a spinster of twenty-eight self-interest is nothing to be ashamed of. It is a duty. So we accept your decision. Be off with you!"

"Here! No! Wait a minute!" Poumphrey tried to make a grab at the girl as she turned and started to walk away.

Jinny cried out at the same moment. "Oh no, please, Mitty."

"Let her go," said Mrs. Abel. "Don't be stupid. She's quite right."

"She has no means of transport."

"She can catch a bus."

"They've been taken off this route."

Poumphrey had caught up with the girl and they were walking quietly together towards the entrance to the hotel. She wasn't the slightest bit excited or upset, as he expected. She just kept on saying he was a big man of affairs. He had always been that, of course, but she could see now, after the way he'd talked that afternoon, he was going to be even bigger and more important. He was the sort of man who became Prime Minister.

"I insist you don't go. If you go now I'll go with you."

"All right, Gogo! You know, I really am fond of you." She slipped a hand into his. "And your health seems so much better," she added, inconsequentially. "I'm sure you'll live for years and years."

"Perhaps it's time for us all to go. Let's go back and collect the others."

The Constituency Committee had been in more or less continuous session since the morning and it had been chance that Poumphrey's turn had come with the tea and biscuits. There now seemed to be a break because Poumphrey noticed some of the Committee stretching their legs on the terrace. He overheard a man say, "There's a sort of political meeting going on in the hotel and I've just been told by one of the waiters they're going to come out and make an announcement." This man had nothing to do with the Committee. He was just sitting under one of the coloured umbrellas with two other people. "They're going to name a candidate for the next election. What constituency is this anyway? The boundaries have been rearranged, or something."

Poumphrey took Mitty back to where Jinny and Mrs. Abel were waiting, and said, "We can't go now. There's a rumour the Committee are going to announce the candidate."

"I'm surprised you have to depend on rumour for information of that sort," said Mrs. Abel.

"Surely they would have asked you to stay if there was to be an announcement?" Jinny had been fussing about, looking for a chair for Mrs. Abel.

Mitty's arm was still being gripped, rather tightly, by Poumphrey just above the elbow. "Isn't it exciting!" she cried, "I'm just so happy to be here to see Gogo's triumph." She made so much noise people turned to look at her. "Fancy me even knowing him." She seemed to bear Mrs. Abel no ill-will for what she had said—perhaps she had not understood—and actually went up to her once she was seated, and said, "I could see the twinkle in your eye."

"Twinkle?"

"Now that Gogo's well again everything else seems sort of funny."

"Why do you let her call you by that silly name, Edward? What twinkle?"

"You had a twinkle in your eye. You've got a real sense of humour. Why do you call him Edward? You say I shouldn't call him Gogo. Well, I like it. His name is Arthur really. You call him Edward."

"I think Gogo is a very good name for him", said Jinny, "though it's not the one I'd use myself."

Mrs. Abel said it was an absolutely ridiculous name.

Poumphrey was on Mitty's side in this matter of a name, not because he liked it but because at that moment he wanted everyone to be happy, particularly Mitty because she thought he was so marvellous and because she had brought him back to life. He did not understand how she had done this. It wasn't as though he had been drowning or experienced an electric shock; nothing so obvious as the kiss of life, or what you call it. Without knowing what she was doing she had put an exploratory hand into his and led him back from wherever he was.

They were standing in front of Mrs. Abel who had the sun full in her face. She touched her lined pink and white face with the back of her hand, tidying strands of hair out of the way, and smiling as though to congratulate the world on having come up to some expectation she had privately formed but never thought to see realized.

"Do you know who I am?" she said to Mitty.

"You're Mrs. Abel."

"I'm somebody who tries to speak the truth when I see it."

"Oh," said Mitty, after a pause. "Well, yes, of course."

It occurred to Poumphrey Mrs. Abel was choosing this moment to claim she was his mother. It was inappropriate but in the general euphoria a certain slackening of discipline was only to be expected. She was pleased with the way he had spoken to the Committee and saying, "Edward is my son," would be a way of showing it. After all, he had done damn well!

But if there was anything of the sort in her mind she checked herself and went on talking to Mitty as though they were alone. "If I'd been in your position I would not have been talked into coming back."

"In a way I think I understand him," was all Mitty could think to say. "We talk very openly, you know. He told me he was going to be reborn."

"He would need a mother for that."

"That's just what he said at the time."

Poumphrey had been much too busy looking round for the expected messenger to pay any attention to this chat. If they were indeed going to announce him as the candidate they'd want him up front somewhere.

Instead, he saw Grice. Grice's presence was not exactly unexpected since he was one of the other candidates. Elaine must be somewhere around too but knowing what an emotional chap he was Poumphrey would have expected him to clear off home after the undoubtedly poor showing he must have made. He was a bit old-fashioned. He might have wanted to hang around and shake Poumphrey's hand. He had, however, entered the greenhouse and was now mooning about, inspecting the plants. And yet he wasn't really inspecting them. He was mooning about, that was it. Something had gone wrong and he was keeping out of the way. Trust Grice to think of concealing himself in a greenhouse, where everybody could see him.

"Excuse me," Poumphrey said to the women. He went along to the greenhouse, opened the door and walked in.

"Hallo." Grice apparently knew who it was without turning round. "I expect you know who the candidate is to be. It's a chap called Partridge."

The place was full of pelargoniums—pots after lines of pots

of red pelargoniums, different kinds of red pelargoniums, and white pelargoniums, and red and white pelargoniums, and pelargoniums bearing small scarlet flowers on long stalks, and others with big, rich flowers; there were bronze crinkled leaves and green leaves, hairy leaves, smooth leaves. Angel fish stood to attention in a glass tank, all facing one way. The place stank of pelargoniums, bitter and medicinal.

"Partridge?"

"Insurance broker. Good chap, I'm told."

Grice had turned round now and was looking at Poumphrey. "I suppose you know that if it hadn't been for you I'd got it all tied up."

Poumphrey was so shocked he wasn't taking in what Grice said. He could only stare at him and repeat what he was saying. The reek of these plants was making him sick but he did not want to go outside because at least it was warm in the greenhouse. He was very cold but common sense told him it was warmer inside than out.

"If it hadn't been for me?"

"You seduced my wife! Apparently the member for this constituency shouldn't have that sort of wife."

"But you told me——"

"You bloody liar, I didn't. I didn't. You've done me out of this constituency. You've done yourself out of it and for the same reason, or you would have done if you'd ever been a strong runner, which you weren't."

"I did you out of the seat? Me?"

"You were never a runner so far as the Committee was concerned. I was."

Grice's face had the kind of pallor that made the hair that grew on it seem artificial and stuck on: the moustache that slipped away from the corners of his mouth like gravy, the sideburns. What little wet blue eyes the man had! He had pursed up his mouth as though to spit.

Poumphrey hit him squarely just below the nose. The teeth grated on his knuckles and Grice went back among the pelargoniums, bringing down pots and shelves, ending up half lying across a bench with the back of his head resting against a splintered pane of glass. Even when Grice had stopped falling the clatter went on. Pots seemed to be jumping off the shelves in sympathy at the other end of the greenhouse.

Poumphrey came out of the greenhouse. Everyone on the terrace was looking in that direction. He took no notice. He charged between the tables making for the entrance to the hotel. He was just going through it when who should appear but Elaine herself.

"A chap called Partridge has got it," he shouted at her.

She looked at him, a bit startled by his manner. She was wearing an enormous, absurd, white hat, like a cowboy's with what looked like a dead rattlesnake instead of the usual sort of band. Her suit was white, too, with bits of leather hanging from it. The get-up didn't suit her. It made her seem pale and big eyed. She did not say anything and would have walked past but he caught her by the arm.

"Don't you understand?" He didn't give a damn that everybody was watching. He just didn't give a damn about anything now. "I'll have to find another constituency. If it's true, that is. You seen Plaistow?"

She tried to remove his hand from her arm. When he tightened his grip they both looked at it and saw the blood on his knuckles. Even now she said nothing. She fought to get away and Poumphrey realized she was cutting him. Why?

She lit up like magnesium. The sudden and totally unexpected blaze of white light made Poumphrey cry out; and what came into his mind, ridiculously, was a strip of the Syrian Hauran where Raouf once took him to picnic on whisky and cold chicken. The road to Damascus was what the bright light immediately put him in mind of. He could taste the chicken and the whisky. He could see the tawny hillside run away down to trees and green grass. The press photographer was at him again. He had a flash light that went off with the brilliant vehemence of total revelation.

Which was why Poumphrey came to treasure this print. The *Mirror* and the *Sun* were the only two papers to carry one. It showed him apparently fondling Elaine. His right hand seemed to be resting on her upper arm while she was apparently caressing it with her left. In reality, as he well knew, she was trying to tear his hand away and the expression on her face, as she looked up into his, was not so adoring as a trick of light made it seem. Her lips were parted in what readers might have supposed a controlled ecstasy. Not so. He was a realist. She was furious. That was not the point. The expression on his own face was the point. In the most matter of fact way it was the gaze of a man who had seen the light.

The caption said neither Arthur Poumphrey nor the husband of Mrs. Grice (photo above) had been selected by the East Dene Conservative Association to contest the impending by-election, and that Mr. Grice had been involved in an incident in a greenhouse leading to the breaking of some glass. As a photograph of the nominated Partridge was not printed it was clear to readers that the story was not about the selection of a candidate. It was not a story about anything, though professionals would have detected it was the beginning of a story.

In the illumination of the photographer's flash light Poumphrey saw that Mrs. Grice was cutting him for political reasons. What Grice had said before hitting the pelargoniums was sober truth. Having come straight from the greenhouse, to this encounter with the man's wife in the entrance hall of the hotel he was able to deduce she knew it was sober truth too.

A mistake. She cut him—as came out eventually—for his bad performance in bed, and would have cut him if Reggie had been nominated, if he himself had been nominated, or even if she had known about the Plaistow strategy that made any nomination other than Partridge's quite impossible anyway. Poumphrey was sexually incompetent in a way that had humiliated her. That was enough. She never claimed to have a head for politics. She cut a man on a more personal basis.

Poumphrey preserved the photograph as a record of the

moment when, as a consequence of the political indignation shown by Mrs. Grice, not to mention her loyalty to her husband, he saw the truth about himself.

Being a lawyer, Grice did not sue.

* * *

A part of the break-up that he now viewed, with some incredulity was this bit, immediately leading up to the interview of candidates at the Clarence, when he was busy trying to summon a Board meeting in his own house. Rogers had been all for his forgetting about business and politics. Generaille still came along from time to time, though—Rogers clearly regretted allowing the man to intervene even on an amateur basis—and said he was in favour of any course that led the patient to direct his psychic energy away from his own person.

"That is why I'm so much in favour of enemies," Generaille had said. "They externalize. You must cultivate your outside interests, dear."

There had never been any question of the East Dene Conservatives holding their selection committee in Poumphrey's house: Poumphrey always envisaged himself descending upon the Clarence with an impressive supporting cast—wife, of course, Mrs. Abel, now that he had had further talks with her and realized she might look impressive, Mitty, because her presence cheered him and gave him confidence; a nurse in uniform whose presence would demonstrate what he had been through and what determination had been necessary to bring him before the Committee at the right time; and Rogers himself, if available, even Generaille.

But did he really have this silly idea, even in the small hours when he couldn't sleep? An entourage that included medical attendants would not impress the Committee. It would dismay them. He was letting his oriental experience lead him astray. Yet it must have taken a strong hold on his imagination at some time or other for him to be remembering it now.

The Board meeting was different. That was reasonable, even practical. If the Board wanted to kick him out the least they could do was say why, in his presence at a properly constituted meeting. They had such meetings all over the place. There was no reason why one should not be held in his house if he was not well enough to go to the City. He was well enough. He just wanted to show his power and it was maddening the Board just sent a crate of champagne with a message to forget business for six months.

That afternoon (he remembered the coincidence) he thought he would phone Todd and ask him to come round again. He wanted to get at him because he had a suspicion Todd hadn't been party to this resignation demand and wanted to talk business. But Todd was tied up in some way. His secretary, rather surprisingly, was not even sure where he was.

One certain sign that he was better was his ability to look back on that particular afternoon without being worried. Of course he had been sick, but he was better. He had lost his temper and that was another good sign. He came out of a spin. He was absolutely fine (just angry) when those press photographs were taken; and the fact he could look back without worry at the afternoon when he tried to phone Todd, and then Todd came, just showed he was O.K. again now.

He had slept, woken up and was thinking he'd play his record of Elgar's second Symphony when he heard these footsteps on the stairs and wondered who had been let in. He had a quick ear for footsteps. He remembered footsteps better than faces. He remembered the way a man walked better than he remembered the man himself; he just did not know these footsteps. When the man came through the door he saw it was Todd. He looked like the old soldier on the Greys cigarette packet. That took you back. He had never forgotten the Edwardian seriousness of that rectangular moustache.

"Nobody about so I came straight up. You look fine, anyway."

"Good of you to come," said Poumphrey. "Why does

the Board want me out, that's what I want to ask you."

"You've earned yourself a bit less work." Todd took the black chair. "You don't need all this stress."

"I can take it."

"What I'm calling in question is achievement itself. And ambition. And work. Work is the drug of the well-to-do."

"I've never been one of these single-minded tycoon types," said Poumphrey. "Why do they want me out?"

"You haven't been kind to yourself. Be kind to yourself. Ease up. Buy yourself a flowered shirt, or something. What sort of ties do you wear? Well, get some big, bright ones. Stop being ambitious. Stop worrying. Stop being nervous. Let us sit quietly for a few minutes and enjoy nothing happening."

"They want to kick me out. You want to talk me out."

Todd leaned back in his chair and allowed himself to go all limp. He closed his eyes and Poumphrey, leaning well back in his own chair, was able to look up and see the clouds passing over the skylight. Cars could be heard swishing along the road so he guessed it had been raining. Apart from that it really was very quiet.

"You're making a mistake. I don't need soft soap. Will you answer my question?" Poumphrey could hear himself breathing and his heart beating.

Todd brought out phrases, such as, "Let us be still." Long pause. Breathing. Traffic noises. "Just let go." Pause. "Let go of our plans." Pause. "Our ambitions." Pause. "The world does not depend on us." Pause. "Let it go." Pause. "No need even to daydream." Pause. "Be still."

Poumphrey tried not to daydream but all he could think of was his resignation and whether, after all, he wasn't a fool to fight it. If they didn't want him on the Board, well to hell with them. He had his pride. "It's political pressure, isn't it? Over Damascus."

"Let go," said Todd. Pause. "Don't be afraid." Pause. "We

may be hurt but we need not be afraid." Pause. "If the pain is too much, we die." Long pause. "That's all."

Poumphrey said, "I don't get any actual pain. It isn't that."

If he had expected any comment on this he did not receive one. He had the impression his remark had been brushed aside. Maybe he had responded on a rather trivial level. The chap wasn't actually talking about immediate pains.

"I've never been afraid of my own death," said Poumphrey. "Only other people's."

"Those who are with us are more than those who are against us." Long pause. "Be still." Pause. "Let God be." Very long pause. "Creation is with us." Pause. "Let us enjoy the presence of God." Pause. Pause. Pause. "Be still and know that I am God."

What other people's death? Only his father's. Everybody else had seemed immortal. But he had known his father was going to die.

After some time Poumphrey heard the other chair creaking, opened his eyes, and saw that Todd was standing up and examining his collection of records. "I see you're interested in music. Strange that you and I have this in common too. I daresay we're the only two members of the Board who'd ever be caught at the Festival Hall."

"You talk like that," Poumphrey said. "But you don't believe it. Why don't you prise yourself out of the City if you can talk that way."

"The City is just a game to me," said Todd. "You and I could play this Parthian game if we wanted to."

"Nobody else is for it."

"I am."

Poumphrey thought this was a straight lie at the time, because Todd had clearly been trying to manipulate him; if there was one thing he could not stand it was the suspicion he was being manipulated. Todd must have studied him from a distance.

"I'll tell you the game I'm going to play," said Poumphrey.

"It's called Silly Buggers and I'm not resigning. I regard the Board's attitude with real concern. I'm concerned for the Company. We've never given way to political pressure like this before."

"There is political pressure," Todd had gone prowling about the room. He had a smile on his face but he was working his arms and shoulders as though to prevent stiffness settling in. He looked tough, even aggressive. "But that's not the main reason the Board thinks you ought to take a rest. You're so bloody disruptive."

Todd had so much surplus energy he circled about the room like a plane round an airport jettisoning petrol before an emergency landing. "You're the sort of chap who commits himself totally. You haven't even got any hobbies. Marvellous in a way. But you ought to ask yourself what you're running away from."

"I don't play games." Poumphrey had climbed out of his chair and joined Todd in his prowls. He never dodged a challenge. They did not move about together but cut a morris dance pattern of retreat and advance and circling, all in fairly slow motion.

"Naturally," said Todd. "The F.O. don't like unorthodox negotiations. What particularly annoys them is that it seems to have paid off this time. If you'd made a complete balls that would have given them a lot of satisfaction. But they claim it'll make the Syrians impossible to negotiate with next time. I don't take this view. I'm an admirer of yours. I'd like you to know that."

"I'm going to circularize the shareholders." Poumphrey shrugged all this off. Todd had some deep plan, no doubt, but he was clearly a bit touched. Talked like a Quaker. "I'll shake the Company to its back teeth."

Todd said he didn't think this would be necessary if Poumphrey would lie low for a bit. "The trouble is you do play games in a way but they are sometimes the wrong sort of games. A lot will depend on whether you know when it's the right time for lying low. That's what you should do right now. And trust me."

The first flash came when he was looking more or less directly into the camera and he was so dazzled it affected his sense of balance, which was one reason why he clutched Elaine's arm so tightly. By the time the second flash hit him he was already falling into a brilliant pit.

"Be still," he thought. Pause. "Let go." Pause. "Be empty." Pause. "Though the earth should change, though the mountains shake in the heart of the sea, though its waters roar and foam, the nations rage, the kingdoms totter." Pause. "There is no need to move." Pause. "Relax." Pause. "It's all a bit of a game."

He remembered letting Elaine go and how she was not there when next he spoke to her. He could not see anything, he was so dazzled. He cupped his hands over his eyes. He seemed to be falling through sharp patterns of white light. Someone was holding him by the arm but he shook himself free and pushed through the crowd.

"Poumphrey, I'd like you to meet Partridge," he heard somebody say in a very level bass voice. His hand was being shaken. The noise seemed unbearable.

"Be still," he thought. Pause. "Be empty." Pause. "Know that I am God." Pause.

That had been Plaistow's voice. Plaistow was now making the formal announcement that Partridge had been adopted as the prospective Conservative and Unionist candidate for East Dene and a few people, not many, clapped.

A man was complaining to someone, the hotel manager probably, that he had ordered tea in the garden half an hour ago and it had still not been served.

Although his eyes still hurt Poumphrey was beginning to see again. There was a strong, sweet smell. He was standing by a shelf where there seemed to be a lot of light. On this shelf was a small silver jug of lilies of the valley. He could see them quite clearly and precisely. He picked the jug up to smell the lilies better and it gave out a cold, secretive wink that made him gasp because of the way it struck into his eyes.

"A pain is just a pain," he thought. Pause. "I can bear it." Pause. "Let go." Pause. "Let it be." Pause. "Be still." Pause. "Let it go." Pause. Pause. Pause.

6

His wearing of dark glasses dated from this time. So did his increased hairiness. He agreed, too, that he was really rather a fat man and ought to be wearing more generously-cut clothes. He began by not shaving or having his hair cut for a month. His whiskers grew an unpleasant saffron colour and when he studied himself in the mirror he thought he looked a real bum. Jinny didn't say anything. Mrs. Abel didn't say anything. Even Mitty, when she came round, didn't say anything. They all seemed to think he needed tolerating a bit.

Later he had his hair cut properly, but he liked to wear it long, Southern planter style of the eighteen-sixties, with a moustache that grew wider, yellower, as the years went by; so he looked like a mangey tiger and his beard, he expected, would grow sandy and straggly, a beard to claw as he stared into space and saw, in his mind's eye, desert landscapes, sea shores and mountains. He saw Greece from an aeroplane, from the Gulf of Corinth to Olympus, and the high snows in the thin air and breath-taking sunshine. He saw places, not people; broken stone pillars at an abandoned site, that sort of thing. He cut out alcohol altogether. He drank barley water and lemon juice instead. He ate a lot of fruit and padded about his room in bare feet. His dreams were so agreeable he was ashamed of them. A man who had been defeated as he had been defeated had no right to happy dreams. He just didn't care what happened, so long as he spoke the truth. He wanted to confess. He wanted this so badly he had to check himself from confessing to things he had not actually done.

To Mitty he said, "I am a middle-aged man sucking your young blood."

To Mrs. Abel he said, "You put the fear of God in me."

To Jinny he said, "We never had any kids but I've got a son and it's time you knew about him."

As for Elaine, he went on thinking she cut him because she blamed him for Grice not getting the nomination and then compounding the disappointment by failing to get it himself. If he had she might have switched horses. He really thought she was that crazy to have a husband in the House of Commons. What other explanation could there be for turning her back on him at the Clarence? At that moment she could not possibly have known he'd bashed Grice in the pelargonium house.

With Grice himself he had a correspondence; because he wanted to apologize for carrying on with the man's wife, for knocking him down in that greenhouse, and so on—and he wanted to explain that he was a different man these days. Who better to make this explanation to than Grice? He wrote, mentioning St. Paul.

Grice wrote back a very nice letter, really. He said he was sorry Poumphrey had had such a time of it. He bore no resentment. It was the first time in his life he had been felled in this way. No harm done. All experience is an arch, etc. Then he ended up, "Of course, if I'd known you had this physical trouble I'd never have come to see you in the way I did. When Elaine told me the truth I felt a bit of a fool."

Poumphrey did not think this did justice to the transformation that had taken place. He wrote back to say that when he had mentioned St. Paul he did not wish to imply that he was making a direct comparison—there was, in the photographer's flashlight, a physical explanation for the sudden brilliance. He wasn't blind, of course. He just could not see very well. For a long time he had this feeling of being dazzled. That was why he wore dark glasses.

Poumphrey could tell from Grice's reply that the fellow thought he was round the bend. Grice offered to come round and talk about music. His previous visit had been based on a misunderstanding. Anyway, on that visit he had noticed the record player and the records. He tape-recorded broadcasts and as a result had a lot of rareties he'd be glad to share. He said that listening to good music persuaded him that Freud was wrong in suggesting that sex was as important as all that. There was so much propaganda about sex nowadays that anyone who hadn't an appetite for it was bound to feel inadequate. It was a passing phase. Lots of great people had been sexless and he didn't think Poumphrey ought to worry about it.

Poumphrey wrote back, saying that no doubt there would be a Freudian explanation for the crisis he had passed through. He was a human animal and he functioned as such. That was not the point. He had lived a life of illusion and now wanted a life of truth. That was what counted, the truth. He didn't know what else counted, really. He wanted to see people as they were and himself as he was.

He certainly didn't want Grice to come round and discuss music. He was more interested in the visual arts these days. He went to the National Gallery. He went to the Tate. He removed his dark glasses and, screwing up his eyes, peered at the canvases. It occurred to him the change he had lived through was a change in the way of perceiving. Once people and objects had seemed what he had needed them to seem. He had been like some Ancient Egyptian who represented people in profile and their eyes as though they were looking straight at you; and their hands held up to show they had five fingers. The world he had seen was the world he understood it to be. Now it was as though he had invented perspective and adopted an appropriate humility in the presence of nature. The bowl, when not seen from above, was not a circle but an ellipse. A foreshorted limb was a frightening thing to set down on paper. That was the sort of experience he was going through. Nobody understood.

He corrected himself. It was quite possible that everyone understood. It was possible Jinny understood. It was possible Mrs. Abel understood. He wasn't so sure about the value of raising the question so far as it concerned Mitty. But the truth of the matter could only be established by observation. He did a lot of observing from behind those dark glasses.

Be still, anyway, and know that I am God.

Be gentle with yourself. He thought of himself as being surrendered naked to a universe quite different from anything he could deduce from self-scrutiny. He had to look at *it*, the universe. This was painful. Music was not painful and that was another reason why he gave it up. It was the most self-regarding of the arts. He ought to have been some sort of scientist. In the hot weather (it turned out to be a splendid summer) he went walking on the Heath. He smiled at a lot of people and knew the impression he was making. They thought he was tight or simple. He heard singing in Hampstead Church one day and went in. But he came out quickly. Bach was a mistake. Art was a mistake.

* * *

"My first husband was a disappointed man, too," said Mrs. Abel. "His favourite quotation was, 'I strove with none for none was worth my strife.' That was rubbish. He was just weak. He did not compete. For him to say, for example, that I was not worth his strife was absurd. I was more intelligent than he was and I had a greater capacity for enjoyment. He was going to kill me once. He said he'd kill me and then he'd kill himself. That shows how negative he was. I don't value worldly success as a good in itself. But when it makes people cheerful and good company and gay, obviously one likes to have successful people of that sort about one. I suppose I'm a bit of a Calvinist. I've always had a sneaking suspicion that to be successful and godly were one and the same. You could almost say I have a theological objection to failure, especially if it is accompanied by self-pity. Do you pity yourself, Edward? You've had more of a set-back than he ever did."

"Your leaving him must have been a bit of a blow," said Poumphrey.

"It did him a service. He was one of those melancholy men who have no cause for melancholy and are not happy until they find it. I am quite sure I provided this man with enough resentment to fortify him for the rest of his life. Unlike you, everything about him was in a minor key."

"I'm in a major?"

"You had big expectations and they came to nothing. That's what I call failure."

"He was quite happy actually."

"Nonsense."

"Yes, he was, wasn't he, Jinny? He married rather a nice woman."

"I'd heard she was extravagant and rather empty-headed," said Mrs. Abel.

"Yes." Poumphrey thought this over. "That was what he liked. He never felt sorry for himself, anyway. She was very rich. They made a good couple."

"I'm not interested," said Mrs. Abel. "I'm too old. My leg hurts."

* * *

Darling Gogo (Mitty wrote from her Villaparty holiday on the Costa Brava) Darling Gogo, I thought the sun always shone here but there's been rain and haze. I don't know what my state of mind is. If I were at home I know I should be miserable but I'm on holiday and that means I'm happy. You told me always to say everything that was in my mind. We have a launch and we all go water-skiing, or try to. Certainly I'm no good at it. I can't stay on the skis. We eat a lot of fruit and the wine isn't charged for, so I get a bit tight and in fact we all get a bit tight. There are only two married couples. Give my love to Jinny. She has been very sweet to me. She is a good woman. It isn't every wife who would be so nice to one of her husband's girl friends even to keep him going through a bad patch and all the disappointments you've had.

I sometimes wonder whether you understand what a remarkable woman she is. Except for these married couples the rest of us are on our own and we sit up half the night in a club here. Everything is very free and easy. Pierre drives the launch. It's surprising he's not Spanish, he's a Frenchman. He's always fishing me out of the water. We all went by coach to a bull fight but Pierre said he'd sit in a bar until it was over. Actually I stayed with him because his English is quite good and he's always laughing. Today is really hot and we had to sit in the shade. I've always been careful but deep down I'm very miserable, though I don't show it. I'm not naturally sexy. I don't think I'd ever be really casual about it. You'd like Pierre, though. I like him, I think. He's so determined.

I'm writing a real letter not a postcard because, after all, I said I would and I sometimes think you are my best friend. You understand me so well and if I got into real trouble I know you would help. Jinny would help, too. I have the feeling I could always come to you and Jinny. Is Mrs. Abel still with you, I wonder. Please give her my love and say I'm having a marvellous time.

Pierre says he likes older girls and I must say I've never known anyone so attentive. You can imagine the horrible things the other girls are saying. I don't care. They are just jealous. You can get drunk on this local champagne without a hangover. I'd like this holiday to go on for ever. I heard a girl laughing this afternoon. It really rang out. After a bit I realized it was me. You get rather beside yourself in this heat. The light is dazzling. We are going to a party tonight. There's another big house on the hillside opposite with a swimming pool and it's run by the same agency. It gets a bit riotous and it's only a matter of time before the Spanish police raid the place.

Pierre says it's not just a holiday affair and that he is going to see me afterwards, but it won't be that way and in my heart I know it's all awful and I shall be ashamed of myself. I couldn't stop him, Gogo. The other girls are as bad, or would be if they could. You know what I mean, though. Some of them are really plain.

You know what I am. I have to say just what is in my mind because I don't like keeping bottled up. I can't stand secretive people, can you, Gogo? I just love everybody to know about everything. Girls are always doing silly things on holidays but I'm the silly-billy who says so, I mean actually lets on about herself. Do you think this means I've no self-respect? I think it is so important to have dignity. I'd be so upset if I thought that Pierre did not respect me. I should feel awful. Must close now, hoping you are continuing to make progress. Love to Jinny and Mrs. Abel.

Mitty.

* * *

"This meeting of the Board is extraordinary in more ways than one," said Lowther. "For one thing it is held in my house and not in the company's Board room. For another it has been convened at short notice and is additional to the normal meetings of the Board; so it is extraordinary in the conventional sense of the term. As you know, it has been called at the request of Edric Todd. We're all here except Edgar and Herman. They're on holiday. My secretary is not here. There'll be no minutes, except those I write myself and get you ultimately to sign. Now the extraordinary—in the common meaning of the word—thing about this meeting is that one of our number has engaged himself not to speak."

They all looked at Poumphrey who was wearing a white linen bush shirt, open at the neck and rather smart trousers in small black-and-white check. They had noticed that he wore no socks, only what looked like slippers in basketwork. His beard was about six weeks old at this time and his hair hung down like a sheep dog's. He grinned at everybody, utterly relaxed, looking doggy and friendly in a way that clearly alarmed everybody except Todd who said, "Arthur and I have been having some long talks. It was his idea he wouldn't say anything. Mind you, he'll answer questions. But his line was that if he didn't speak you wouldn't hold it against him."

"It seems a bit irregular," said Lowther. "It puts the rest of us at a disadvantage."

"Well, it's the way he wanted to play it," said Todd, "and as the Board has called for his resignation it didn't seem unreasonable to me that we should tell him why. Arthur's oath of silence is just to make it clear he's not going to argue or state his case, or anything like that. He just wants to listen. He wants to hear why the Board wants him to go. He's not aggressive about it."

"Didn't you tell him?" asked Nightingale.

"He wants to hear it from the Board sitting as a Board."

"What were we doing, for Chrissake, last time this matter was under discussion? Arthur was present. He knows the name of the game. I'm sorry but I think this meeting is totally unnecessary. Let him circularize the shareholders. We know how futile that is, the way this company's equity is held. We've been into all this. It's distasteful." Nightingale was a hairless, clean-looking man who when he was angry looked as though he had just had a very hot bath. The little fringe of white hair at the base of his skull stood out against the glowing, almost steaming, red skin. "The company is more important than personalities. O.K. I know Arthur's been ill. That was the only consideration that brought me along tonight."

"Arthur's been ill," Todd agreed. "That's the starting point. But he's fine now and he just wants to listen to what we've got to say."

"Well?" said Lowther, who was the chairman and felt he ought to be taking a grip on the proceedings.

"Arthur wants to know the truth. He wants to know what we think of him. He's not going to defend himself. He's hitting bottom."

Lowther was suspicious. "He's not going to confess, is he,

and thank us and say his faults are acknowledged." Lowther liked his joke. "We're not bloody Maoists here."

"I wish Arthur wouldn't just sit there saying nothing." This was Drew who was quite sure Poumphrey must go, though he liked him well enough; he just didn't care for the inquisitorial atmosphere. "Unless this is some sort of therapy," he added, as an afterthought.

"Arthur's fine. He doesn't need any therapy," said Todd.

"I'm not going to play any part in the humiliation of anybody, even if it is at that person's request," said Drew.

"Arthur would be grateful if you'd just speak out. There are one or two thing's he's authorized me to say. He's not angry about the Board's decision and he certainly doesn't bear any resentment against anyone. Arthur has had an experience. As a result of this—well, illumination I'd call it, I guess—he's just about committed to getting to the bottom of things. I don't know what we've got to be uptight about it."

Poumphrey just sat there, looking round, smiling and rubbing his face now and again. It made a surprisingly loud rasping noise.

Lowther drew a lot of air up his big nose and held it for some time, his chin on his chest, while he thought and drummed with the fingers of both hands on his splayed-out knees. They were not sitting at a table. The Board was in arm-chairs. "I'm out of my depth, I must confess," he said. "Arthur is *persona non grata* with the Foreign Office, the Syrians have said they'll never let him set foot in the country again and he has this way of personalizing issues at the Board so that we get involved in interminable arguments with a lot of heat in them. He is too much of an individualist for an organization like ours. And basically it's no good having a negotiating director who hasn't the confidence of the Foreign Office. It's as simple as that."

"It isn't just his known views on the desirability of a merger with Parthian?" Todd was making notes as he spoke.

Nobody spoke so Lowther got up and opened a cabinet. "There's whatever you like. Who's for booze?" He looked at

Poumphrey. "You're the guest of honour, Arthur. What'll it be? Scotch?"

"Tomato juice," said Poumphrey, speaking for the first time.

"Merger, you call it," said Nightingale. "Take-over is what it would turn out to be."

Nightingale helped to dispense the drinks. Poumphrey was scruffier than any of them. At the same time he looked ruddily healthy. Above those yellow whiskers the cheeks were brick red. He gave out a curious, sweet smell, too, like stored apples.

"We want to be clear this isn't political pressure," said Todd.

"He just won't be supported by the F.O., that's all."

"That isn't what I call political pressure. That isn't government pressure, just saying that, is it?"

Everyone was now standing, except Poumphrey, and Todd leaned with one hand on the back of his chair. "When I was a kid I can remember once looking at a lot of people in their sixties and seventies and being amazed. It was a family party. They were grandparents and great-uncles and aunts, you know. We were a big family. Well, I was amazed by them because I knew, and they knew, they were all going to die pretty soon, it was in the nature of things, but they went on laughing and talking and drinking, as we're drinking now. I wasn't going to die for a long time. I was seven, or eight, or whatever it was. At that age one feels immortal. But all those oldies were on the edge of the grave and I remember being really quite astonished, I really marvelled, at the jolly way they were taking it. Well, here I am. I'm sixty-four and I'm drinking and talking."

Lowther came over to Poumphrey and said, "You sure you're sticking to tomato juice? You can rely on us to do the right thing financially, Arthur. We're paying your salary for five years. You're a young man."

Poumphrey never said anything but "Tomato juice" that evening, not even when Drew, after a few whiskies, began talking about the Iraq Petroleum Company and saying the native intelligence in the organization was supplied by expatriate Palestinian Arabs, which meant it was bound to be virulently anti-Zionist at the local level. It was a great disability for any oil man, nowadays to be thought an Israeli sympathizer, or partly Jewish, or anyway, you know!

"The F.O. doesn't take this seriously, not so far as Arthur is concerned," said Lowther who had been listening carefully. "Let's be honest, it's a factor."

"No, not at all. What really sent the F.O. up the wall was the way Arthur compromised that fellow in the Syrian Ministry of Foreign Affairs. Raouf what's his name?"

"Raouf Omra," said Todd.

"What happened to him?" asked Nightingale.

"Not absolutely certain but they're pretty doctrinaire in Syria these days and one theory is they just shot him."

Nightingale was amazed and said, "Why doesn't anybody tell me things? I didn't know that was why Arthur was out. I thought it was because we didn't like him."

Todd turned on him savagely.

* * *

Jinny had had her hysterectomy quite early on. They never talked about kids after that except when Jinny said she did not like them. The subject usually came up when they were staying in some hotel where kids were making a bit of a nuisance of themselves and Jinny would say something like, "Assuming the human race has to perpetuate itself there ought to be a better way."

They never even discussed the possibility of adoption. Jinny didn't like the look or feel of babies. She didn't know how to talk to small children. Her attitude wasn't natural, and because it wasn't natural it couldn't be true. Behind it all—Poumphrey now saw—there was quite possibily an unacknowledged yearning for a family and if he had only done as he had wanted, adopted a baby or two and a nanny to cope, life might have been different, they might have been happy. Jinny would have discovered kids were lovely. He was fond of children. He was cut out to be a father. He saw himself playing cricket on the beach with his big family; or walking into the lounge of some hotel on the continent with his teenage daughters, tired but merry after their sight-seeing; and people would look up, saying, "There's that English family again." Jinny didn't feature in all this.

She might, after her first resentment, have taken to an adopted baby, especially if it were pretty and turned out to be intelligent. But the idea never seriously came into his head and Jinny took up with Black Africa. Perhaps these blacks were her children. Perhaps that was the nearest she would ever get to confessing she wanted babies of her own. Maybe they could have adopted a black baby. To satisfy Jinny, he guessed, it would have to be a genuine African-born baby, none of your British-born blacks of West Indian descent. At the time when adoption might have been a genuine possibility for them the Korean War was on and there must have been a lot of Korean orphans needing a home; later, of course, there were the Vietnam orphans. Jinny might have overcome her dislike of children if they had been Korean or Vietnamese but he suspected the only real welcome would have been for a real black baby from Africa with the flies still gummed to its eyes and mouth.

"Why didn't you tell me before?" That was her reaction when Poumphrey told her he thought he had a son living somewhere in the North of England. No shock or outrage. Just surprise that he should have kept quiet about it for so long. He thought that maybe she supposed he was still ill, or lying, or subject to some delusion and in need of being humoured and understood.

"Well, she's married, you see. She's got other children and her husband thinks they're all his."

"But you know differently?"

"Yes."

"She doesn't want it known?"

"No."

"Then there's no more to be said. Or done."

"Don't you want to hear about it?"

"Of course not. Why should I?"

"But don't you want to know how it happened?"

"No."

He was incredulous. "I've been nursing this for years and I I want to get it off my chest."

"It was before we got married?"

"That's right."

She thought for a while. "I don't see this is any business of mine but if talking about it will make you feel better."

He said it was when he worked for Northern Refineries. They used to have management conferences, usually at big hotels in the country and at Gleneagles that year wives and girl friends were invited along too.

"Why wasn't I there?" said Jinny.

"Wasn't your father ill?"

"He died in 1950."

"I don't know why you weren't there. I got friendly with a couple and I remember the woman, she had her hair treated so that it looked silver, talking behind her husband's back about him. She told me she married him because he'd have been upset if she didn't. And she'd never let him touch her. They didn't sleep together. It was weird. I mean, why should she tell me all this? She said he was just physically unattractive to her. That's how I know the boy is mine. We made love one afternoon when the rest of the party were at a film show. She sent me the announcement of birth cut out of the paper nine months later."

"You believe this?"

"I'm just telling you what happened. It isn't a question of believing or disbelieving. The boy was christened Mark Frederick."

"How do you know she and her husband had more children

later on? Did she send you more clippings out of the paper?"

"As a matter of fact she did."

"So you haven't kept in touch?"

"No. I don't know where they are. The last I heard was about twelve years ago. They might have emigrated for all I know."

"Did she know you married?"

"Yes."

"How did you let her know?"

He hesitated. "I sent the announcement clipped out of *The Times*."

Jinny laughed violently at this, a bit hysterically he thought. The news had come as a greater shock than she liked to pretend. Jinny did not understand herself. Dragging the truth out into the open, as he had done, would make her look at herself as much as it made him look at himself. They were stripping off illusion and deceit, both of them.

"I didn't realize you were so innocent," she said.

"Innocent? I know what happened."

"If this woman wasn't sleeping with her husband and then she had a baby how do you think she'd explain that?"

"To her husband, you mean?"

"Yes."

Once this would have been enough to put him in a rage but a man who was purging himself of myths and self-deception had to be ready for calm explanations. In a way he was glad Jinny asked these questions. It showed she wanted to arrive at the truth too. He was just puzzled she wasn't upset to learn he had a son when she had failed to provide him with any children at all. He reckoned she was still fighting unwelcome news.

"I'd always supposed she started a normal sex life with her husband to cover up."

"Or he forgave her," said Jinny. "He might have been besotted. A man who'd have been upset if she didn't marry him might be so much in love he would have taken anything just to keep her."

This had never occurred to Poumphrey and he was pleased with the idea. "Then they had children of their own. In a way I started their marriage off."

Jinny seemed to be enjoying herself in a way he found explicable only in terms of shock. A woman didn't go on giggling, normally, when her husband tells her he'd got a bastard.

"Perhaps there were other management conferences," said Jinny. "I mean, after you left Northern Refineries. Perhaps she sent a whole lot of clippings from the paper and her husband just had to put up with it."

"She didn't just send me a clipping. Later on she sent me a photograph."

"What was their name?"

"Puddifoot."

Jinny began shrieking and blowing her nose so violently Poumphrey went and put his arm around her. "I want you to forgive me, Jinny. I must see this boy."

"Don't be such an utter fool," she yelled. "Fancy falling for a story like that!"

"I've got to know what I've done. It's not a story. A man comes into the world. He's got to know where he's come from and what he leaves behind. I've got to face this boy. He's my flesh and blood."

"The woman seduced you, and I'll bet you weren't the first."

"I'm sorry to have hurt you, Jinny."

Jinny quietened down and went to tidy up her face in front of a mirror. "I'd like to have ten minutes on the phone with Mrs. Puddifoot. Have you still got that photograph?"

"I suppose so."

"I don't suppose for one moment the child was yours. The woman was lying."

Poumphrey had had to shake his head sadly at this because he knew differently.

There had been a heavy thunderstorm earlier and the rain had been thudding down for some time. Now in the late afternoon, it eased off and they could hear cars swishing up the hill and water dripping from the leaking pipe just outside this sitting-room window. The comfortless wet of high summer seeped into his mind. Another way of putting it would have been that Jinny's worry crept on him like damp. July was autumnal. It was only half-past five but there were lights on in the house opposite.

What was the good of it all? He knew that was what she was thinking. He would meet this boy and no doubt the boy would know nothing of his origin. He would have to be told. Perhaps Mrs. Puddifoot would create difficulties. Absurd he couldn't remember her first name. Iris? Daphne? He had an idea it was Greek. No matter what pain the confrontation might bring it was better for everybody to know the truth—the boy himself, Iris (might be Diana), the husband, Jinny and he himself. Jinny was prepared to brush the truth under the carpet. That was her immediate reaction. But as time went by Poumphrey knew she'd think about this boy and he'd be all the more worrying because of his vagueness. That was the way myths were born. Poumphrey knew. He had walked with this one for years.

But it was going to be bloody unpleasant, going up to Dewsbury or Wakefield, or some place like that and meeting your bastard son for the first time and shaking hands with a cuckold. Perhaps they were all dead, killed in a car crash. He didn't see it that way, though, it would have been too easy. He'd have to get on to the Northern Refineries and check up on the Puddifoots on their payroll. Once he had the address what would he do then? Write? Telephone? Just go? Take Jinny with him? Nothing would be evaded. No sparing of feelings. No evasion, no false delicacy, no dishonesty, no hypocrisy; nothing but the great cold gale of truth.

* * *

Instead of going north he drove south, to Chichester, from

where a message had come saying that Mrs. Abel was in hospital. She had been taken ill some time previously. They had thought it odd not to have heard from her.

"I've come here to die," she said when they were shown into her private ward. She looked very clean. Her head and shoulders were supported by several pillows, so much so that she was almost sitting upright. Her grey hair was parted in the middle and ran, straight as running water, to her shoulders. She reminded Poumphrey of a picture he had once seen of Liszt as an old man. Over her feet was a cage to take the weight of the bedclothes and she invited Poumphrey to lift them and describe what he saw.

"Go on," she said, when he hesitated.

He lifted the bedclothes and saw that one of her feet was discoloured and almost black.

"My heart is so inadequate the circulatory system is not working. In a few days my kidneys will cease to function and then I shall go into a coma. This is not very interesting in itself." They had to bend down to hear what she was saying.

"Feet are not important. Legs are not important. They can be amputated and the trunk goes on living, but to what purpose? It's bad enough being diabetic with the use of all one's limbs."

"I'm sorry to see you like this."

"Hallo, Jinny. Kiss me!" she said. "I just passed out and the next thing I knew I was here. I'm dying. I quite insist, my dear."

"I daresay Sister has other ideas," said Jinny as the Ward Sister came in. "You must come and spend your convalescence with us, mustn't she Sister?"

"She's looking much brighter, today," said the Sister. "She's got quite a touch of colour, hasn't she? This nice room with all the sunshine. Flowers. Everything as it should be. Don't tire her now. She's such a one for talking. Not too much excitement. No, we don't talk of convalescence these days. Once she's out of here she'll need to take it quietly a bit."

"Tell them I'm dying, Sister," said Mrs. Abel. "I hate conversations that are based on false assumptions."

"We're all dying, Mrs. Abel."

"Stupid creature," Mrs. Abel said as soon as she had gone.

"I hope they're treating you well." The day was so hot Poumphrey was wearing an open-neck shirt, slacks and some bedroom slippers in purple leather. Jinny had tried to persuade him to put on some proper shoes but he had insisted they were just right for driving. Indoors at home he had taken to walking about naked. It relaxed him. It left him free. A man, when he was naked, could think only of the essentials. Jinny said he looked like one of those wooden figures with weighted bottoms who always returned to the vertical however you hit them; he had this same glazed expression on his face too. There was no question of driving about in a car naked but by wearing bedroom slippers he felt he was indicating his real frame of mind. He took them off and showed them to Mrs. Abel who was not interested.

"You want the truth, well this is it!" she said. "A gangrenous foot."

She was lying there, quite helplessly, but the attack was as real in its way as when she had lifted her walking-stick and prodded him in the stomach, so that he fell and struck his head. She did not need to spell out again that message about taking himself too seriously. "Human kind cannot bear very much reality. You'll have to settle for some sort of self-deception. St. Paul settled for self-deception. If impossible things were not true then we were much to be pitied. Which is as much as to say we were to be pitied. I've always chosen my illusions for myself, because I believe nothing and know nothing and expect nothing. My old carcase is rotting about me. But I summon myself. You are my son and you forgive me and you love me. I make up my mind to it. When you come to it reality is just a black foot. I choose to say I am dying and you are my son. It isn't human kind not bearing much reality. That's not how I'd put it. They choose the reality that is as near the limit of pain as they can bear."

Jinny helped her to a drink and Poumphrey watched the streaming hair fall back as the lined face came forward and the lips fastened on the rim of the glass. She had stopped talking but he could still hear her slow, faint, croaking. He was upset. He didn't know what to say. He was trying to be truthful. Why couldn't she be truthful too?

"I don't see what there is to forgive you for."

This made Mrs. Abel laugh, Jinny wiped her face with a flannel and then dabbed at it with an airline eau-de-Cologne pad that she found in her handbag. She explained it was left over from her last trip to Geneva where she had been for some conference. Mrs. Abel wanted to know which conference. Jinny replied that it was to do with the supply of textbooks to schools in certain African countries.

Mrs. Abel went on laughing as she held the eau-de-Cologne pad between the finger and thumb of her right hand; as much as to say, "Well, if the delegates all got eau-de-Cologne pads at least that is something." And she may have been thinking this. But when she lifted her eyes and looked at Poumphrey she said, "You're right, Edward. There's nothing to forgive."

"Why do you dislike me so much?"

"Dislike you?" She stared at him. "You're a fool, aren't you? See, you're making me cry." The tears welled up and flowed copiously down her cheeks. She made no attempt to wipe them away but lay there staring at Poumphrey as though the familiar had been made strange and needed studying.

"Can't you shut up?" Jinny said to him as she got busy with the flannel again.

"It doesn't matter. I just wanted to know, that's all." Poumphrey was surprised she'd been distressed by his question. "This isn't a moment for hypocrisy."

Mrs. Abel blew her nose, took another drink, and then said calmly, "Tell me again about all those eyes you saw."

"We're talking too much." Jinny began extracting the dead

roses from the vase. "We'll go away in a few minutes and come back this evening. We don't want to tire you."

"Tell me about the eyes," Mrs. Abel repeated.

When he had first told her about the eyes she had not seemed to pay much attention. In early August Jinny had been up in the first-floor sitting-room with a lot of students listening to a Zulu poet, Mrs. Abel and Poumphrey had been sitting in the garden on the other side of the house to be away from the noise, and there had been a sudden spectacular thunderstorm. They scurried indoors. The Zulu poet made almost as much noise as the thunder and after a while, when the storm had moved away, all they could hear was his voice, a high, ritual chanting, and the steady downpour of rain.

Poumphrey said that one of the delusions from which he had suffered was to do with brown eyes. He had only to see a certain type of brown-eyed man—rather large eyes, widely separated—and it didn't matter whether they were fair haired, or dark haired, or bald or whatever; but to him they were all the same person. While the Zulu poet chanted and the rain drummed Poumphrey stood in the little back parlour overlooking the garden with Mrs. Abel watching the lights come on in the houses through the trees and the clouds over the rooftops crack and re-form against a remote, bright, thin, blue. He talked of the different disguises this person adopted. It was absurd. It was comical. No doubt everybody had some trivial illusion. He had never mentioned this before but now he wanted to bring it into the open. The brown eyes, he said, signified a kind of awareness of him. Behind those different faces, hidden in those different bodies, was the same individual Being. He always recognized this Being by the brown eyes.

"Friendly?" Mrs. Abel had asked.

Poumphrey did not know about this. There was an M.P. he had met on a plane, and a Syrian general, and a member of the Board, and, so far as he could remember, a man called Trapp who used to teach him at Cambridge. Poumphrey said he was going to see each of these men again and establish that he was no more than he purported to be. Yes, they were all quite friendly. They had all seemed interested in him. Poumphrey did not know quite how to express it.

"You don't mean you're actually going to check up on them to make sure they are not the same person masquerading in different ways? You would need to assemble them in the same room and at the same time. Then you'd be sure——" He never knew when she was laughing at him.

He said he wasn't that crazy. He knew that they were quite different men who had no connection with one another except in his own mind; but he wanted to see them again.

So here, since she asked him to, he talked about the eyes again, and she said yes, everybody was crazier than they liked to confess to; she herself could never quite rid herself of the idea she had a mysterious royal origin.

"I don't have these feelings," said Jinny.

"Oh, you must do." Mrs. Abel leaned back with her eyes closed. "Think!"

"No," said Jinny. "I think we ought to be going now. We'll come back at about seven."

Mrs. Abel seemed to be asleep, but she whispered that life would be intolerable without delusions.

To kill time Poumphrey and Jinny walked across the playing fields. Mrs. Abel's remark about delusions took him farther than he wanted to go.

* * *

The most recent brown-eyed man had been Chairman of a constituency committee in the east Midlands who wrote to say his brother lived in East Dene and had given him an account of the splendid show he had put up when seeking the nomination there. At this east Midlands constituency they were looking for a strong candidate to contest the next election and if Poumphrey was interested this fellow—his name was Pritchett—wanted him to come and have lunch at the Athenaeum. For this encounter Poumphrey wore his Chairman Mao outfit which consisted of a tieless blue cotton shirt buttoned at the throat and blue cotton slacks. The shirt hung outside the slacks. He wore white tennis shoes. Pritchett took a pretty big whisky before lunch. Poumphrey watched this behaviour carefully and contented himself with a tomato juice. The eyes were usually on him, and as soon as the meal had been ordered Poumphrey said, "With a name like yours you must be of Welsh descent. I should like to investigate your Pritchettness."

Pritchett was a bit staggered by this and tried to laugh. He was a fresh-faced man who plainly spent a lot of time out of doors. "Pritchettness? I suppose so. I don't know what you mean, really. Actually, it isn't a Welsh name. Do you never drink? I mean, are you a teetotaller? Good thing. Very wise. We're both big men. People know when we're in the room. A good thing in politics. Well, drink water if you want to. I'll have a pint of draught. Bloody odd way of conducting things in East Dene, I hear. Still, their misfortune may be our good fortune. My brother put me up to it. I say, if you don't mind me mentioning it old chap, that's a funny get-up. I don't know they'd like this in our neck of the woods."

"You've never set eyes on me before, have you?" asked Poumphrey.

Pritchett laughed. "Wouldn't swear to it. You're not a member here?"

"You don't really know me?"

"That's the purpose of this lunch, getting to know each other, you see. Our man's taken a job with the Steel Corporation. You've seen the story in the Press. He's a shit. Why don't we get down to business straight away? You're interested in the constituency? Of course, it's a Labour seat. There'll be a fight. Majority two thousand. Marginal. Our man's in next time. You see what I'm getting at? What d'you mean, Pritchettness?"

The eyes were the same and there was something about Pritchett's manner that revealed he was putting on an act. His behaviour could not be explained as the ordinary nervousness of meeting a stranger. To Poumphrey it appeared a deliberate pose. Common sense told him it was not a pose. There was no presence inside the skull, looking out through those brown eyes; just a man, just Pritchett. Poumphrey was enjoying the game of establishing whether there was a mask or not.

"I've a feeling we've met before. We know each other, don't we?"

"Honestly, old chap. I'm always meeting people, you know. If we've met I apologize for not remembering. Perhaps it's the beard."

"You don't remember?"

Poumphrey held up his two hands, palms out, to conceal the lower part of his face and his beard.

"No." Pritchett paused with a spoonful of vichyssoise half-way to his mouth. "It's my brother you're thinking of. We're not unlike."

Poumphrey lowered his fork, stared at Pritchett, and saw him visibly dwindle like a witch whose spell had backfired. It was the first time he had had the experience of seeing the Eyes —and he could have sworn they were the real Eyes and they recognized him—only to find the face in which they were set take over. Engulf them, almost. Pritchett did not have to prove he was Pritchett. He really was.

"I don't know that I'm interested in seeking nomination. East Dene was a turning point so far as I was concerned. You've not heard of my illness? I don't know that I'm cut out for politics. Render unto Caesar, you know."

"My brother said you were absolutely splendid. I quite agree about Caesar. What the House wants nowadays is the occasional prophetic utterance, and all that. Have I understood you? Tell me, have I put my finger on it? You see, I know what the Party and the House are in need of. Render unto Caesar! I say, I like that. Who said it? Where does it come from? Of course, it's Christ. I was on the point of saying. He knew a thing or two. Am I reading you? Do I know your mind?"

Poumphrey had accepted the invitation to lunch in order to

test himself. It would be a way of establishing whether or not he was still interested in a political career. That, he already knew, pretty well. But when he saw the brown eyes, he realized that he had the opportunity to make an even more important test. As soon as he established the man was merely Pritchett and there was no other intelligence looking out of that skull Poumphrey put his fork down, rose to his feet, made his excuses and walked out of the dining-room. He was sorry about having to deny himself smoked trout. Pritchett was too amazed even to call after him.

* * *

Jinny said, "It's pathetic the way she just has to see herself as your mother."

She was driving. Poumphrey, at her side, had switched off the car radio. "Let's get out and walk a bit. I think I know where this goes to."

They had been on the road to Selsey. The sun was high and hot but under the elms where they parked the shade was cool. They could smell the sea. They followed a path through the trees and came to what looked like a long pond, separated from the sea by shingle. The sun glared, the pond was dead blue, the shingle scoured and purple-pitted but brilliant against the pallid wash of the Channel. To the left shone the brown estuary water. On the other side remote white houses flickered among the trees.

"When you stayed with her that time I came down and looked at you."

"You did?"

"Yeah. I got into the garden late at night and watched the both of you through the window."

"Why didn't you come in?"

They sat on the shingle and tossed little brown pebbles into the lagoon. He found the branch of a tree that had been so long in the water it might have been the antler of a deer. He used it to scrape among the pebbles as though, if he only scraped enough of them away, he would find what he was looking for down there. He just found more pebbles, wet ones.

"Listen", he said, "I'd like to tell you what happened from my point of view and we'll see if it squares with what you remember."

"You mean that time I stayed with her?"

"When you ran out on me, yeah, back in April, that's it. You ran out on me. You went down and joined her at Sidlesham. I couldn't take that at all. I was bloody angry. I might have killed you. I could have done that." He searched his beard with his fingers and wished it had been thicker. So far as his fatness permitted he sat erect and cross-legged. There was strain on his knees and if he sat as upright as he liked he could not see his crossed ankles for his belly. "I don't know why you did it. But I don't care." He made a quick gesture. "Don't tell me."

"Anybody living with you deserves a break from time to time."

"I accept that. Don't go on."

"I don't understand why, if you did come down, you didn't show yourself. You're not lying again, are you?"

"You'll be able to judge for yourself."

He left Jinny and went walking along the shore—a barefooted, middle-aged man, wet to the knees of his blue cotton slacks, carrying his purple slippers in his left hand, the sweat showing up in patches on his shirt, screwing up his eyes against the glare of the sea. He was wondering how serious the black foot was. He was wondering, if Mrs. Abel were really dying, whether, at the last, she would break out of her too well-guarded position and tell him—well, what? Oh, God knows! She must know! Something!

He had started to put on weight again. The funny thing was that although the flesh expanded the skin did not split. He ought to feel tighter all over but on the contrary he was looser. His cheeks wobbled. He liked wearing as little clothes as possible. His bones had enough to wear in the way of flesh.

The sea had always fascinated him. He peed in it. Three or four yards out the water was silky. It lifted long backs to the sun you wanted to stretch out and scratch, like the backs of cats, sea cats that purred and spat their pleasure. He was a poor swimmer. He knew that the beach shelved sharply and if he walked after the cats he'd be out of his depth. He thought for some time about walking out of his depth and then went back to Jinny.

"I'd like to tell you what happened", he said again, "as I saw it. And then I'd like to know whether you remember it differently."

"Remember what?"

"I'm trying to tell you."

Jinny looked smart in her blue trouser suit, a bit like a sailor and it occurred to Poumphrey the outdoor life might have suited her more than the existence she led; he saw her busy with horses—she looked a bit like a horse—or pulling in the nets. She'd look almost sexy on some mannish activity. Maybe she just wanted to be a man and that was what was wrong with their marriage. He could see her as a sexy peasant or fisherman. But any woman who knew she couldn't have kids would trick herself into believing she was secretly a man. Jinny had certain advantages. An unmistakable fine little moustache, for example.

"You played Canasta down there, didn't you?" he said.

"Yes."

"And *she* wore a green sort of dress and over it she wore a white stole. All I remember about you was the Bahrein comb. You were wearing the Bahrein comb, weren't you? You had your back to the window and she was facing the window."

Jinny still did not know whether he was serious.

"You've got to remember that if you were peeking at us through the window one particular evening we wouldn't have been aware of it. I wouldn't remember any particular evening when we were sitting the way you say. But it's possible."

"You really didn't know I was watching? Neither of you?"

"I've only got your word for it you were there. I suppose that's good enough. No I didn't know you were there. If she did she didn't say anything. And she would have said something, wouldn't she?"

He said he would have to spell the whole story out and he wanted her to seize on any detail that, in her recollection, was wrong. So far so good. She hadn't denied the card game, the green dress, the stole or the Bahrein comb. But this was information he could have picked up. He knew Jinny had taken the Bahrein comb with her, he knew Mrs. Abel had a green dress and a white stole because she had worn them on other occasions; and it was well known she liked Canasta. He could have deduced what he would see through the window at Sidlesham without actually going down there.

"It was pretty late. Not many lights in the village. I parked the car in the yard, and expected one of you to come out because the back door was open and there was a light over it. But nobody came out. I thought maybe you were watching television and hadn't heard the car so I walked into the kitchen. And I tell you what. I remember what it smelled like that evening. It was warm and wet. There'd been a lot of rain. No moon. You couldn't go wandering about without a light. I could smell the dead rain and mustiness and a sweet smell, it might have been lilac. In the kitchen it was sweet too, like a dairy. I could hear you talking in the sitting-room and I knew you hadn't heard the car and you weren't watching any show. I just wanted to see you both without being seen. So I went round the side of the house. I took my shoes off."

Jinny was incredulous. She sat up straight. Her lips were tight and her eyes enormous. "Well, I seem to remember the doors being left open. Mrs. Abel said she liked air to circulate. There were warm evenings. A lot of early moths came in."

"You see?" An old woman leaving the back door open to ensure the air of a warm spring evening flowed through her house was not a detail he could have hit upon by accident. It must have been the way it was and he could see Jinny appreciated the fact.

Poumphrey said he stood on the outside, looking in at the two women playing Canasta and as he remembered the scene, he said, there was a bowl of daffodils on a table just behind them.

Jinny shrugged. There were always bowls of daffodils at that time of year.

"I could hear what was being said. Although I was standing back. I stood back because if I came too near the window the light would shine on my face and you would have seen me. I was very wet. My feet were horrible. The bushes were wet and I just got drenched pushing through them. Anyway, though I stood back, I could see all right and I could hear what was being said, so I suppose there was a window open somewhere. It wasn't the window I was looking through. That was the big picture window and, of course, that can't be opened. But there was an open window. There must have been. I could hear every word, and of course, I could see. I could see Mrs. Abel bring out that album of photographs."

"What did you hear?"

"She showed you these photographs. I couldn't see them. Naturally I couldn't, but she was talking about them. They were taken in the States, and they were mainly to do with her husband. That engineer. They were photos of her engineer husband, as I remember. That right?"

"Yes."

"Well, she spoke about him."

"Right on the nail." He detected the note of scorn that often came into her voice when he was irritating her but she did not know how to get back at him. She wasn't interested in what interested him, namely what had happened on that particular night. What chiefly struck her was (he could see) that as usual he had behaved like an idiot. Instead of being natural and making his presence known he had spied on them. So naturally she was scornful.

"A bit later on", he said, "you stood up near the window, and you were so close I thought you might have seen me."

"I didn't see you."

"There wasn't much light shining out from the room. I've got to agree about that. It was a black night. I remember the rain had stopped but the water must have been still running out of the bushes and off the roofs and down the drainpipes and gutterings. I could hear this running water and wind. I heard you tell Mrs. Abel that in spite of everything you loved me."

After a pause she said, "I remember something of the sort."

"I'm not holding you to anything, Jinny. I'm just trying to establish what actually happened. You said something about——"

"Yes, I could well have said that."

They understood each other.

"For Mrs. Abel's benefit, not necessarily because it's true?"

"She's very vulnerable. I wanted to help."

"I love you, anyway," he said and lay back on the pebbles in the hot sun, throwing arms and legs wide, eyes shut, sweat trickling through his beard and between the folds of belly flesh.

"Is this all you wanted to say?" She sounded so cross, in spite of what he had just said he marvelled that he had said it and meant it. It was true. That was all that interested him nowadays, the truth. She was still a bitch but he loved her. Which was another way of saying that, deep down, she wasn't a bitch, that he remembered when he liked touching her, that he wanted to touch her again; and that her bearing towards him was such, or what he instinctively assumed her bearing to be, that he felt better about himself. That's what he meant by love. At the moment it worried him she was so annoyed about the way he had eavesdropped.

"No. I stood there and I had the funny feeling my father was standing there too."

"Your father?"

"A man with a beard. As it might be me, as I am now."

"But it was an illusion?"

"Sure it was an illusion."

"Then why are you talking about a man with a beard?"

"I don't know."

"Is this why you grew a beard?"

"Could be." He began laughing at the recollection of the way he had put his shoes on over his wet socks and there had been so much moisture in the car the windows steamed up. "You believe I was there, anyway?"

"It isn't worth arguing about."

"Then Mrs. Abel showed you these snaps of this midget husband of hers, and how they'd met and all that. And it came out she'd never been married to anyone else, nobody at all."

"You must have been out there in the wet some time."

"You don't deny she met him when he was in the American Army. He was stationed at Southampton Docks and she met him in 1918."

"Yes, she said something like that. He wasn't very good to her."

"Why should I have to learn things like this by accident?"

"By dishonesty, you mean."

"All right, dishonesty. But it's true, isn't it? She fell in love with this Yank Movement Control major and after the war they married and went to live in the States. That is the complete history of Mrs. Abel."

"That's right."

"It's true what I heard about this Movement Control major?"

"Yes, if you like."

"Then you admit I was outside that window. All this is fact? It really happened?"

"Yes."

"You couldn't have known, then, that I knew. Why didn't you tell me?"

"She particularly asked me not to."

"She didn't know I was outside that window?"

Jinny shrugged.

Poumphrey sat up so quickly that momentarily his head swam. He was dazed by the brilliance and the heat and the constant hissing of the sea. He looked at Jinny through half-closed eyes, blazing in purple and yellow against a kaleidoscopic background of shifting trees and sky and a black lagoon. He fished the dark glasses out of the pocket of his shirt.

"But I've got it right, haven't I? She said what I said she said. My memory's not playing tricks."

"No."

"I'm cleaning the old memory up. I like to remember things as they were."

"How else can you remember them?"

Poumphrey stood up and said they ought to be getting back to the hospital. He was thirsty and they spent some time finding a cottage where they did teas in the garden.

"She can't die," said Poumphrey. "I'd find it bloody intolerable of her to die."

Jinny sat watching him drink tea and eat scones with butter and strawberry jam. She herself took nothing. "She could last for weeks."

"Jinny, I really remembered what happened."

"If you say so."

"She didn't talk about my father at all."

"How could she?"

"I got the message?"

"Yes," she said. "Yes! Yes! Yes!"

* * *

Cooper, when Poumphrey had called on him at the Foreign Office, had been evasive and suspicious. The wintry gleam of pleasure that came from knowing Poumphrey would never again be negotiating in the Middle East faded when he realized the man was talking of going to Damascus to put flowers on Raouf Omra's grave. He had made difficulties about seeing

Poumphrey; they were nothing to the defence he would have put up if he had known what was really in Poumphrey's mind.

"We don't know he's dead. He was one of a number tried last June. Khazin was certainly shot. Jaliyah on the other hand has been seen about the place. It seems your name was mentioned."

"And I'd like to do something for his family."

"You're taking it on yourself a bit, aren't you? We don't know how important or how trivial a part his dealings with you may have played in his trial. We don't know what the charges were. If you want my private opinion they weren't all that important."

"I just want the truth." Poumphrey wished to spare Cooper's feelings, so he didn't wear his Mao outfit. He wore an old, loose-fitting suit that looked as though it had been cut out of sail cloth, a silk cravat, with blue-and-white daisies on it, and suede shoes. His thin, sandy beard was so long it waved when he moved his head sharply. Cooper had not so much as blinked. This was his way of saying he had heard of Poumphrey's illness and sympathized.

"You won't get that, Syria being the sort of place it is nowadays. We can't stop you going but it's a crazy idea. If Omra is still alive you might even do him a lot of harm."

"The information was he'd been shot. This is accepted by my Board. So you don't have to break it gently. I just want to know the worst. You didn't just make it up that he was shot, did you?"

"He was court martialled and found guilty."

"What of?"

"I'm sorry to say you were mentioned as the foreigner he dealt with. If you turned up in Damascus we couldn't guarantee your immunity from trouble."

"I'd risk that. I know Asraf. He's an old friend."

"They'd never give you a visa, anyway."

"Say something helpful."

"You're here at your own request."

"You can't tell me anything?"

"Nothing. If we do get something I'll give you a ring."

Poumphrey thought that if he couldn't get into Syria he might at least go to Beirut. He just wanted to know what had happened, that's all. And how it had happened. And what Raouf thought of him. And what General Asraf thought of him. And he wanted the Syrians to know he had never been mixed up in Intelligence work. Once in Beirut there was usually no trouble getting to Damascus.

"Do you mean", Cooper had said when he put some of this into words, "you're ready to risk not only your own neck to demonstrate you were misrepresented at Raouf Omra's court martial, but you are, if Omra is still alive, ready to risk his too?"

"Yes."

The wintry gleam returned to Cooper's worried face. The lines round his mouth softened. The change of expression persuaded Poumphrey Raouf really had been shot, and that Cooper knew it for certain, and that he was only playing along in this speculative way because it was his idea of a tease. "Take my advice, forget him."

"I reckon I'll go to Beirut and look about a bit."

Cooper brought his shoulders up. He wanted to look comically deprecating but he only succeeded in a pantomime cringe. "Out of sheer vanity you're ready to run the risk of even further incriminating this unfortunate man. My advice to forget him seems pretty innocuous compared with that."

"He's dead. You know it."

Cooper pressed a button on his desk. "We really don't know for certain."

"Even if he weren't I'd not be blackmailed by you into staying away. Or even by him."

* * *

Get-well cards, flowers, cables, fruit, flowed into Mrs. Abel's room and every day Poumphrey examined them carefully to identify their new tributes and exact information about their source. Cousin Francis in Windsor, Ontario, sent a number of cables and wrote a confused letter in spidery handwriting which Mrs. Abel asked Poumphrey to read aloud to her. It was mainly about his bees and a visit he had just paid to New York where he had met—well, it didn't matter whom he had met.

Poumphrey wanted to brush all these cards and cables and presents on one side because, as he saw it, he was capable of providing all the tribute she needed. And the more she thought of them the less capable she was of summoning the strength to give him the Great Message.

He had an absurd idea she had a Great Message, a stunning piece of information, some Total Revelation to communicate. He knew it was absurd. He and Jinny put up at a local hotel so that they could be on hand at all hours. If only he caught her at the right moment she would utter. He supposed he reached this crazy calculation because she seemed ready now to talk to him as though he really were her son. She was weaker every day.

She gave him the name of her solicitors in London and said they had her will in their keeping. There was a codicil. Poumphrey just wanted to stop her talking about such trivialities. Tell me, he wanted to say, what is really in your mind. There was a primitive idea that when people died they knew everything. His own obsession was as silly as that. But he could not escape it. He watched her thin crinkled lips. He kissed them. By now they had fitted up a drip to compensate for the failure of the kidneys and he sat watching the liquid wink in the flask above her head.

One day, in his absence, Jinny told her about Raouf Omra and when he came in—she seemed surprisingly strong that day—she said he was not to think of going to Syria.

"If you take my advice you won't go looking for that bastard of yours either," she said drily. He was amazed by these two injunctions and said nothing.

"I want you to go to the house and bring me a box." She spoke slowly. Her voice was stronger than for some time. "It would appear to be leather, but in fact it is a metal box covered with thin leather. It is on the top shelf of the cupboard in my bedroom where I keep all my old books and things. The key is with me here."

In case of surgery they needed somebody's say-so, apparently, and there was no guarantee Mrs. Abel would be in a fit state to give her permission. The doctor was a young Negro from Trinidad. He said he did not think it would come to that but he wanted to know who he had to turn to.

"Come to what, for God's sake?"

"Well, surgery, you see. An amputation."

Jinny did a lot of the driving these days. No doubt she was buoying herself up with the thought of the funeral. He could see it would be a real comfort to her. He honestly thought he was a better man for seeing this simple fact and accepting it.

Even so, he was a bit shaken when Jinny asked, as they drove to Sidlesham, "Poor old dear! I wonder if she's left a directive against cremation."

He wanted to shout out at her but instead he sat in silence reflecting that he was a better man for having overcome so many illusions and so much selfish fantasy and self-deception. He would not have liked to say this to Jinny because she might have laughed at him. And it would not have been easy to explain why his acceptance of her love of funerals was such a moral achievement. You had to be as mad as he'd been to know what order of achievement this was. Anyway, she'd deny she liked funerals.

They drove past Mrs. Collier's burnt-out cottage.

"Why did she reproach me over that?"

"She just wanted to get at you."

"In the night", said Mrs. Abel when they returned with the box and he sat at the bedside holding one of her hands, "it was like—I don't know what it was like. It wasn't like anything. It just *was*."

He stood up at this, releasing her hand, put a napkin under her chin and tried to get her to take some unsweetened orange juice. She could scarcely move her head. On her upper lip were silvery hairs which he had noticed before. Jinny sat at the back of the room talking about—of all things—dahlias. The dahlias in the garden at Sidlesham were a wonderful show. Mr. Prossor sent his regards and good wishes for an early recovery.

"It just *was* and it was very real." Mrs. Abel did not take any of the orange juice nor, indeed, even open her eyes. "A steady beat like footsteps on a hollow ground. It was walking. Somebody was stepping steadily behind a—it was behind something but I knew I would see him."

"You're supposed to take a lot of fluid." Poumphrey tried to push the rim of the glass between her lips but she wasn't having any. "Do drink, there's a good girl."

"I can't tell you," she said. "On the other side of the wall was the steady beating."

"It was your heart."

"I didn't want to come back."

Poumphrey kissed her on the forehead and she whispered, "Wipe my face. There, that's lovely. That's cool. That cool flannel. Last night," she whispered. "Just the beating. There were no distractions. I thought *this* is real."

"You were dreaming. You're better now."

"I've always thought, behind the veil."

"What d'you mean, behind the veil?" Poumphrey was waiting for the Utterance.

"Where's the box?" she asked.

Sister came in to take her temperature and pulse. When she had gone Mrs. Abel tried again to talk about the night. "I was alone. But in this place it was silent. No sound, just pacing, you see? There was awareness, by somebody else of me. I was in a state of recognition. I mean, I was recognized."

Jinny came over and tried to calm her but her eyes were open and her right hand lifted and pointing.

"Yes?" said Poumphrey with the orange juice still in his hand.

"The key is on a ring in my handbag, over there. See?"

While Jinny opened the handbag and looked for the key with which to unlock the box—and Poumphrey had no interest in it whatsoever, he wasn't interested in papers or locks of hair, or whatever it was old women kept locked up—he said, "I saw all Greece from an aeroplane once. The meteorological conditions were quite exceptional."

"What's that got to do with it?"

Poumphrey was at a loss. He didn't want an argument. He did not know what he had meant really. The recollection of seeing snow on the Greek mountains from Delphi to Olympus came into his mind when she struggled to tell them of the way she had listened to her heart beating during the night. And again, when he had seen her pointing.

She seemed to understand his confusion and said, "It was a maze only you couldn't see the walls. I was watched. It was more real than you. It was more real than this bed. It was real. It was——"

"When you're better we'll take you down to Cornwall."

"Don't talk like a fool."

"It was your heart beating."

"You don't know what real is."

She seemed to be drawing quite crazy remarks out of him. He did not want to argue. He wanted her to be easy. All right! he didn't know what real was. Nobody did. It didn't mean anything even to consider such problems.

"Rubbish! It's the only way to keep sane. Sane people choose the right kind of delusions. Pilate wasn't a fool. What is truth? Eh? What is it then? Your bastard won't give it to you. You know that, don't you? Nor Damascus. Truth! Certainty! When hot for certainty in this our life. You have to choose the most comfortable uncertainties. Open the box."

Jinny was opening the box and lifting out documents and letters tied up in red ribbon; and finally a miniature painting in an oval silver frame. The blank young face was presumably that of her late husband, the engineer. He guessed as much, anyway.

"Understand", said Mrs. Abel, "I don't believe there's anything after. When I'm dead I'm dead." She sighed. "I'd like to see a photograph of your father."

* * *

The bedside telephone rang. Poumphrey was so confused he could not find the receiver in the dark and Jinny switched on the light. He assumed it would be a call from the hospital but in fact it was from London, for Jinny, and she took it sitting bolt upright with her blue nightgown slipping over one shoulder. She sounded rather pleased.

"It's Mr. Samsun," she said to Poumphrey. "He wants to know the latest on the VC10."

The shock had made Poumphrey sweat. Still half asleep he looked at his watch. "It's half-past three in the morning."

"Africans go to bed late," said Jinny. "He's just had a cable from Addis Ababa. What shall I tell him?"

There was to be a conference of black writers and artists in Addis. Jinny had been trying to organize a charter flight from England for the forty or so friends of hers who wanted to go but there had been a hitch because they did not constitute a bona-fide club; only a club could, apparently, arrange a cut-rate charter flight. Jinny was in such despair that Poumphrey had telephoned around and found he could hire a VC10 for £6,000 over an eight-day period. But forty or so people were not enough to fill it. In order to please Jinny he set about trying to increase the party by inviting some of his own friends along —the Grices, for example, Todd and the other members of the Board, Collison and his wife—but there were no takers. The delegation from Britain were so important that the date of the conference depended on when they could arrive.

"It's a bit problematic, Mr. Samsun," Jinny said. "As you know we've a dear friend very ill."

"How the hell did he get this phone number?" Poumphrey demanded.

"He says the conference has to be before October 1st because the hall is booked after that and the government's offer of free hotel accommodation runs out. He wants to know one way or another, are we going or aren't we? Look, Mr. Samsun, I'll ring you back later in the day. We're tired now. What? Well, he's doing his best." She replaced the receiver. "He seems very cut up. It's understandable."

Poumphrey could not sleep after this and in a muddled sort of way he went on debating with himself why his friends had not wanted to go to Ethiopia with him. As he had explained to Jinny, it wasn't as though he had not changed. He was a simple, direct, unpretentious sort of chap these days. He bore no resentment against any one. He wasn't furious with the Board, or the East Dene Constituency Committee, or even with Grice and his wife for that matter; he just wanted to show them all how straightforward he had become. They thought he was still the old Poumphrey, of course, and that they would be in for a lot of talk and exuberance. A misconception. He had become rather silent. He had been really puzzled why everyone was so prepared to miss a jaunt to Ethiopia—fantastic country, marvellously beautiful—when it would have cost only about two hundred quid each all in. He had said there was no need to go to the conference. He'd arrange to fly about the country in little aeroplanes while Jinny and the blacks were busy at the conference. But there had been no takers.

"Look," he said to them, "I'm different now."

* * *

That afternoon he left Jinny in Chichester and drove home to look out that photograph for Mrs. Abel; though, as he reflected, when he began fishing in drawers and cupboards the family had never been strong on photographs. Some people had photographs in silver frames standing on desks and little tables.

But not the Poumphreys. They didn't even have a family photograph album. It was not wanting to dwell on the past.

If you dwelt in the past your life was haunted and as Poumphrey walked about the house—ostensibly he was looking for this photograph but really he was just walking about the house—what he liked was the way it had no special atmosphere or promise. The rooms had been exorcized. He had been exorcized. He slopped about in his white knitted jumper, his blue cotton slacks and sandals, feeling open and receptive to whatever might happen. He felt cheerful, even about Mrs. Abel. If he ever tracked down that son of his he'd feel cheerful about him too. Even if they had nothing to say to each other a little more truth would be let into the world. And if he reached Damascus and told the authorities the truth about Raouf and himself that would be one illusion the less. Poumphrey opened and shut drawers, looking for a photograph of his father; he went to the bottom of trunks, dragged out books, boxes and folders. He was rooting out all the lies and the illusions and the self-deceptions.

"My boy," he'd say, "I'm your father." The kid might be a bit stunned, and so might he for that matter, too, but guilty secrets had to be brought into the open.

All the time he was looking for a photograph in a folding leather case. He remembered it well. Two leather panels hid the photo as if it had been an ikon in its case. His step-mother carried it on her travels and propped it open in hotel bedrooms. It didn't mean anything. Mrs. Abel? It wouldn't mean a thing to her but she was dying. You don't know this man, do you? he would be able to say to her at the last. Confess that you never set eyes on him in your life and die with a cleansed mind, like mine. This man died on January 4th, 1956. He was nothing to you. Look! The face is strange.

The phone rang and he hesitated about answering it because he thought it would be Jinny to say Mrs. Abel was dead.

The ringing ceased and, after a pause, started up again. Poumphrey picked the receiver up and found himself listening to a man's voice. "Hallo, is that you, Poumphrey? This is Collison here, remember? They said you weren't in the office. I'd like to talk to you about one or two things. Would it be all right if I came round?"

Poumphrey thought of Collison on that flight back from the Middle East and again in the Quo Vadis and he had a very clear picture of the little head, the black, close-cropped hair and the brown eyes.

"No, it isn't convenient. What do you want?"

"Money."

If Collison had phoned five minutes before or five minutes later he would have had no answer. The fellow didn't seem to realize how lucky he was. "You in trouble?"

Collison explained that he had many links with India. At the moment he was trying to raise money for a Performing Arts Centre in Bombay. In particular he wanted five thousand pounds for an air-conditioned mobile recording van which would tour rural areas and tape folk music and he thought that Poumphrey with his interest in culture and history would lend a sympathetic ear.

"How do you know I'm interested in culture and history?"

"I shall never forget the way you spoke about Greece."

"That's true."

"Anyway, this is what I wanted to come round and talk to you about."

"How much to you expect me to fork out?"

"You, personally? Well, five thousand quid. They'd paint an acknowledgement on the side of the van."

Poumphrey did not know how to convey that he was a changed man these days. At one time it would have been possible to appeal to his vanity but now the thought of a recording van trundling round India with his name painted on the side was an embarrassment.

"Do you often ring people up and ask them for five thousand quid?"

"As a matter of fact I do."

Poumphrey thought a bit and then invited Collison to come round, not because he had any intention of parting with five thousand quid but because he wanted to see the man's face again, more particularly the man's eyes. He'd put him in a chair and inspect him.

"Money means nothing to me," he said. "It isn't that. The way I feel now I'd be ready to give away everything I've got and beg, or be a hermit. But I've never gone for folk music and foreign languages and trying to be a Red Indian in the way you have. I just think that's running away."

Collison arrived half an hour later and Poumphrey was disappointed by the small impression he made with that head and those eyes. True, they were brown but they seemed to lack the special awareness, the informed watchfulness, that Poumphrey now realized he was on the look out for in spite of his cult of unclouded realism. The house had been exorcized, but there was always the possibility of some new enchantment.

"Thank you for seeing me. I wouldn't have recognized you behind that beard. They tell me you're a bit of a hippy these days."

Poumphrey ignored all this and went on studying Collison who was wearing vaguely hippy gear himself—sandals, brown velvet trousers and a pink frilly shirt open to the waist. Around his neck was a chain that supported a medallion over his hairy belly. Poumphrey could not make out what was inscribed on this medallion. Had he still been politically active he would have liked to know what Labour M.P.s got up to in the summer recess and asked questions about this medallion.

"I'm not a hippy," he said. "I've just settled for being what I am."

"Bit depressing that, isn't it?"

"Life's just some bloody great fancy dress ball so far as you're concerned," said Poumphrey. "Now me, I'm a contemplative."

Collison went on for some time telling Poumphrey about Indian music and how it had no system of notation so that for centuries it had been maintained only by the master and pupil link which, for a variety of reasons, was now being broken. He said that unless somebody like Poumphrey coughed up money to record it there was danger of a lot of great music being lost for ever. Even now it might be too late.

"Let it go," said Poumphrey. "Let it all go."

"When we were flying over Greece you wouldn't have spoken about a cultural inheritance like that."

"You don't understand, old boy. I've changed."

"Well, if you can't manage five thousand what about four?"

"No, not a bean. Listen, Collison. There's something uncanny about you. So far as I know we've met how many times? Three? There was that Bournemouth conference, there was that time in the plane, and then we met up in that restaurant."

"You mean it seems more?"

"It seems I've always known you or somebody like you. There's some aura. Do you know what I'm talking about. It isn't just you. Other people are involved. It's enough to make anybody believe in reincarnation. Now, what I'm getting at is this. Do you recognize anything in me?"

"Not in that sense, no."

"You don't feel that inside my skull there's an intimate of yours staring out?"

"Not at all."

"What I'm saying doesn't ring any kind of bell?"

"No."

"I'll think over this Indian van. I might give you a fiver for old time's sake. You'll have to excuse me. I've got to visit somebody in hospital." Before Collison went Poumphrey tried again and without success to persuade him to join the trip to Addis.

* * *

Jinny was sitting in the hotel lounge when he arrived.

"How is she?"

"She could talk quite clearly."

Poumphrey nodded. He sat down and put the brown-paper covered parcel on the table and said he supposed there was no point in waiting. He had the photograph. He'd have a cup of tea and then they'd go straight up to the hospital.

"She'll have to confess she's never seen him in her life before."

"What if she doesn't?" said Jinny.

"She'll have to be challenged."

"What do you mean?"

"I mean I shall have to help her to face the truth."

"It would be unforgivable," she said.

"You mean *you* wouldn't forgive me?"

Jinny hesitated.

"There's no one else," he said.

"You don't count her?" Jinny took out a handkerchief and blew her nose because that was the second time recently he'd said he loved her. "Or do you mean she's dying and doesn't count?" Unexpectedly Jinny began crying. She knew that he would think she was crying over Mrs. Abel, and she was in a way.

"We're making a fuss about nothing. You see, it'll all turn out to be nothing. Nothing will be said. Nothing ever is about really important things. Shall we go?"

"I'm not coming."

"Why not?"

"I couldn't bear it if you're going to be beastly to her."

Two hours later he was back from the hospital, minus the photograph, looking for Jinny. She was not in their bedroom nor any of the public rooms and he eventually found her in the garden.

She was sitting right at the end of the terrace, catching the last of the sun. It had been a dry, sullen month of cloud and dust but now a different wind blew and there was this late sun glaring round the corner of the hotel. A paper bag blew against her foot and she bent down to pick it up and screw it into a ball. The air smelled of dry stubble and roast meat from the kitchen. The August stubble smell came from the scoured, bright field at the end of the rose garden, quite peppery in the pink evening.

Poumphrey made towards her slowly and warily. She was wearing a yellow headscarf and had been reading a paperback which she put down as soon as she became aware of his approach. The way the headscarf framed her face gave it a pathetic watchfulness.

"What happened?" she asked.

Poumphrey sat down and beckoned to a waiter. "What'll you have? I could do with a drink myself."

No, Jinny did not want a drink.

Poumphrey ordered a pint of draught bitter and said nothing until the waiter returned with it. Poumphrey took a sip and put the tankard carefully down. He did not care for beer and could not think why he had ordered it.

"Well?" said Jinny.

He began scratching uncomfortably among his beard. "It's all right. I showed her this photo. As a matter of fact I'd forgotten this particular photo. I showed it to her. It was as strange to me, I suppose, as it must have been to her. No, stranger. We talked. You're right about her seeming brighter. We just left it she was my mother."

* * *

The door of her room had a glass inspection panel. Standing in the corridor and watching through this window Poumphrey had hesitated. She seemed to be asleep and in the absence of any nursing staff Poumphrey did not know what to do. She was well supported by pillows, sitting rather than lying. Her dentures were out and her cheeks sunken. She wasn't so much pale as floury. An inverted glass flask was suspended from a metal stand between the bed and the wall. From time to time a bubble floated from the bottom of the clear liquid in this flask and burst in a tiny, silent explosion; a white tube ran under the bedclothes where, as he knew, it was plugged into her arm. Under the cage with the sheet over it at the bottom of the bed he could see the two feet as black as bog oak.

He opened the door quietly but her eyes were immediately open. They were small eyes, withered by the years. Behind her were gauze curtains. Her left arm being trapped she lifted her right arm, smiling, and when he bent near her she put this arm round his neck. He kissed her and thought that when she was properly awake he would show her the photograph. Or, perhaps, if she didn't ask for it he wouldn't show her the photograph at all.

"I'm ashamed to say I soiled the bed. Disgusting." She was only whispering. It was a very loud, penetrating whisper and Poumphrey drew his head back. "You'd have thought a woman my age could wait for the bed-pan. The nursing sister was neither surprised nor displeased. And she should have been. She behaved in a very conspiratorial way and I didn't like it. When a wrong has been committed I think it should be faced."

"Doesn't seem a wrong to me."

"Dirty woman!"

"You're feeling rested, I hope."

"Where's the photograph?" she asked.

The old man, if he had been there, would have urged him to take it all very gently. His father, at that moment, seemed real and because he was real someone to feel impatient with. The lids of Mrs. Abel's eyes were puffed. Poumphrey actually reached out a hand and touched the lower lid of her right eye. His father would have done that. But his father would never have unwrapped the photograph as he was doing now. He would have lied. He would have said he could not find it.

He remembered his father nailing some trellis to a wall and hitting his hand with the hammer. It must have hurt like hell. He came down the ladder and went and sat on a grass bank, holding his broken left hand—it turned out he had smashed a small bone—in his right and not saying anything, not making a sound, in fact, but smiling. He just took whatever life served out and smiled and was happy. At times he was really insensitive.

Poumphrey put the brown paper in the waste-paper basket and that left him with just the case. His intention had been to hand the whole thing to Mrs. Abel but he had forgotten she could not move her left arm and so he had to open the case himself. It was very like opening an ikon. The two flaps lifted to reveal the coloured face.

"Show me," she said.

It was a crude, primitive, coloured photograph of his father made, possibly, in the early twenties. Basically it was a black-and-white photograph but it had been touched up with colour, amateurishly and coarsely. The close little beard was a kind of yellow ochre, the long, legal cheeks, pink as a child's and the eyes were brown.

He remembered the picture all right, but he had not remembered it until that moment. The reason he had always kept the flaps closed was the ugliness. It was a comic-strip face. The eyes were brown like toffees. Mrs. Abel was waiting but he did not know what to say or do. The face looked up at him with the smiling intentness of a marionette.

How could they ever have kept such a travesty?

"See!" he said, and showed the picture to Mrs. Abel.

"Yes, that's him." He had to hold the picture before her face. "Though I can't see very well without my glasses."

Poumphrey had been about to say, quite gently, that it was the picture of a man to whom she could not conceivably have been married. The time had come to stop deceiving herself. Instead, he began defending the picture. For all its crudity it conveyed a more vivid impression of the man his father had been than a more natural photograph. It had the innocent truthfulness of a child's daub; and nothing else, no other photograph, no painting, could have caught the unblinking stare of those eyes as he remembered them and as he had seen them, here and there, imposed on this face or on that face, in different countries, or in the dark, in dreams, long after they were dead and their real light had gone out and he was alone. He had not known, all these years, what he was looking at.

He had tried to be truthful and found himself naked. "He had remarkable eyes."

"There must be a curse", said Mrs. Abel, "for those who laugh at the old and the sick."

"I'm not laughing at you, my dear."

"Yes, you are. You're laughing."

"I'm not laughing at you."

"You mustn't make me laugh, either. Stop! Please!"

Poumphrey closed the flaps over the photograph and put it down beside the spectacle case and the tumbler with the dentures. He was laughing, now, because she was laughing, and she was laughing because she had found him out. Did she know how?

"I'm glad I saw those brown eyes too, Edward." After a long pause. "I'd have liked to live. Take it from me, dying as an experience is vastly overrated."

There was trouble with B.O.A.C. about hiring a VC10 to take a party from Heathrow to Addis Ababa direct so the party had to make its own way to Vienna where Poumphrey had arranged a charter flight with Aeroflot. This meant that on a sunny autumn morning he was able to look down at Greece again, and say, "Look, Jinny! It's very clear." What cloud there was floated in compact, white shapes that threw sharp shadows on the brown and blue mountains. No snow, even on the peaks and high, hanging north-facing shoulders.

Jinny had never been to Greece.

"That's the Gulf of Corinth," he said. "All that land over there is the Peloponnese. Down there is Delphi. You can't see it, but it's down there all right."

He was on the point of saying what he had to Collison, there was the cross-roads where Oedipus killed his father. But he didn't.

After a while he said, "I once told my father he was a failure."

"He wouldn't have heard."

It was true the old man often didn't listen when you talked to him, but this was one of the times he did take notice.

So, here Poumphrey was, flying with his wife and about a hundred blacks to Ethiopia, while his mind went back to that occasion in the office overlooking Kingsbury Square where, to be fair, he hadn't actually murdered his father, but he had said to him—and, he Poumphrey must have been about twenty; he was still at Cambridge—looking about this office, at the framed company certificates, at the box files with their faded labels, at the confusion of papers on his desk, at the stacks of documents tied up with pink tape and thrown into a heap on the floor, looking at all this, and remembering the heat and the airlessness because of the sealed windows and the stink of his father's Turkish cigarette: "I suppose you'd be thought a failure."

"What would you think?" his father had said, leaning back in his chair. Cigarette ash fell across his grey waistcoat with brass buttons. Poumphrey had been embarrassed. At this distance of time he could not remember what had prompted him to say his father was a failure. Perhaps it was nothing more than the sight of that disgusting office. Perhaps there had been a row about money. He was doing well at Cambridge. Spoke at the Union. Perhaps this was the first time he realized his father was just an inefficient country solicitor whose wife had run away from him.

"I wonder when it was", said Jinny, "that people began talking about success and failure. When money-making came in I suppose. Your father wasn't very competitive."

"I didn't see it that way," said Poumphrey. "Anyway I wasn't thinking just about money."

"What would you think?" his father had said, his face foreshortened because of the way he was leaning back, one eye closed against the smoke from his cigarette and his mouth, a bit masked by the beard, showing itself to be slightly twisted.

"Yes, a failure," Poumphrey had said brutally.

The old man was amused. What saved the day was his sense of humour. Nothing more passed. He hadn't asked for any elaboration.

At the time it had seemed self-evident that what the hell was the use of being a solicitor if you weren't at the top of your profession? Poumphrey hadn't murdered his father, but he had not been with him when he died. He had been abroad, in Bahrein actually, and he received the news by cable. In the foreshortening of the years it seemed there had been no opportunity to say he was sorry. That would have been clumsy. It was no good saying he was sorry for speaking the truth, if it really was the truth. He ought to have found something else to say.

"What did he say?" Jinny wasn't really interested.

"Nothing much."

"What did he look like? I mean, how did he take it?"

Poumphrey thought back again. "Amused. Pleased."

"He just took it as evidence you meant to get on in the world. Parents do that sort of thing. He just thought, talking the way you did, you were set on being Prime Minister."

"I was too." It interested him that Jinny should talk with such confidence about the way parents thought. What did she know about it really? She was even less of a parent than he was. He liked the idea the reason his father was relaxed that afternoon was the way his kid showed spunk. But Jinny's remarks made him wonder what his own son, assuming he had one, would say in similar circumstances.

Assuming he had one. He put it that way because Jinny still argued Jane Puddifoot was a liar. Jane. He remembered her name now. Not Greek at all. Assuming that she had not lied, assuming he did go north and find this boy who'd be roughly the age he was when he'd told the old man he was a failure; what would the boy say to him? "You sound a bit of a failure to me. You wouldn't have turned up now if you weren't. What are you trying to prove?" Would he say that?

Not impossible. It was failure to have a son of twenty and not catch up with him until the boy was smart enough to ask difficult questions.

"What would you think?" he'd say to the boy.

"Yes, I suppose you *are* a failure," the boy would undoubtedly answer. Poumphrey could imagine himself tilting back in his chair, turning his head away, riding the punch.

If only Jinny and he had kids and seen them grow up, to be beastly and say cruel things to him he'd have known for sure the old man smiled because he was thinking of something he, in his turn, had said to his own dead and unforgiven father.

He wasn't going to look for the boy so the occasion would not arise. Say it had, though, and the boy blurted out what *he* said to his father. The answer would have been, "No, I don't see it that way. In my book I've had a kind of triumph."

The middle-aged solicitor with a cigarette in the corner of his mouth could have said the same. He didn't because the bright boy in front of him would not have understood. He tipped his chair back and watched the cigarette smoke drift up to the fly-spotted plasterwork on the ceiling, he closed those brown eyes—which Poumphrey had not inherited—and they both waited in the legal, dusty silence. He sat up, sighed, looked at his son out of those rather close-set, humorous eyes, and the silence had gone on. For years. They had not quarrelled. Father had not taken him seriously enough for that; the silence of the solicitor's office had, after all, not been absolute. Traffic noises dreamily penetrated the unwashed veils of the double-glazed windows. In the same muffled way another world was always signalling. The sounds and signs had been barely detectable, particularly to a man like Poumphrey who was bad even at remembering faces, let alone eyes.

Aeroflot provided free vodka and by the time they sighted the Libyan coast singing and rhythmic handclapping, in which Jinny joined, became so noisy the flight captain sent a message to say he could not hear what traffic control was saying into his earphones. Jinny was every bit as gay as she had been at Mrs. Abel's funeral. She walked up and down the aisle talking to everyone by their first names. Poumphrey took his shoes off. Few of the other passengers would have thought he looked particularly triumphant. On the contrary. He was not joining in the singing. He wasn't clapping. He wasn't even drinking.

Some time later the blackest man in the party moved into the empty seat next to Poumphrey and what he said made Poumphrey think that people might always be saying profound things in his presence but he didn't notice because they had no immediate bearing. Some such theory was necessary to explain why this man made such striking remarks. Otherwise the coincidence would have been too great.

"Your wife is well known for her cultural activities." He had a reverberent New England voice of a kind that gave Poumphrey a slight headache. Later the American revealed he was now domiciled in the Congo Republic where he was running a literary journal on U.N.E.S.C.O. funds. "But you're the only white man with us. You along for the ride?"

It was unusual to see an American as black as this, the shiny blackness of a piece of washed coal and Poumphrey had the feeling he *was* coal. His small round head was bald on top and a strip of grey, close, Astrakhan curls ran round three sides. He had big bloodshot eyes and a lot of grey hairs on the backs of his hands.

"You could put it that way," said Poumphrey.

"You don't really know?" His name was Spinner. Clearly, his intention was not to be provocative. He just registered that he was in the presence of something that could be taken to illustrate an argument. No, it was more than that. Poumphrey's lack of any real justification for flying to Addis—and Spinner by a series of sharp questions elicited as much—provided a text from which many lessons could be drawn, in the manner of a minister in his pulpit and Spinner might well have once been just that: Spinner knew why he was flying to Addis. Everybody else in the plane knew why they were flying to Addis; they knew because they were black and African (for the purpose of his argument Jinny was black too) and the crew knew why they were flying to Addis. But Poumphrey did not know.

"We have here a paradigm of the contrast between the old white cultures and the new. We, in the new rising culture of black Africa have social and political objectives which everyone understands. No doubt we wallow in anarchy from time to time, but we are on our way. Our objective is to secure enough for all to eat and to secure justice and freedom. This sounds terribly boring, as you would say in England. No doubt it is all too obvious. You understand what I am saying? We emergent blacks have loyalties and an awareness larger than our individual selves. But, for you, this period of historical development is in the past. You have no idealism nor any political or social objective larger than hanging on to what you have gotten into your hands."

The smoke from Spinner's little cigar drifted into Poumphrey's face and he reached up to adjust the air vent that would drive it back again. "I've no theory of history myself."

"O.K., that's a theory of history! You don't believe in spiritual absolutes or transcendence because you've been corrupted by Freud. You dwell in your irresponsible solipsist psyche waiting for messages from the unconscious. Now, what does your unconscious tell you about this flight to Addis?"

To begin with Poumphrey had been annoyed by this kind of talk but as time went by and he could no more stop Spinner talking than he could stop the cigar smoke from drifting into his face—the air vent was not working—he grew interested. He did not like being categorized as a degenerate white waiting for truth to well up from the depths of his psyche. Truth was not something that welled up from anywhere. You went out and established it. Truth was discoverable by an act of will.

"My wife wanted to help a lot of people attend this Congress. I just fixed up the transport. Men do that sort of thing for their wives, you know." Even Poumphrey thought this was not quite on target. "I've been ill, too," he added.

"You look very well to me." Spinner turned his head and examined Poumphrey's face carefully. "Just a few broken blood-vessels in your nose. Good circulation. I can see you've lost weight."

"You a doctor?"

"I was, once. Then I was a lawyer. Then I was a preacher. Now I am a man of the future. That is doctor and lawyer and preacher rolled into one. And I have a sense about people. I sense a culture without a sense of direction and you as an embodiment of it."

"You could be right about that." Poumphrey repressed the thought he must have grown in moral stature to be capable of such humility.

He went off to the lavatory and sat there for some time. The events of the past few months were an allegory of some larger truth towards which he had unconsciously been striving. The tussle over the East Dene nomination, the pressure to resign from the Board, the death of Mrs. Abel, they all hinted at some profounder truth. What?

The eyes! His father rose up and addressed him. His career, his marriage, his ambitions, his failure, his success, his triumph —dear God! he thought, I see in a glass darkly. On her death bed Mrs. Abel had been taken, by him, to the point where she ought to have said, "I am not your mother," and died calmly. Instead of which, she was able, with a mother's authority to stop him from going to find out whether Jinny was right and Mark was not his son after all. And she stopped him from going to Damascus. You can't know everything, even about yourself, she seemed to say.

He hadn't even known the old man was dogging him. It was true. That crude photograph of his father was shocking. The idea that he might ever get at the truth about anything now seemed naive. You got rid of one illusion only to accept another. The good life consisted of choosing only the right kind of illusion: you cultivated the most desirable state of mind your circumstances allowed. Even a lust for truth was fraud.

He sat on the lavatory seat as the jet flew over Africa, thinking the Biblical yearning of bowels was more than just a figure of speech. He thought of the death of Mrs. Abel. She knew when she was going to die and had asked him to go away while she did it.

He had gone into the corridor and when he returned some ten minutes later the Sister was closing her eyes. Why had she died like that? What did it mean? Why should he have acquiesced in the idea, finally, that she was his mother; and worse, fallen in with her view of Mark and Raouf. Let them go, she had seemed to say. You don't know why I am asking you to let them go, but believe me it is for the best; and his confidence had been so rocked by the brown eyes looking up at him out of the crude photograph Poumphrey had thought, "I give up. Behind the last veil there is always another one. This is as far as I can get." Let them go, she had said. It reminded him of Todd saying, "Be still and know that I am God." "Let the world go. It is not your responsibility."

By the time he returned to his seat lunch was being served and Spinner was eating a huge piece of rare steak. Jinny was tucking into duckling. Seen through the window the continent ran wrinkled and tawny below them in the cloudless light.

"You wouldn't agree Black Africa thinks of white culture as its father?" Poumphrey said to Spinner. "Because if it does it's a poor look out."

"I deplore metaphors of this kind."

"You may deplore it but a man's view of his father and mother must be as basic as you can get. Even when they're dead they're still there. And they can still be there even when you never knew them in the flesh."

"I assure you we do not think of white culture in this way. Come to our discussions in Addis." He turned weightily. "Mrs. Poumphrey, it is a great pleasure of course, a real privilege, to have your husband as one of our company. But I cannot stomach his racialist line of talk."

"Me, racialist?"

"Arthur's mother has just died," said Jinny. "At least Arthur thought of her as mother. We were supposed to send the ashes to her sister-in-law in Rhodesia. But we couldn't because of U.D.I. Ashes come under trade sanctions."

"If only other governments were as firm as the British!" said Spinner. He worked meat from between his teeth with a fingernail. "Do please accept my sincere condolences." Spinner put down his blood-stained knife and fork and extended a right hand in Poumphrey's direction. "The Lord has given and the Lord has taken away. When a man loses his mother the very cord of life is cut. Have you children? But I gather she wasn't your mother in fact."

Neither Poumphrey nor Jinny answered and Spinner picked up his knife and fork once more. "My mother's grandfather was a slave. Just think of that now. Well, she's still alive and she takes a keen interest. Have you ever thought that what chiefly upsets a man about his parents is the way they raise questions about his identity? He is the same as they are and yet he isn't. I sometimes think it would be healthy if no man ever knew his parents."

Poumphrey decided to sleep instead of having lunch. He tried to imagine a society in which people knew nothing of their parents, and saw them wandering about like spirits searching for bodies to inhabit.

Instead of sending the ashes to Rhodesia he had a small grey marble urn locked in the safe at home. Jinny did not know. One day he might tell her. Angry letters had arrived from the Rhodesian sister-in-law.

These he had sent to his solicitor because what angered Mrs. Rewbridge was not the failure to implement that direction about the ashes in her sister-in-law's will—they were to be scattered over the waters of some Rhodesian river where those of the sister-in-law would eventually follow. What made her wild was the new will Mrs. Abel had drawn up in the summer of that year leaving her entire estate to Poumphrey, who was referred to in the document as her 'dear young friend, Arthur Edward Poumphrey'. Mrs. Rewbridge was challenging the will on the grounds that her sister-in-law was mentally incapable when she had made this substitution for an earlier testament in Mrs. Rewbridge's favour. The estate was about £160,000. This was of less interest to Poumphrey than the fact she had given it to him. How it would turn out legally he did not know but if it came to a deal he thought he might want to hang on to the ashes. They were all he really wanted.

At the time he had gone down to register her death he knew nothing about her will; but when the Registrar sat waiting, his pen poised over the appropriate space in his ledger where the informant's relationship to the deceased had to be entered, Poumphrey hesitated only momentarily. "Son," he said. Anything less would have been a failure of love.

Penalties were threatened on the declaration, which he now signed, about the giving of wrong information; but this part of the certificate had little legal importance and his conscience was clear. He had been wrong thinking he could get at the truth by an act of will. Nobody liked uncertainty but there were times you had to accept it in preference to something worse: a truth that would lead to even more uncertainties.

Over the Sudan he had another exchange with Spinner. Jinny was up in the first-class compartment talking to some journalists so Poumphrey felt free to say, "Never ask a couple if they've any children. If they have they may have gone to the bad and if they haven't there may be painful reasons. As a matter of fact my wife and I have no children."

"I'm sorry to hear that," said Spinner. "I've eight, four boys and four girls."

"I used to think I had an illegitimate son," Poumphrey wanted to be helpful.

Spinner waited but Poumphrey said no more and went off to look for Jinny.

He did not attend any of the sessions in Addis. The first three days he was happy to sit about in the sun. Later on Jinny and he would take a few trips. They might fly off in little planes to remote places and Poumphrey had some scarcely worked-out plan for visiting the old rock churches he had heard about. He would rather see those than go about looking at animals or mountains and gorges. The altitude and the dry heat suited him. He slept like a log at night and nodded off comfortably during the day too. He was sitting on the hotel terrace reading the airmail edition of *The Times* when he heard someone calling his name and looked up.

He did not recognize Todd immediately. For one thing his presence was so unexpected. For another he was wearing a white suit and a big bright tie with a pattern of monkeys and palm trees. He dumped a brief-case in one empty chair and sat in another, leaning forward to grin at Poumphrey.

"I was in Nairobi. Knew you were here. My spies. Thought I'd break my journey."

"Nairobi?"

"There could be big petro-chemical business in these parts."

"You're not active on Murex's behalf, then?"

"As a matter of fact I think like you. I'd like to see Murex moving out of the oil-vending business altogether and turning over to industrial exploitation. I tell you frankly, I know this doesn't shock you too much. It would mean an upheaval."

"What's brought this up?"

"Lowther was dead against transforming the company in this way as you know and one had to tread carefully. The time may be ripe for proposing the election of a new chairman. Somebody who wouldn't regard the change as a downgrading."

Poumphrey ordered some tea for both of them. He thought of Spinner's accusation that he sat about waiting for revelations from his unconscious. He had contradicted the man but now he had the feeling just such a revelation was on its way. A big feathery tree at the other end of the terrace was bright with birds, white ibis no doubt, and something must have happened to scare them because they all took off in ragged, clumsy flight, like blossom, breaking across the blue sky.

"You know I'm no longer a member of the Board. You're being a bit free with company secrets aren't you?"

"When does your resignation take effect?"

Poumphrey thought. "I suppose I'm still on the Board until the end of the month."

"You see what I mean?" Todd stood up. "Come on. Let's go into the hotel and send a cable withdrawing your resignation."

"Why should I?"

"Because you're the new chairman we're going to elect."

Poumphrey was vaguely aware that behind all this was some shabby manoeuvre. For the moment, he was incapable of analysing it. He had an unexpected thrill of almost physical lust. He just knew that Todd had suddenly revealed what, all along, had been his one objective: not a seat in the House, not love, not family, not mother or son or friend or charity or a yearning for any kind of truth. Just this: being Chairman. He tingled.

He knew that if Todd talked in this way to him he must already have talked to his own Board in London and to certain chosen members of the Parthian Board too. He would never have opened up in this unguarded way if it was not now clear for Poumphrey to seize what, from the beginning, he had been intent on seizing. He was confused by the realization this was what he had wanted from the beginning, the chairmanship. He had agonized for it.

No good saying he'd gone a bloody funny way about it. This was the sort of man he was. He arrived by running away.

"No," said Poumphrey. "Sorry, it's not on."

"Why not, for Chrissake? Don't tell me you never saw yourself as chairman. Lowther is three years past retiring age anyway. You've been ill. O.K. You're fit now. Don't tell me you haven't been playing hard to get."

"I couldn't do it."

"All that balls about putting up for Parliament. You never meant us to believe that, did you? Nobody in his right mind goes into politics. For God's sake, don't disillusion me. You wanted Lowther's job. No?"

"Yes."

"Then what's happened?"

"Rule me out," said Poumphrey. "I thought your advice to me was drop out and be still."

"This is different."

"How?"

"Look. I was never pushing any sort of quietism. Or perhaps I was. There is a time for quietism and a time for action."

He walked back to the hotel with Todd and then went off to take a shower. Jinny was changing when he came out; and she said, "Oh, I saw Mr. Todd in the hall. What an extraordinary coincidence. He says he was in Nairobi but he came up here to persuade you to stand for the chairmanship, but you won't, or something. He seemed upset. You will, won't you?"

Before he could reply Jinny went off for a shower and when she returned he was in trousers and shirt trying to knot his black bow because these African cultural conferences, Jinny had warned him, had their formal moments. When Jinny took off her bath hat she had nothing on but her dressing-gown and it struck Poumphrey she had the figure of a youth; a bit broad across the beam, maybe, but no tits to speak of.

"We're going to have a pan-African intellectual review in English, French Swahili, Amharic, and Arabic, edited by Mr. Spinner," she said. "If you were chairman of Murex you could put up a bit of money. They get enough profits out of Africa."

She was in a funny state of near-sexual excitement that had nothing to do, Poumphrey realized, with her state of undress or his proximity; it was this conference. She really felt she was somebody and achieving something. Even the end of her nose had lost its red flush. Perhaps it was the dry air, but anyway she had no catarrh. She even looked attractive.

She knotted his tie and he kissed her, a bit to her surprise.

"For the past few years I suppose I've wanted Lowther's job."

"So you *are* standing?"

"No."

"Why not?"

She didn't care whether he was chairman. She was thinking of this pan-African *Encounter* and whether she would be nominated to the editorial board. Poumphrey had no illusions about the extent of her interest. A flame-coloured western sky with a black mountain slope propped against it showed up through the window; and on the lower slopes of the silhouette were inky trees, like spiders.

He could see she wasn't quite herself. Tipsy with the excitement of this congress, she sat at the dressing-table looking at herself. Just the knowledge she was in Africa was enough to make her vibrate with happiness. He was jealous and the jealousy made him go and stand behind her, his hands resting lightly on each shoulder.

"Wouldn't make a good chairman," he said. "Todd and the rest of them ought to know that. The fact they don't shows how incompetent they are. I'm a nut."

The confession was so momentous he actually felt he was at the centre of some physical displacement. Weight was being moved about. Gravity wobbled. He spoke in a light, teasing tone—after all, wasn't he sliding his hands over his wife's little breasts?—but he really did wonder whether the floor had moved. Did they have earthquakes in Addis?

From her reflected face in the mirror he could see she was looking up at him; and he saw again that she, too, had brown eyes. He hadn't looked at them in this way for years. She had very round, beautiful eyes, so brown they were black in the light from the dressing mirror. She lifted her head to be kissed and he saw the real eyes.

Incense was burned in the corridors of the hotel to kill odours. The smell of it had penetrated to their room. The curtains were covered small faces copied from holy pictures; and there were little cupolas and towers and trees and birds and monkeys. What with the incense and the curtains it was like making love in a church.

He said he'd make a rotten chairman and again he felt this powerful erotic stirring. Jinny could scarcely be expected to get any sexual kick out of the way he was now able to trample on the last of his illusions. He did not know what was turning her on. Not him, he suspected. Black Africa, probably, in some perverted way.

"Don't shout so much," she whispered.

"I didn't know I was. I'm O.K.," he said. "Are you O.K.?"

He had taken her dressing-gown off and lifted her up. She wasn't that big or heavy and it surprised him how soft and clean and young her flesh was, smelling of lily of the valley soap and talcum powder. She was like a great big, silly, giggling girl, not like Jinny at all, as she reached up and undid his tie.

She stroked his beard and then, delicately, his belly and thighs as they lay on the bed. He wondered whether she really stroked him or, in her mind, the Congress. He kissed her breasts and left thigh. Her eyes were bright. The gentle touching and kissing melted some last damming rock in the flow of feeling.

She whispered. "What are you crying for, Arthur? There's nothing the matter." She put a thigh, protectingly, across him. "Everything's fine."

And everything was fine. They made love as they had when first married. The spell was broken; he was free, loving and potent. She cried out and he kissed her open mouth.

The bedside telephone rang. It was ignored. It stopped ringing. Some time later it rang again. It was ignored. It fell silent. After a while it rang again, and Poumphrey picked it up.

"It's for you." In fact it was Spinner to say their absence from the dinner table had been noticed. Were they all right?"

"He wants to know if we're all right," Poumphrey said.

* * *

Todd hung about for days, not really believing Poumphrey meant what he said. They had an audience with the Emperor together with six Chinese, an Egyptian and a Brazilian Jew. They had their photographs taken with one of the palace lions. They went swimming in the hotel pool.

Eventually Todd said he was flying to London the following day and he really wanted Poumphrey to realize the kidding had to stop. It was yes or no.

"You know I've been through a rough patch," said Poumphrey. They were sitting by the pool, drinking martinis. Or, rather, Todd was drinking a martini. Poumphrey let his warm in the sun.

"I've never seen you looking so well."

"I'm all right."

"The whiskers suit you. You're O.K."

"I had really bad things happen."

"What sort of things?"

"Oh, things. Couldn't be sure what was what."

"Not all that uncommon."

"My eyes are O.K. now, that's one thing."

There were pauses between these remarks because it was three in the afternoon, the sun was hot, and Congress murmured in the distance like an aeolian harp. The breeze stirred in the trees and floppy shrubs. The high, mountain air was thin and, at the same time, stupefying. Sounds travelled from a great distance. Poumphrey had the slightly transported feeling that hearing music a long way away often gave him.

"Chairman of——" and here Todd mentioned one of the great industrial empires, "thinks he's a reincarnation of an ancient Egyptian."

"No harm in that. But you couldn't have a chairman who couldn't tell the difference between what was happening and what he thought was happening."

"You'll have to spell this out."

So Poumphrey told him he had once overheard a conversation in unusual circumstances and every time he recalled the conversation it was different.

"Why d'you keep recalling it then?" said Todd, after a while.

"Well, misunderstandings had to be cleared up. A chairman's got to be more on the ball than that."

"This wasn't a business conversation?"

"No."

"Purely domestic?"

"Sure. That doesn't make any difference."

"The Chairman of——" and here Todd mentioned another great industrial empire, "has had a conversation with a man out of a flying saucer. It doesn't affect profits."

"That's not the same."

"Look!" said Todd. "You're spoiled. If everybody in the City who got confused now and again packed up there'd be a lot of work to go round among the others. And not just the City. My brother thinks he's got a glass stomach."

"I'm not that daft," said Poumphrey.

"And he runs a building society."

Poumphrey stood up. The conference hall on the other side of the square was a long way away but the sounds of the afternoon had changed and Poumphrey, looking across the valley, saw the members of the Congress beginning to come out of the great doors and pour down the steps. He took off his dark glasses. He couldn't see Jinny but in the hope she might see him, he waved.

"Even I", said Todd confidentially, "get followed about by animals. I've never told this to anyone, but a white dog often follows me about. It tries to get into my house. The fact is everybody has something. Some people hold their heads on in case they fall off. Tchaikovsky did. Ever notice old Green at a meeting? That's supposed to be his trouble."

Poumphrey thought he would swim about a bit, dress and walk down to meet Jinny. "You're just trying to cheer me up."

"The really bad ones never tell," Todd said.

"And I don't need cheering up."

"Some of the top Japanese business men go in for Zen relaxation and passivity at week-ends. That's all I was trying to sell you. I thought you needed it. You can't tell me a bit of mysticism gets in the way of their productivity. Perhaps an interest in these matters is *my* eccentricity," said Todd. "And the dog." But he still could not persuade Poumphrey he was any less fitted to be chairman of the company than these other nuts were to be chairman of theirs.

Poumphrey dived in, swam to the other side of the pool and then kicked off again, floating on his back, his eyes shut against the sun. They didn't hurt any more. He could see pretty well these days. He remembered as a kid peeing in a bucket outside the back door and his mother coming out and scolding him. No, not his mother. Then his father came. Neither his father nor his step-mother would have anything to do with him after he peed in the bucket.

The chlorine in the water brought it back. Bleaching powder had been shaken into that bucket; and he could see it all clearly and how he went into the shrubbery near the place where he had buried a dead squirrel and where there was a bitter smell from the leathery leaves. He remembered being called, out there.

Oh, it was years and years ago. He could see the white plastering of powder in the bucket as clearly as he could see the blue tiles at the bottom of this pool, with fish on them, and lions and giraffes. He was being called again.

He remembered how he ran out of the shrubbery and into the house. No, his father and step-mother had not called him. He was still in disgrace. Then who had called? Who was calling him now? He went back into the shrubbery, and through the shrubbery to the open field, listening. He was listening again, now. It had been a woman's voice, he thought.

How had he been called? A shouted endearment. D-a-a-a-rling! As a mother might call, he supposed. But there was nobody in the field, and that was just about the only place, except for the garden anybody could have been. He just never knew who was calling, and whether it had all been a mistake, but he remembered the voice, which was a kind of woman, he thought.

He didn't scramble out of the pool to see who was calling him now. It would have been like going out through the shrubbery and into the field again. Nobody would be there—nobody who could be found, anyway.

But, naturally, he thought of Mitty swimming in some Spanish pool with her Pierre, of Elaine splashing in the bath with him, and of Jinny at the window looking out at the night to say, "Love," and of ashes in a small, cold, grey urn locked away.

A long time later, weeks, it might have been months, they had been back in England a long time, she said, "Of course, you know, if you ever met your real mother——"

He was surprised, because it seemed to him he had.